Bones Beneath the Soil

TJC Howard

BONES BENEATH THE SOIL

For Ellen
All my love
Always

You carved your name on my heart;
Take my hand and dance with me in the blood that flows.
- Matilda Mueller

All deaths appearing in this narrative are a matter of public record.

To aid reader clarity, a table of births and deaths has been provided as an addendum to the main text.

She smiled at me again today

S he smiled at me again today.

She smiled at me and I felt the same excitement as I did the first moment I laid eyes upon her, all those months ago. A warm, visceral *pull* strong enough to make me weak at the knees.

She didn't *know* she was smiling at me, but I still think it counts.

Hannah never sees me. She doesn't even know I'm here, despite the fact that I am the first thing she looks at when she wakes in the morning – dewy eyed and mussy hair'd - and the last thing she looks at before she wraps herself beneath the eiderdown at night and drifts off to sleep.

I don't sleep. At least, I don't think I do. I don't think I can, but then again, I've never tried.

I don't *think* I've tried.

But why sleep when there are a million and one other things to be done? I watch Hannah sleep, counting the deep, heavy breaths which underscore her blissful slumber. I spend the hours gazing at her beauty.

Hannah has 124 eyelashes on the upper lid of her left eye and 121 on the upper lid of her right eye. She has 43 freckles of varying shapes and shades across her nose and cheeks, although there are slightly more on her left cheek than her right. They are often hidden when she forgets to take her makeup off before she goes to bed.

I am not obsessed, though.

There are other things I do during the hours of darkness. Sometimes I gaze wistfully out of the parlour window downstairs, imagining myself standing in one of the pools of light cast by the lampposts in the street outside like some hardened film noir detective. Sometimes I sing sweet songs to the empty swallow's nest tucked high amongst the roof-beams in the eaves of the loft.

I avoid the creeping dark in the back bedroom.

Sometimes I lower the pressure in the central heating system.

But I always, *always* return to my Hannah.

I love her so.

I wish she was dead.

Like me.

Family

Hannah and her family move into my house a few months after the old lady whose home this used to be passes away. I think her name was Agatha.

It seems strange to me now, that such a vacant bundle of flesh and bone had a name. Cruel almost. Like giving a homeless man a welcome mat to place outside the cardboard box in which he huddles from the cold, the nominal homeliness of the gift in stark contrast to the tattered blankets beneath which he shivers. The fact that the old woman had a name served to highlight how little like a person she really was.

At least, that's what I think.

Hannah's parents seem really pleased with the house when they move in. They call it sweet, and charming. The estate agent smiles at them through polyester teeth and shiny skin and resolutely avoids telling them that an old woman died in a puddle of her own fluids in the very dwelling whose cornicing they are now admiring.

One of the few interesting things about being dead is that my knowledge of the world and its players seemingly extends beyond the here and now. Paltry succour it may be, compared to the bliss of heaven eternal, but it affords me some minor entertainment in those moments when I deign to use it.

Take our good friend the estate agent, for example. He may stand before me in the parlour, but I also see him during a night out with a group of friends in a dingy little bar in town a few days later.

"You don't ever tell them someone died in the house," he says quietly, his stomach is full of vodka and Redbull and cheese-covered chips.

He is beginning to experience the creeping doubt that perhaps his friends do not particularly enjoy his company and wonders whether he is just, fundamentally, a bit unlikeable. "No one enjoys being reminded of their own mortality on a daily basis," he continues, to no one in particular, while slightly-too-loud soft jazz plays over the bar's out of date sound system.

His talk of mortality is a bit rich, considering seventy-eight hours earlier he'd been standing in the parlour in the exact spot that my coffin had rested in the days before I was buried all those years ago, playing online bingo on his mobile phone.

He is killed in a traffic collision three months later when his company car skids on a patch of black ice into oncoming traffic on the M4 motorway just outside of Reading.

My coffin had been small – which was to be expected – and white. Inside, pale and peaceful, I wore a bright blue dress which matched the sprigs of bluebells which my little sister had handpicked from the garden and tied in little ribbons to the ends of my little wooden home. I did not care for it, but this was probably not particularly surprising.

My mother had always thought of the dress as my favourite and had insisted I be buried in it. Truth be told, I had always found it rather uncomfortable and had disliked wearing it enormously, but I had never gotten around to telling her that. It was too late now, and so my dead body would be shrouded in scratching lace and cotton for all eternity, or at least until the worms ate away enough of the fabric to make the thing wearable.

My parents wept with a grief that rose and fell with each breath and the bitter taste of guilt in their blood which would remain until their dying days.

A gloomy pastor with a long black cassock and bad breath explained that I had gone to a better place, but really I was in the pantry at that point, so I guess it could be argued either way. There certainly weren't choirs of angels, but there was a victoria sponge cake.

Hannah's parents like my house. They like the original parquet flooring, and they like the flow through from the front parlour into the dining area and they like the spacious back bedroom. The creeping dark is more noticeable in the daytime – although it is altogether worse at night – but both

Hannah's parents are so overcome with like for the 'charming, spacious, period three-bedroom, two-bathroom, semi-detached in a quiet neighbourhood' that they failed entirely to notice the strange sense of chilling dread that permeated the back bedroom.

They make it their younger daughter's bedroom. This is probably fine.

Hannah's parents are called Terry and Debbie. They are paper people, thin and flimsy and gossamer to the touch. Pointless, sitcom people, no more real than the shadows that flutter at the corners of your eye when you are particularly tired.

Terry is tall and balding, with a large pot belly. He laughs too much when he is around strangers, and not enough when he is around his own family. He drinks Guinness and masturbates to 1970's pornographic films on the internet whenever he finds himself alone at home.

Debbie is NOT tall and NOT balding. She does not like the people that she works with, a fact that is made sadder by the fact that she runs her own florists. She no longer sees the joy in flowers that she once did and has started to feel trapped and resentful towards the business. *After all,* she thinks to herself daily, *what other choices are open to me? It's not like I can go back to college and train to be a pastry chef now, is it?*

She *could* go back to college and train to be a pastry chef. She won't.

Terry and Debbie do not seem like particularly bad parents, but I think, on the whole, I preferred mine. Terry and Debbie are not dead, which is definitely something they have over my parents, but beyond that – and despite every horrible thing they ever did - there is nothing I would not do to see my parents replace these two beige people who have infested my home.

They are beige in the way they talk to each other; they are beige in the way they are redecorating the house. They are beige in the way they make love in the night, and they are beige in the way they sit around the breakfast table with their children in the morning.

"Pass the orange juice, please," they say to each other. They yawn and pass the orange juice.

"You need to cut your fingernails, Lily. You've scratched yourself in the night."

Lily is Hannah's younger sister. She is twelve and she did not scratch herself in the night.

"Do you need a ride this morning, Hannah?"

I sit amongst them, beside my love, and slowly sour the milk to punish them for being tedious. It is difficult to see how someone as perfect as my Hannah could ever have been the product of these empty people.

My parents were never beige. My mother had a smile that lit up the world, bringing ships home safely through the storm-tossed darkness. I can remember, so often, being filled to the brim with her smile and her warmth and her scent, sloshing around inside me, filling the emptiness within me from my toenails to the very tips of each strand of hair.

My mother's father had been a head chef in an expensive London restaurant and had instilled in his daughter a love of cooking and baking which ran deep and red through her veins. To say she cooked was to say that others breathed – she would not have been herself without a mixing bowl beneath her arm and flour blossoms in her hair.

No matter what day of the week, or what time of day, the house would be filled with scents both savoury and sweet, tantalisingly, wondrously delicious – to my young mind I lived within a story-book gingerbread house, such was the total immersion in edible delights that saturated the walls and floors and ceiling of my home.

My father was a bear of a man, as huge as my mother was slight. He had a laugh that brought dust down from the trembling rafters and was quick to hug and hold. With a bottle in his hand, he would sing too loud and too long and too large – deep, soulful songs from the old country. He cared so much for my mother, my sister and me.

Too much, perhaps.

My father was a man with quick emotions and contagious moods, he filled the house as much as mother's cooking ever did. He had a knack for knowing when your mood was sour, and would *swoop* down and enfold you in his broad arms, squeezing out all doubts and fears that cobwebbed the mind.

The home of my childhood was a happy one, filled with joy and laughter and life. Not a month went by without my mother and father throwing open the front door for friends and family, warmth and light and music spilling into the streets in open-armed invitation to all.

Even now, if I close my eyes and concentrate, the wallpaper and woodwork exude the scents of perfume and cigarette smoke, the twang of alcohol and sweat of rooms fit to burst with the rhythmic sounds of dancing and laughter. Images cloud my mind – lipstick glossy mouths stretched wide in raucous exuberance; thick, pink fingers clenched around cigars the width of a baby's thigh.

That strange sense – as a child – of glimpsing the parallel world of adults so far removed from that which they seemed to inhabit day by day. That tell-tale glimmer that, perhaps, life did *and could* go on without you. An unspoken knowledge that would become very real only a few short years later.

And the dancing. *Oh,* the dancing. My parents' love for each other was lyrical, above all else, and they only needed the *suggestion* of music to embrace and dance. Whether it was in wild abandon or gossamer-light steps, mother and father's bodies would pick up the beat and follow it, moving as one.

"Another!" my father would cry once the music was done, and cigar clamped between his lips, he would spin my mother once again, laughing and loving together as another record was placed upon the player or another song announced.

They would dance for each other, or they would dance to entertain. It wasn't until much later, when I had little to do but observe, that I realised how hollow their exuberance was. How little depth there was to the raucous laughter. How my father could never take *no* for an answer.

Sometimes, at midnight, I find myself dancing their dance in the living room, threads of moonlight piercing my skin as I sway to the music of long-forgotten orchestras from a wireless that hasn't existed for over seventy years.

I choose to remember my parents as they were - happy - before my death. Before they lost their daughter. Before the fruit dropped, rotten, from the family tree.

It is a painful thing to watch your family move on without you.

It is more painful still to watch them fail to move on at all.

The Unfortunate Twelveness of My Death

I was twelve when I died

Which was
Terrible

Not the dying, as such,
(Although if I remembered more about the closing of my days I might have more to say upon the matter)
But the twelveness of my death

Twelve is a pretty wretched age, in my opinion,
Neither child nor adult,
Bored by youthful folly,
Yet without the rigidness and responsibilities of adulthood,

And an eternity trapped within that score of years did not
sit well within my youthful heart.

And so,
With a release of spirit
And relaxing of the soul
(Though words alone make shallow reflection of physical
practicalities)
I aged.

Along with my sister,
My mother,

My father,

For half a dozen years or more, I grew alongside them all,
My sister grew taller,
Grew older,
And wiser,
My parents smaller,
Older,
Weaker,
Before my eyes,
While I grew,
Unseen before *their* eyes.

Until I reached the age of twenty-one

And change for change's sake drew to a halt.
(How long could the process of ageing have continued?
- is there a me somewhere, stalking these rooms, wiz-
ened,
    bent and skeletal, root-twisted joints and balding pate
    adorned with trails of silver)

I became the young woman I had always wished; I
changed
    and moved on.
    If I could do it, why couldn't they?

Sisters

Hannah has beautiful veins. While she slumbers deeply, curled beneath the bedsheets, I imagine the brilliant dark red of them strung out across the sky – my love portrayed as a sparkling new constellation in the heavens.

My love throbs with each scarlet thread which courses beneath Hannah's porcelain skin. Bloodcells jostling and cavorting on their merry way like giddy schoolchildren at the ringing of the afternoon bell. Ninety thousand miles of glistening beauty, carrying within them each perfect breath inhaled through the perfect lips of my perfect Hannah.

I could watch them all night.

Decades before, and here is a little girl who never gives the veins in her body a second thought. They serve their purpose, run pinkly blue beneath her skin, and flow with excitement and adrenaline as she dances with her papa.

She is twelve years old, this girl, and they dance together loudly - raucous jazz music terrorising the otherwise quiet afternoon. Held tight in her father's arms, the girl feels safe, pressed tight against his grizzled chest, inhaling the spicy scents of aftershave and cigar smoke. Their feet skip in time, and they laugh and laugh, and the father twirls the girl in the parlour in which they dance, blood pumping, hearts beating in time.

The girl's mother is busy in the kitchen preparing supper but is by no means ignorant of the joyfulness which fills the adjoining room. Indeed, it brings a smile to her face and fills her heart, and sure enough, she soon finds her feet moving in time across the terracotta kitchen tiles.

Agatha – the girl's younger sister – sits curled up in the large green armchair by the window in the parlour. She pretends to read the book open in her lap and tries to swallow the feelings of jealousy that prickle behind her eyes at the sight of her sister occupying so much of their father's precious time. The blood within *her* veins seems to run a little cool, and she shivers slightly and watches the cavorting before her with a glassy smile. She hopes that, by being a well-behaved girl, she will be invited into the next dance. If she is good, she may even get to choose the song.

The father dances because he fears there may soon be very little to dance for. There are rumblings on the continent, political unrest and sands shifting under the feet of good men, who suddenly find themselves on the wrong side of battle-Iines being drawn many thousands of miles away.

Herman Mueller has recently lost his job.

His is a name which rings with enough Germanic undertones to qualify for dismissal from the factory floor, despite having left this notional homeland when he was barely more than a child. Nonetheless, his protestations fall on ears wrought deaf by nationalistic bluster, and he finds himself treated with suspicion – if not outright hostility - and the fear of hardships ahead grips at his heart.

He has yet to tell his family the bleak news.

The girl only has eyes for her papa, but his attention is split between the apple of his eye and a glass of amber-rich liquid which sits upon the sideboard.

Dancing is thirsty work, after all, and as the trumpets of the past reached their crescendo, the father stretches too far, his fingers grasping outward, and he spins his daughter a fraction too fast and a fraction too far.

In one triumphant motion, the father feels the cool glass against the palm of his hand, his grateful fingers closing around the much-needed drink. A drink which would quench so much more than mere thirst.

But as one hand grasps, the other loosens and his daughter tumbles clumsily from his embrace. Her feet skip unsteadily across the wooden floor as she tries to right herself, but the dance was too frenetic and the music bounces still and she is unable to keep her feet steady.

Her little sister notices - the first real grin of the day sliding readily across her face as her eyes light up in expectation of her sister's embarrassment. There is no meanness in her joy – it is so short lived, anyhow – but merely the recognition of a sudden shift in the focus of the afternoon's entertainment.

The girl lands with a thump against the hard wood floor. Her calves and buttocks smart against the parquet. Her back jars. Her elbows graze painfully against the linen of her sleeves as they shift upon impact. In the split-second before the girl's head swings back against the floor, she looks up at her father in shock and surprise only to see that he is still holding onto his drink. She notices the light glinting off the amber liquid it contains as, with a dull, damp thud, the sharp stone corner of the hearth around the fireplace enters the back of the girl's head.

It takes a moment or two for the pain to register and I look up into the concerned eyes of my family, desperately embarrassed, keen to get standing again as soon as possible.

"Are you alright, kitten?" my father asks, distress slurring his words slightly, as my mother comes into the room behind him.

"Yes, yes, I'm fine, Papa," I manage, pushing myself up by my elbows. With this action, pain begins to make itself known and my head starts to throb with such an intensity that it makes me feel quite sick. However, I am too focused on dismissing the whole event to pay much attention to physical discomfort.

"Oh, there's blood!" Agatha gasps, pointing at the grey stone around the fireplace.

I can't turn my head properly to look, but I can tell from the concerned look that passes between my mother and father that there is certainly more blood there than they would have liked. Which was *any* blood, really.

"Come, take a seat on the settee, darling," my mother coos, wiping her hands nervously on the apron tied about her waist. "Let's have a look at you!"

I make my way over, my father supporting me with one arm around my waist. "You are such a wild thing when you dance, kitten!" he tries to laugh. "You nearly broke the fireplace!"

I grin at him as I take a seat and feel my mother's fingers probing the back of my head gingerly. I instinctively take in a sharp hiss of breath as ice white razors skitter across the skin of my scalp.

"There's quite a lot of blood, Herman," my mother mutters.

My father's eyes flash bright. "It is a head wound, darlings. They bleed so, you know this!" His forced joviality almost manages to hit home, although I can tell from the paleness of his face that he is worried. "I'm more concerned about the damage to the fireplace, eh, Aggie?" He repeats, nudging my younger sister playfully, but she merely holds onto his broad arm and looks around at me with wide, haunted eyes.

My mother sighs, and picture her looking up at my father thoughtfully. Then she delicately pats me on the shoulder. "Let's get you cleaned up, sweetheart, and see what we've got to deal with. Agatha, darling, I've got some bandages under the sink, could you grab them for me?"

My sister climbs down from behind my father and makes her way out of the room as my mother helps me get up. I can feel my pulse pounding in my head by now, I can almost imagine my skull expanding and contracting with each thud of blood that my heart manages to push around my body. There is a strange, broken-glass sensation between my eyes which makes it difficult to see, and the fragrance of supper burning in the stove wreathes the air in the hallway as I make my way gingerly up to the bathroom.

***

Lily - Hannah's sister- is twelve years old, the same age I was when I died. Despite this, I do not think we would have been friends, even I had been alive at the same time as her.

My darling Hannah has used the move to a new house as a reinvention of the self. A cleansing of the child and a growth into young adulthood. There is little evidence within her bedroom of the child she once was, it remains an excitingly blank canvas as she sets about figuring out who she might be.

I wish I could be part of that journey with her. Help her, guide her hand in self-discovery. So far, however, she seems to disregard my attempts at reorganising her geography coursework and making the fairy lights above her bed flicker in the night as mere annoyances. Why won't she see what I'm trying to say?!

Hannah's bedroom is a Zen Garden of tranquillity compared to the riot of artistic and emotional temperament on display in her younger sister's bedroom. I try to stay away from the back bedroom as much as possible, for obvious reasons, but I do not understand the preponderance of pastel colours and glitter and doe-eyed boys with which she covers her walls.

Another wedge between us would be her love of drawing. I have never been particularly artistic - save for those moments when I am overwhelmed by Hannah's beauty. In these moments, I feel the urge to scratch out her likeness with my fingernail in the moss which grows underneath the paving stones in the back garden. Lily, however, is always drawing. She copies pictures of singers from magazines and doodles cartoon animals in the margins of her homework book. She fills notebooks with images of dark-eyed shapes with blooded mouths which she hides from the other members of her family. No wonder she screams and cries in the night, but then again, I never had felt-tipped pens when I was growing up, so who knows?

I am determined not to be too ill-disposed towards Lily however, as it is clear that Hannah loves her very much.

Hannah and Lily do not seem to need to share their parents in the same way that I had to share *my* parents with my sister. Hannah is – after all – a young woman and so hers and her sister's requirements on their parent's time are bound to be different. The relationship between mother and daughter, father and daughter are on completely different levels when the daughters in question are both entering and leaving their teenage years respectively. They suckle on completely different and individual parental teats, each receiving different and individual familial enrichment from their parents, while Agatha and I squabbled and fought over the same teat like angry piglets, slipping and writhing in the pigshit and filth of childhood while our mother and father wallowed nearby like a pair of hairy, overfed sows.

I remember staring down into her cot soon after she was born. The house still smelled of blood and cigar smoke – my mother and father's individual contributions to the introduction of new life into the family. I watched her lying there, pink and mottled, and told her in no uncertain terms that I was not willing to share my parents with her for my entire childhood.

How correct I was.

Perhaps it is ironic then, that my sister was the last person to see me alive, and the first person to see me dead.

***

The veins that serve the brain have a diameter one fiftieth of an inch. As I lay there, listening to my parents argue outside my bedroom door, these narrow little tubes, filled as they are with blood cells and plasma, began to transport inside them the tiny fragments of bone which have become detached from the minute cracks and fissures cobwebbing out from the point of impact at the back of my skull.

"We have to call for the doctor, Herman!" my mother's voice rings out, shrill and tearful.

"Nonsense!" my father replies. "When I was a child, we fell like this all the time, my darling. You don't think she's tough enough?"

"Oh, don't put this back on me! We both know the real reason you don't want me calling the doctor!"

My father splutters. "I don't know what you..."

"The drink, Herman!" she shouts, cutting him off. "You were drunk when you dropped your daughter – you should be ashamed!"

"No!" There is anger in my father's voice, although as he continues, he tries to hide it, badly. "No, you do not get to speak to me like..."

My mother cuts him off once again. "You don't want to take the blame for your daughter's injury Herman..." She paused and dropped her voice low. "Or maybe there are other reasons you don't want the doctor seeing our girls, eh? Maybe other marks not so easily explained away...?"

"Don't you dare..." my father's voice seems to bubble from within his chest, quiet and unfocused.

I try to listen further, but my head hurts too much. Already, the little shards of bone have begun their excoriating journey through my veins, each sharp little edge carving tracks through the soft tissue of my brain.

By the evening, the infection has already set in, quiet and poisonous and insidious.

By the following morning, it hurts to open my eyes to look up at my mother's worried face.

By the following evening, a fever holds me in its clammy grip.

I had died the moment I had fallen from my father's arms, although it took a total of six days, fourteen hours, twenty-seven minutes and three seconds for my heart to stop.

My father doesn't visit me once in all that time.

Roses

R oses grow from thorn'd limbs,
     Their beauty fragrancing the air.
Their colours bright – pulsing reds and beating pinks,
Velvet petals whisper gentle secrets,
Confessing love, adventures yet unplayed.

Yet sharpened stakes beneath bring forth blood,
Though charitable minds would cast doubt upon
deliberate motives.

The constancy of love is as a rose, my love,
Delicate and red, it leaves its mark.

Hannah, my love - the first night you sleep in this house you cry yourself to sleep. You mourn the life you have lost – the friends left behind, the opportunities unexplored.

The house around you, not yet a home, feels empty. Its walls are unadorned, mementoes of happier times still squirrelled away in cardboard boxes with only the barest of essentials plucked from within to make those first few hours manageable.

You do not want your family to hear that you are upset – your parents are stressed enough about moving house as it is – and so you bury your face beneath the eiderdown and sob silently in the darkness.

You do not realise it, but the quivering of your chest mirrors the twinkling of the stars in the night sky which is visible through the window of your new bedroom, the tears that squeeze from between your tightly closed eyelids the exact shape of those shed by my mother on the occasion of my death, and the blood that pumps through your heart the exact colour of the roses that used to grow in the back garden before the war.

You are a symphony.

I fall in love with you tonight. You share your sorrow with me and no one else. Come the morning your tears will have dried upon your cheek and remain hidden from your family. But for now, they pour unbidden, direct from your soul and the well of darkness it contains. I envy you, my love. The emotions you feel, the redness of your eyes and nose, the dampness of your pillow, these are things I can no longer experience.

I cannot recall the last time I cried. Some childish folly, I would guess. A grazed knee, stubbed toe, or sibling squabble which sent me rushing to my mother. Perhaps I never felt so deeply in my short life as you, my love. Another experience which was stolen from me in my youth and kept behind locked doors forever more.

But through you, I am enriched once more. Through your sadness I am made whole again – your tears nourish me like the crops in the field.

When troubled sleep finally takes you in its embrace, I try to kiss the tears from your still-wet cheeks, but to no avail. A gentle frown crinkles your slumbering brow, however, and my heart skips a beat.

My home, my heart – you are welcome to both, my love.

I hope they both bring you peace.

***

Entertainment

The screen is warm and bright. Neutral hues comfort the viewer - safe, cosy, comforting. Rest here awhile, they seem to say.

We watch a man and a woman stumble through accidental interactions scripted to convince us that there are emotions of some sort beneath their generic white chests.

And I thought Hannah's parents were bland...

The woman is the living embodiment of the word 'disgruntled': a televisual warning that perfect hair and teeth do not a perfect life create. She once worked in an office of some sort - we saw a glimpse of it a million years ago when this film first began - and now she is in a small town which seems to consist solely of bakeries and municipal community centres. People smile at her with dead eyes, their bright, cheery conversations starkly undercut with hate or pity.

Many people seem to dislike this woman, although no one comes right out and states this as a fact.

Except of course, the man. He is ruggedly handsome - if you like that sort of thing - and has clearly suffered some sort of terrible childhood trauma which has irrevocably damaged his ability to communicate appropriately with someone for whom he has feelings.

He appears to be employed as some sort of coffee shop owner-slash-handyman-slash-local politician? Whatever he does, he is clearly indispensable to the small town, as the woman cannot go anywhere without him appearing like a smiling, be-stubbled wart, deriding and insulting her with every word spat out of his face hole.

Maybe he had a distant, alcoholic mother? Maybe he was sexually abused by a violent father? Whatever the dark tune to which his soul dances, it seems to have left Mr Rugged with the impression that the way to a woman's heart is a systematic grinding down and belittling of every aspect of her life and personality. He judges her for the shoes she wears, her source of income and her lack of understanding of small-town living, whilst never acknowledging that he, himself, *would be equally out of place were he to be suddenly stranded in a cosmopolitan setting as alien to him as this home-spun back-water town is to her.*
Black ice runs through his veins in place of normal human empathy.

The woman plans the man's death, that much is clear. We, the viewer, cannot help but stand at her side. With every wince which clouds her face at another barbed word, we see in the flicker of her expression the desire to leap across the bonnet of his pick-up truck and gouge his eyes out with a blunt spoon in front of an audience of jolly old men, wide-eyed little girls, and nosy spinsters.

In my heart of hearts, I hope that, before the final credits role, the woman will burn this wholesome town to its very foundations – a brunette god in business casual - punishing them for their hubris and thinly veiled hate. I can see her now, flames sparkling within her deep brown eyes, ash smudged across the tight skin of her perfect cheeks, standing amongst the smouldering brickwork and wooden beams of the town hall, petrol canister still gripped tightly in her perfectly manicured hand.

I would not watch such nonsense if it were it not for my darling Hannah. She sits cross-legged on the edge of her bed, the eiderdown wrapped around her knees as she paints her nails a brilliant, vivid blue. Such a beautiful colour, so vibrant and *alive*, there is nothing she does which is not heaven itself. My darling's hair hangs in deep auburn curls about her shoulders, and I wish to run my fingers through, to lift the soft locks to my lips and plant just one kiss.

Her dressing gown slips down one porcelain shoulder, her flesh so sweet and scented and I rest my cheek against her, my arms around her, listening to the sweet music of her breathing, feeling the comfort of her pink towelling robes beneath my fingers. Goosepimples rise upon her flesh beneath my cheek as I breathe in the strawberry scent of her soft hair. We sit there - entwined - she mine, I hers as we watch little lives lived out upon little screens.

For a moment our viewing is interrupted as the image before us freezes and a small green shape bobs up upon the glass screen of Hannah's mobile telephone. Gingerly, taking care not to smudge her still tacky-wet nails, she thumbs the message and her eyes crinkle with loving amusement as she reads. It is obviously a message from Callie, Hannah's best friend.

I am absolutely *not* jealous.

Hannah's fingertip tip-taps across the screen in reply, before the lives of the woman and the man play out before us on the small screen once more.

There are many little screens within my home now, far more than I ever thought possible or necessary. The old woman who lived here before had very little in the way of technology. There had been a television in the parlour, of course. A huge black beast of plastic and glass whose dusty gaze took in all that was laid before it, reflecting back the distorted image of a lonely, solitary life.

Had the television set known, as it had stood witness, solid and redoubtable for oh so many decades, that it would one day sit passively watching over the slowly, desiccating corpse of its owner? I was glad, in a way, for the television.

As long as it sat there, watching the deceased move from one plain of existence to the next, the burden did not fall to me.

There were no small screens when I was a child, but now there are so many! Each member of this family seems to have at least one or two, disgorging information and entertainment at their fingertips. It seems, sometimes, that this house is filled with little glass screens and glowing lights and humming wires transmitting and emitting their bright, harsh lights.

There is no true dark within the house anymore, unless you count under the stairs or within the back bedroom.

***

The screen shines with rich, dark blues and dazzling gold. Luxury and glamour entice the viewer – brilliant, exciting, enthralling. Witness here: The Birth of a Star, the colours seem to say.

While Hannah sits upstairs in her bedroom, her mother and father sit in the living room, at either end of a large settee set out before the vast flickering television. The show itself is just a distraction to them – a pseudo-comforting background noise against which their evening plays out.

Upon the television screen, a tragedy begins. A pretty boy in his early twenties stands dead centre on a vast black stage. Busy lights flash on screens behind him as he closes his eyes in concentration and sings.

He sings to an audience of millions, although he tries not to think about it too much. Panic grips his mind if he lingers too much on all the pairs of eyes and ears which are currently giving him their undivided attention.

So, he sings instead to his mother, who sits backstage in a wheelchair, watching her only child with awe and pride and fear etched across her face in equal measure. Their life has been hard, God knows, what with the cyst she had developed on her spine and her husband leaving the two of them to start a new life with a widowed trumpet player from Ashby de la Zouche. She reaches up and squeezes her own mother's hand, seeking reassurance from the tiny elderly lady beside her – the singer's Nana – with whom they had been forced to move in with when the bailiffs repossessed the family home due to her falling behind on the mortgage repayments.

She watches her son singing soulfully on stage and prays to a God she no longer believes in – they need a win.

But despite the glitter and gold, the appreciative audience, the nodding judges and the sweet emotion of her son's voice, he will not win this competition. He will come second, beaten to first place by a girl group with marginally more polished voices and significantly more marketable attractiveness.

Disheartened, the boy will drink too much at the television show's after-party and enter into a conversation with an understanding letch of a record producer whose warm voice and cold eyes will attempt to persuade the boy of other paths to fame and fortune in the music industry.

The boy is neither as innocent nor as naïve as some might think, but alcohol and the bitterness of failure flow through his veins and later that evening, in a surprisingly well-turned-out private bathroom, the boy will get on his knees and earn himself a record deal and a lifetime of trauma.

And the boy will become a minor success. He will sing songs that appeal to middle-aged women and his first song will reach number two in the charts – although he will never manage to reach number one. He will be no stranger to the record producer and his friends, and he will drink to forget. He will have his face on magazines and his mother and Nana will be so proud of him and part of him will resent them so so much for the role they played – no matter how minor – in his degradation.

He will experience the pleasant numbing sensation of cocaine for the first time on his twenty-fourth birthday and will slash his wrists with a kitchen knife on his twenty-sixth.

His funeral will be embarrassingly small.

Debbie, Hannah's mother, watches the show, her attention split between the manufactured drama playing out upon the screen and the magazine which lays open on her lap. The room is dark, but a table lamp throws a pool of yellow light across the pages in front of her, illuminating a half-finished crossword puzzle. Distractedly, Debbie taps the black plastic lid of the ballpoint pen against her teeth, and mulls over the answer to seven down.

It is not the singing competition on the television which is causing her to have difficulty focusing, however. Her mind is occupied with other things.

She is worried about her family. She is worried about her daughters and her husband and whether the move was the right thing to do, given the circumstances. While Hannah appears to have coped well with such upheaval in her final year of college, Debbie thinks, Lily does not seem to have settled into her new school at all. The young girl has become withdrawn from the rest of her family, choosing instead to spend her free time in her room away from others. Never a particularly robust looking girl, Debbie has seen her daughter become pale and sickly looking and wishes she could *connect* with her somehow. Debbie doesn't understand – she remembers her own childhood in golden, bucolic shades of laughter and light – a childhood of girl scouts and hobbies and joyfully hanging out with friends. Her younger daughter had none of these things it seems, and part of Debbie wishes she could shake the girl and show her what her life *could* be if only she put the effort in.

Perhaps she has been too busy with the house, she thinks. The summer holidays are approaching. Maybe it would be nice to go away and do something together as a family, she thinks. Maybe that will shift the dark cloud that seems to have settled over them all, like a soot-stained cobweb.

Terry shifts uncomfortably on the settee next to his wife, who casts a nervous glance his way. His head throbs, a crackling pulsing ache which threatens to take over his entire skull. Gently reaching up, he rests his fingertips against his temple, feeling the *thud ludd thud ludd* of his pulse in the veins which seem to bulge out from the surface of his skin.

The sound of rapturous applause blossoms from the television screen and Terry winces in pain – the throbbing in his head quickening in sympathetic rhythm with the unseen audience.

The headache has tormented him for a number of days now. Its wormy little fingers seem to be pulling his skull apart from the inside, pushing into the back of his eyes, down his nose, back into the muscles of his neck. The ache has started to interfere with his sleeping and Terry knows that the disorientation brought on by a combination of tiredness and pain has led to him being irritated and argumentative with his wife and daughters.

Nothing seems to be able to take the edge off the headache – Terry has taken to throwing back handfuls of aspirin as though they were Smarties just to get though the day, staring at himself, red eyed and unshaven, in the bathroom mirror.

"It's just a bug or something that I've picked up somewhere," he mutters to himself, nervously pushing thoughts of tumours and brain inflammations and other worries far down to the back of his mind.

He occasionally wonders whether the headaches have been brought on by the move – not the stress of the situation, he feels too in control of himself for that – but perhaps something in the fabric of the house itself; some long-since banned chemical preservative or paint in the wallpaper or beneath the woodwork. The surveyors had checked the property for asbestos and other nasty surprises before they moved in, but how much did they really know?

As he skitters from thought to thought, Terry comes closer to understanding the cause of all his problems than he will ever know, before another cacophonous musical rift echoes from the television screen and sends his pained mind spinning off into other directions.

As an elderly gentleman in a flat cap and a tweed jacket replaces the pretty young boy in the spotlight on screen and begins to warble his way through *My Way*, Terry massages his temple. *If I don't get a good night's sleep soon,* he thinks to himself, *I'm not sure what's going to happen.*

***

The screen is dark. Dull grey glass reflects the bright overhead light and walls covered in youthful doodles. The room is silent, save for the ticking of a clock and the swell of a young chest rising and falling with slow, measured breaths.

The screen – the phone – sits alone, un-regarded by its owner. There is nothing within it that she needs. Lily has not offered her number to any of the other pupils in her new school – *they would not want it*, the voices tell her – and so the phone rests upon her bedside table, battery slowly dying, as the young girl sits on her bed, sketchpad in hand.

Lily concentrates. That is when her mind is clearest and most at ease. She watches her hand draw sweeping pencil-grey lines across the page with a sweet, sad smile on her face. She watches it as one might watch a kitten at play, marvelling at the focused engagement in front of her while at the same time seeming to lack control over the action.

This is nonsense, of course, and to prove that she *is* in control, Lily stops drawing abruptly, frowning at the pale skin on the back of her hand.

Yes, she thinks, *I am in control.*

She shifts her bare feet beneath her, getting comfortable on the bed. Still frowning – and fully aware that her actions might seem mad to an outsider – Lily moves her hand again to draw. But this time she changes pace, sweeping curves give way to heavy, jagged lines.

Her pencil strikes the page with such force that the structural integrity of the paper is at risk. A droplet of water plops onto the page and her eyes widen slightly. Up until that moment, the girl had not realised she was crying. She reaches up and wipes the tears from her soft, pale cheek.

Beneath the tip of the pencil, the lines on the page take form, almost imperceptibly. Not an image as such, more an *after image.* A sensation left behind – a graphite on-the-tip-of-the-tongue impression.

Pinkness rises in Lily's pale cheeks as she sketches. *I am in control*; she thinks to herself as voices on the edge of hearing whisper their low secrets from hidden places.

Suddenly, a small, insistent buzz echoes around the small room and Lily starts, the tip of her pencil juddering slightly across the page. The young girl scrunches her eyes closed and her shoulders rise as if in pain. The side of her face glows blue as the grey glass screen on Lily's bedside table momentarily lights up.

The blank grey screen returns, and Lily relaxes. As she shifts on the edge of her bed, three small droplets of blood stand out from the pale pink cotton of her nightdress. She doesn't know how they got there.

The Girl in the Mirror

The girl in the mirror with the long black hair
		And the spider eyes

And the skin like chalk
I do not love you

The girl in the dark with the rose bud lips
And the open heart
And voice like silk
I need you so

The blood in the dark with the beating pulse
And the throbbing pain
And the crawling heart
I loved you once

The girl in the mirror with the silent stare
And the haunted eyes
And the scar-flickered cheek
Let me take you by the hand.

On reflection

There are seven different mirrors in my house. In the bedrooms, in the bathrooms, in the downstairs toilet, one above the mantelpiece in the living room. Some spend their days bathed in glorious sunlight, brightening the rooms and bringing a sense of space and openness. Some of them spend their days in the dark, on the back of wardrobe doors, reflecting nothing but the gloom to uninterested shirts and dresses and the occasional moth.

But each of those that can see the light reflect back upon the rooms in which they are situated, innocently tells the story of the day. They are without guile, mirrors. Without agenda or motive, they can only reflect the truth.

I like mirrors. I cannot always see myself in them – it seems to depend upon my mood whether I am visible within their silver surface or not – but I am always there. Sometimes I run my fingertips down the glass, leaving silvery red trails which glisten in the light before fading into nothingness. Sometimes I trace the outline of a heart for my darling Hannah to discover when she showers, but more often than not, the faint marks I can make in the water droplets gather and run together before she has a chance to see my declaration of love as anything other than tracks in the condensation on the glass.

They see me, sometimes, in the mirror. No - not *see* me, that is, perhaps, the wrong word. They sense me? A flickering shadow at the corner of the eye which so readily resolves itself into the shadow folds of a bathroom towel or hanging dressing gown. Nonetheless, I sense their enthusiasm for my presence, even if they do not readily show it. I stand behind them as they wash their face or brush their teeth, staring at them, willing them to catch a glimpse of me. Watching them as they perform their mundane ablutions, oblivious, save for the prickle at the back of their neck giving any suggestion of my presence. Out of boredom or curiosity, I trace the veins at their temples with the tip of my little fingernail or set their skin shivering by the whispering of sweet words in unaware ears. They do startle so easily!

When I was younger, my girlfriends and I spoke of a game wherein we would stare into a mirror in a darkened room in the hope of seeing in the reflection the face of our future love. I never played it myself, a fear hung over the game, for if you saw a skull staring back at you, eyes of fire and a mocking bony grin, the fates had decreed that you should die before your true love was found, and I could never bring myself to carry the burden of that potential knowledge. But I do wonder, one day, that my Hannah might be tempted to play that game, and stare into the mirror with hopes of a hint for whom her soulmate might be. I hover by her shoulder whenever she is in the bathroom, just in case, although she has yet to show any suggestion that she wishes to perform such an act of captromancy.

Still, I will not give up hope. Sometimes I turn the light off when she is in the bathroom, just to give her the hint. It has not worked so far.

***

She looks into the mirror and sees a new pimple, red and sore, by the side of her nose. She sees hairs out of place from her finely plucked eyebrows and wonders what she would look like with a piercing. She wonders which would be more painful – getting her nose pierced or her eyebrow – and which one would upset her parents the most and whether she cares about that or not.

She worries that she is starting to look like her mother and searches her mirror image for signs of wrinkles upon her perfect, young skin. She is beautiful.

It is another morning, and her mother looks in the mirror at new wrinkles and old scars and wonders if her husband still finds her attractive. She wonders if she still finds him attractive. She wonders if she still loves him.

Without thinking, she worries at a grey hair which protrudes from her hairline, thick and unruly. She wonders whether she should dye her hair, wonders whether that would make the signs of aging more or less obvious. Perhaps she should go darker, she thinks. Something dramatic, brunette or red or maybe even a deep, midnight black. She thinks back to the girl she once was: rebellious at heart, desperate to make her own choices and follow her own path. A girl who would have dyed her hair in a heartbeat, if she'd been allowed.

The house around her is quiet, and of everything, this worries her the most.

Early evening, and Lily looks in the mirror and sees very little. Distant memories float reluctantly through the grey of her mind. She thinks of times gone by when she would stare at her face in the mirror for hours, making silly faces and practicing dramatic expressions. She would imagine she was an actor in a blockbuster movie, reacting (ninety percent of acting is *re*acting, darling) to the heroic leading man.

But those once expressive eyes are now red-rimmed and sore-looking, set back in a face fading away to nothing. She sticks the tip of her tongue out anyway and watches her reflection do something remarkably similar. For a moment it seems as though the tip of her reflection's tongue is forked and snake-like, but she dismisses this as nothing. It means nothing. It all means nothing.

Hannah's father shaves in the evening before he goes to bed in order to save himself time in the mornings before he goes to work. He has done this since his daughters were little, and the commute to work had to be managed around drop-offs to nurseries and childminders and the school run. Over the years it has become habit, a ritual carried out with no more thought than brushing his teeth or putting on deodorant.

But he is tired. He can feel it in himself, like a solid lump of iron behind the eyes. He doesn't mean to be short-tempered towards his wife and daughters, but neither can he stop himself from doing it. The fact of the matter is, there is a darkness behind his eyes that he does not see, a darkness that obscures his vision like storm clouds across his mind. And so, he goes through the motions as he shaves: dips his razor into the bowl, peers into the mirror, pulls the blade through the soap on his cheek – leaving behind a patch of smooth pink skin and so on and so on and so on.

A tune crosses his mind, a melody that he does not realise he has never heard before. He hums tunelessly as he shaves and dreams of big band dance halls and the intermingling scents of cigar smoke and brass polish and hot, violent acts of perversion in the darkness.

The silver edge of his razor slips and slices into the soft flesh of his cheek and blood begins to drip from the resultant wound. Pink and red and white and black, the blood mingles with the bristles and foam in the sink. Scarlet trails run down his chin – the cut is deeper than it looks. He does not notice. He does not see the open wound.

***

At approximately half past eight on the first night that Hannah and her family spend in their new house – my house – the skies above darken. Storm clouds gather and the heavens open. There is nothing supernatural or particularly portentous about the sudden precipitation, however. After all, low pressure systems had been working their way across the southeast of England for twenty-four hours beforehand, buffeted by warmer high pressure from the south, so that, by late evening, the skies were a boiling tumult of heavy greyyellow clouds. The first crackle of lightning illuminates the heavens at twelve minutes past eight and at quarter to nine wind speeds are sufficiently high to shake loose a large branch - already dead - from one of the beech trees which run alongside the road outside my house. The storm dies down shortly after, this branch and a few loose roof tiles the only casualties.

The tree branch will hang, dangling from its healthier brethren, for little under a month before being removed by a municipal gardener. By then, the damage had been done.

Emotions

The doctor's fingers are long and nicotine stained. The tip of each digit is bulbous with bitten-to-the-quick nails which lend him the air of a particularly sickly-looking frog.

With these warm, clammy fingers he pokes and prods at my enslumbered form, laying still and silent like the good, dead girl I am beneath his examinations. Despite the fact that I am standing at his side, at least a foot and a half away from the wooden bedframe, I have the strangest sensation that I can still *feel* the doctor's touch against my own cheek. That is, the one on my face here, rather than the one on the body down there in my bed. A muscle memory, perhaps? Some strange vestige of a nerve ending still hanging on in the Great Beyond? It is certainly feel no sentimentality towards my dead body – when I look at it I feel as a snake must towards its skin post-shed (although with less compunction to consume the discarded layers).

I do not care for the sensation, however, and rub my palm against my cheek to displace the unpleasant feeling. It is like an itch in an unscratchable place, or sneeze that will not come to fruition, and it is with more than a little relief that I watch the doctor finish the last of his administrations and stand, impossibly tall in this small bedroom.

His eyes flick briefly between my parents' faces and the open window. Plain linen curtains shift gently in the breeze, for a moment the only movement within the room, the gently rustling sound underscoring my mother's attempt at airing out the room, already trying hard to avoid the awful humiliation of a child's bedroom rank with the smell of death.

"Mr and Mrs Mueller, I am sorry for your loss," the doctor whispers in his deep, gravelly voice, rough from too many years of delivering similar sad little declarations. "It appears the infection from the wound at the back of your daughter's head travelled through the bloodstream, leading to a swelling of the brain tissue. This in turn may have led to her suffering a fatal stroke as she slept. If it is of any consolation, she would not have suffered."

It was true, I hadn't felt a thing. In fact, my mind held no memory of the event in any way, but I still feel irritated at the way that the doctor speaks for me, as if he knew in any way, how death might feel to those who had experienced it. I was not some ventriloquist's puppet for him to emote through for the benefit and reassurance of the living.

With eyes hot and coal black, I glare up at the doctor by my side, at the clammy, yellow skin around his eyes and cheeks, the whiskery shock of black hair perched at the centre of his otherwise balding head.

"I may not have been able to save her," he continues slowly, "even if you had called me to attend earlier."

Over the many years he has plied the medicinal trade, the doctor has learnt to keep judgement well hidden beneath more measured tones but the hyper-attentiveness of their grief ensures that his comment does not go unnoticed by my parents. My mother blushes hotly, her eyes downcast in shame.

There is a curious sensation within my heart when I look at my family, who stand beside my lifeless body as if in practice for the funeral proper which will take place in a few days' time. In much the same way that a severe headache leaves the brain feeling bruised even once the pain has passed, I sense emotion when I look at my family, sense that *something* should be firing in the synapses of my mind but only echoes of emotion remain. They mean so very little to me now.

Which is why I take no responsibility at all for my mother's death a few years later.

My sad little funeral passes with little ceremony. Sleeting rain cleanses the lid of my coffin and makes it shine like polished mahogany as it is lowered into its final resting place.

The ice grey weather beats down upon the few mourners in attendance and sends them shivering hurriedly away from the service, in search of more warming things than the graveside of a dead child. The pastor sniffs pointedly beneath the wide black brim of his dripping hat, looking at my parents as if accusing them of bringing this damp and miserable day down upon us all through the careless act of losing their eldest daughter in late Autumn. *Why not early Summer?* his wet pink nose seems to say.

And so begins the first day of the rest of my…life.

After a few days it becomes clear that this body of mine – such as it is – no longer requires food, water, sleep or indeed any of the other myriad distractions that make up the concept of 'living'. It is fortunate that, despite this, I do not seem to be suffering from boredom. Is boredom an emotion? It certainly seems that it might be, as I move between what remains of my family's daily lives, untouched and above it all. That is not to say that I am entertained by all this, but the lack of any feeling at all brings some comfort.

Time itself also seems to work differently when you are dead. It flows in fits and starts – there are moments when the world around me slows to a treacle-like crawl. The beats *between* heartbeats or the pendulum swing of the clock in the hallway stretch out dauntingly across what seems like hours. This allows me to fully absorb events played out over a few seconds at my own pace – I can take a leisurely stroll through the house and take in every detail, every half-spoken word or revealing expression which would otherwise be lost in the rapid passage of time.

Other moments, however, flit by so fast that I do not experience them at all. I pause to watch a petal detach from its flower and drift to the ground and the next thing I know months have passed and seasons have changed. The flowers before me - the petals - all gone, replaced and the open wound of losing a daughter has scabbed over that little bit more in the hearts of my family.

I have no yesterdays and I have no tomorrows. I have no todays either, come to think of it. I have only now – it is all *now.* As I say, time works differently when you're dead.

I learn more about myself in the days, weeks, months, lifetimes – whatever – after my funeral. As I walk amongst my family, through rooms which seem strangely stretched and strangely empty, it doesn't take me long to realise that I am *invisible* – to others at least.

I look down and see my body, my funeral dress, but standing in front of my mother as she brushes her hair in the mornings, she sees nothing more than a flicker of darkness which she attributes to tired eyes, rather than recognising the figure of her dead daughter before her. When I hold my hand up to the light which streams through the net curtains in the parlour on sunny days, I seem flesh and blood. But despite the way I block the sunlight, my sister sits in the large green armchair reading quietly as always. She may frown slightly at the soft sounds of floorboards creaking beneath my shifting feet but her vision remains unimpeded as I cast no darkness over her.

No physical darkness, anyway.

On emotional levels, there are pitch-black storm clouds rolling throughout the house, while my own lack of emotion affords me to see my family as they are.

As my sister sits and reads, or goes about her daily life, I see a strange sort of rage bubbling beneath her skin. She remains a 'good girl' for my parents, there are no arguments or tantrums, no sullenness to illustrate her inner turmoil, and I can't help but wonder if she has always been this way. I had enjoyed our shared childhoods to a certain extent. We had played together, laughed and told stories in the back garden. Any arguments or incidents of spite I had always put down to our being siblings.

But now, I am not so sure. Her world has changed, that much is true. But does that gentle darkness I see within come from a place of mourning? I am not so sure. There were tears, of course, upon my death. Hot, angry ones which soaked into my mother's skirt as they clung together at the graveside. And after the funeral, Agatha had sat upon my bed, eyes still red and puffy, and looked about my now-vacant bedroom in silent, youthful, contemplation.

But now, only silence remained.

If I cared more, I would watch the girl more closely. As it is, unless her discontent becomes entertaining in any way, I will leave her to her malaise.

My parents are far more watchable, as they fail to come to grips with losing a daughter. My mother and father spend as little time together as possible. They barely spend more than a few seconds in the same room together, save for meal times, and when they retire to their bed at night, a cold wall of silence lies between them beneath the bed covers. The qualities in my father that once made my mother's heart sing now hold it in bitter, twisted brambles. Where once she loved his impulsiveness, now she sees only a thoughtless fool. Where once he took control as head of the household, she now sees that he bullies them all, trampling over their hopes and dreams.

Simply put, my mother is a shadow - she has become a ghost herself. She haunts these rooms as much as I do, but more earthly-bound, doing her duties as a wife and mother in a hushed and pallid state. The only time I see her smile is when she idly tucks a thread of wayward hair behind my sister Agatha's ear or watches her sleeping from the doorway of her bedroom, her back firmly turned against the closed door that once opened into *my* bedroom.

My father does not seem to notice the new sharpness in his wife's eyes whenever she looks at him. He wishes to keep the family together – *keep them going,* he thinks to himself. Despite the numbness of death, I am sure I might feel offended by his attempts at normality if I couldn't see how glazed over with whiskey and guilt his eyes are. The ever-present drink in his hand serves to numb the creeping thoughts which saturate his mind in quieter moments – the thoughts of *what if*.

What if he had held his daughter close to him while dancing?

What if he hadn't taken that drink?

What if he had listened to his wife's pleading to call the doctor?

He swallows these *what if*s, drowning them all in glass after glass of cheap liquid anaesthetic as he tries to convince himself, and the world around him, that his family have done their mourning and moved on. In the meantime, I watch them all crumble and close within themselves, like a ball of newspaper on the hearth.

But comforting falsehoods have a draw all of themselves, particularly in times of high stress. They are tantalising and persuasive, easing the heart and appeasing the mind. They can easily take root and grow to great heights and great depths without anyone noticing that they flourish at all.

I Am

I am

The figure at the corner of your eye

The unseen fingers brushing against your hand as you reach for something in the dark

A whispered name half-heard

A shifting house in the middle of the night

The clanging of air in the pipes

The scent of perfume, of cigar smoke, of baking in the air

An open cupboard

A door slammed shut

The sensation of a spiderweb to the face in the early morning dew.

I am

The face in the mirror as you wash the soap from your eyes

The lost cufflink

The missing hairclip

The hair that stands up on the back of your neck
The swelling sense of dread, the cold sweat, the pounding heart.

I am
Yours, always.

Sweet dreams

"This house is haunted."

The words leave my love's rosebud lips and thud heavily onto the kitchen table between her mother and younger sister. Debbie barely bats an eyelid – she's fully focused on her morning coffee and the gardening catalogue spread out before her - but Lily looks over her cereal bowl with wide, owlish eyes.

A gloom pervades the kitchen. One or two of the overhead halogen lights have flickered out since this family moved into my home and they have yet to be replaced, casting the kitchen table beneath in an unwitting spotlight while shadows congregate in the corners of the room like cobwebs gathering dust. The early morning skies outside fill with bluegrey clouds, dark and heavy looking. They seem to throb with a pulse all their own and I can't help but admire the ease with which they mimic life. If only it was always that easy.

Pressing my fingertips against the cold glass of the kitchen window, I turn to stare at my darling Hannah, letting off from tracing lines of mould along the chipped window putty. Her words echo, coarse and raw, and for the first time since I was twelve years old, I feel an *echo* of excitement.

Perhaps this connection between us – this blossoming, burgeoning love across the spiritual plane – has allowed my Hannah an insight like no other before her. Does she hold the secret of my existence within her delicate hands, a secret that is no longer my heavy burden to carry alone?

My blood pounds loud enough to set off an entire percussion section in my ears. If it weren't for the fact that my heart has been maggot-feed for several decades, its wild thudding beneath my breast would have resounded from room to room, rattling the front door and disturbing the pill bottles in the bathroom medicine cabinet. Clambering down from the kitchen worktop, I see a shadow pass briefly across Hannah's face, causing her to frown slightly.

And for a moment another sensation dredges itself up from the seabed of the past only to wash over me in bitter, salty waves – fear.

If my darling Hannah know me, sees me, senses me, then why would she share this information with her miserable family? Does she not consider my existence as precious as I regard hers? Let this be *our* secret, Hannah, I silently scream. Our own, together, entwining us in its forbidden smoke and let us *be* together. Let me wrap my arms around you and dig my fingernails beneath your porcelain skin and embrace and be one clandestine form before you reveal my presence to anyone.

Why would you share me, you bitch? I certainly do not wish to share you.

Almost beyond my control, my arms outstretch across the room towards my love, aching to hold her in an all-consuming, all-silencing embrace.

As I reach out, I see Hannah's frown lift, and a gentle smile slips across her face. A wave of disbelief rolls through the space where my stomach once resided - how can she smile at a time like this?

"Yeah, it seems like a ghost has taken to moving my make-up around my bedroom," she continues through a mouthful of cornflakes. "Weird that, isn't it?"

The words filter through the buzzing in my ears, and I pull myself to a shuddering halt, the sharp tips of my fingernails mere inches from her throat. I see now, I see the sparkle in Hannah's eyes, the gentle crinkle of skin on her perfect forehead as she stares – not at me but *through* me – to her younger sister, whose downturned expression gives off such a palpable air of guilt it's a wonder that it hasn't taken physical form to fester beside me.

Slinking back to the kitchen worktop, the spectre of embarrassment clangs unjustly in my ears. I barely take in what the family are saying. The first spattering of raindrops begins to hit the windows behind me, little starbursts of water which strike like pebbles against the glass. I shiver involuntarily, despite the fact that I do not feel the cold.

"I don't mind Lil," Hannah continues. "Just put everything back where it belongs, okay?"

Her younger sister mutters a quiet apology, but her mother talks over her.

"*I* mind," Debbie says, sharply. "You're too young for make-up, Lily. You know what your dad and me think."

Lily nods quietly, but glances up to sister, her pupils pinpricks of focused accusation.

"After all," Debbie continues. "You're such a beautiful girl, you know you don't need any of that stuff."

Hannah laughs, but there is hurt beneath the humour. "Oh, and I *do* need make-up, is that what you're saying, mum?"

"That's enough out of you, missus." Debbie turns back to her youngest daughter. "Just stay out of your sister's room, okay Lily? You wouldn't want her going through your things now, would you?"

"What's all this about?"

Hannah's father's voice rings out from the kitchen doorway, and the room seems to darken.

Her mother responds without looking up, quick to dismiss her younger daughter's misdoings. "Oh nothing, don't worry about it. All sorted," she says, turning back to her own breakfast.

"No, tell me what's going on." There is a blade edge to his voice which makes them all turn towards him.

His wife frowns as she looks up at her husband, still stood in the kitchen doorway in his pyjamas and flannel dressing gown. "It's fine love, don't worry," she says, her voice tinged with slight concern.

Debbie can see the change in her husband. He is not sleeping properly, and she knows that he spends the nights tormented by bad dreams the contents of which he does not share with her.

In the artificial light of the kitchen, she sees how unwell he looks, how sallow his face has become, waxy and pale. The skin around his eyes looks grey and tissue thin – Debbie can almost see hair-like veins pulsing beneath the fragile flesh. *Where has the man I married disappeared to?* she wonders as her husband stands there, uneven kitchen tiles creaking slightly beneath his feet, tension rolling off him like billows of dry ice.

Terry turns his sore, tired eyes to his youngest daughter. "Have you been stealing from your sister?" he asks, slowly, tasting bitterness within each word.

"Honestly, dad, it's nothing," Hannah begins, the ancient animal parts of my darling girl's brain sensing the danger in her father and setting out to defend her younger sister without truly understanding why.

Terry shuffles one be-slippered foot across the threshold of the kitchen, and from my position on the worktop I watch the three females shift imperceptibly in their seats, away from him.

"I don't think it's *nothing*," Terry continues, through teeth so gritted it's a wonder little chips of enamel aren't flying from between his lips. He swivels his head uncomfortably to stare at his eldest daughter through bloodshot eyes. "I don't think it's *nothing* at all, young lady. Maybe *you* don't give a *fuck* about respect and privacy and *fucking* morals, but *I* do."

His words, his profanity, strike his family with more force than a sharp backhand across the face ever could, and Hannah's eyes glisten wetly at her father's unexpected attack. Debbie looks up in horror and confusion at her husband. In all the years they have been together, he has never sworn at her or their children, at least, not in anger. He might be cold towards them sometimes, but never *this*. Above all of them, she alone fears the truth. She fears there is something sick within her husband.

"Maybe you'd care more about this *fucking* family if you spent a little more time here," Terry spits these words at his eldest daughter, an ugly sneer stretching the cold, yellowing skin of his face. "Instead of being out all hours of the day and night as though you're *fucking* ashamed of us. What a *fucking* piece of work you are!"

The glistening in Hannah's eyes becomes full and heavy, large pendulous tears forming on her lower eyelids before rolling down her delicate cheeks and soon she begins to silently cry. A protective surge rises in my empty chest. What is going on with me? One after another of these white waveheads of emotion roll and break over me this morning, leaving behind inky, foamy patterns of flotsam across the bleak, grey sands of my soul.

And beneath it all there is something unknowable - a stirring within me? Perhaps. I watch this strange drama unfold and feel torn. There can be no doubt that this stands out as the only interesting moment in the cavalcade of dreariness which is every *other moment* of the few months of this sad man's life that I have been unfortunate enough to witness. But at the same time, there is something in the twinkling of tears in his daughters' eyes which lines my stomach unpleasantly, like nausea. I do not like the way he speaks to them.

Terry raises his arm, jutting out one finger towards Lily. Thin and unhealthy looking as his arm is, it is guided by some unseen strength. Veins and tendons stand up from pale flesh between swirls of coarse hair as he jabs viciously towards his youngest daughter.

Above their heads, one of the remaining kitchen lights flickers momentarily, but all concerned are far too focused on the figure standing before them to notice.

"Stay the *fuck* out of your sister's bedroom," he barks.

He brings his fist down in one hard-swung curve, striking the kitchen table and sending cups and half-finished bowls of cereal clattering. A mug of coffee emblazoned with a picture of a smiling cartoon cactus skitters over the edge of the tabletop and hits the linoleum, where it breaks into several pieces. Terry has broken the fifth metacarpal of his right hand as well, although it will be several hours before he is lucid enough to realise the fact.

"Terry! Terry, what's gotten into you?" Debbie cries, mother-bear instincts finally pulling her from her seat. She rushes to her husband and lays her arm across his heaving chest, holding him back. She places her hand against his cheek, feeling the iciness of his skin. She resists the urge to recoil, the unnaturalness of him raising the hairs on the back of her neck as she tries to calm her husband. "Terry love, stop this," she says, her voice wavering and nervous.

From the kitchen table her daughters watch as she speaks softly to this man who - until this moment – had barely even raised his voice to them in anger. Wide eyed, Lily sits struck dumb by her father's words; her pale face streaked with tears and snot, the bile in her stomach churning as the fight-or-flight instinct runs riot through her body. Hannah – my Hannah, so loving and full of care – reaches across to her little sister and pulls her close.

The man before them lets out a low growl and resists momentarily as his wife gently begins to push him back away from the kitchen, before relenting and allowing himself to be guided back down the darkened hallway, away from the kitchen.

I watch as Hannah gently strokes the back of Lily's hair, as the young girl's sobs break the surface and begin to pitter patter down onto the front of her older sister's pyjama trousers, echoing the drip drip drip of milk from an upturned bowl of cornflakes splashing down from the table onto their mother's empty seat. Hannah plants a loving kiss gently on the top of Lily's head and stares off through the kitchen doorway through which her mother and father have now disappeared. She is more frightened than she has ever been in her life.

"I'm sorry."

Terry mumbles quietly to himself as his wife gently but determinedly leads him back upstairs. He repeats the words again and again, mewling his apologies like an injured kitten.

"That's…that's okay," mutters Debbie, her voice tight with concern. "You're obviously not well, love."

She looks up at her husband, but his eyes do not find hers – he stares off, unseeing as they cross the threshold of their bedroom, which is tastefully decorated in neutral cream and stone.

Once inside, Debbie tries to encourage her husband back into bed. His *sotto voce* apologies dry to a low murmur, his lips moving and twitching quietly, his eyes blank and downcast, as his wife seats him on the edge of their marriage bed.

What was it? she wonders as she grapples with the man she has been married to for over twenty years. *A stroke? A psychotic break? Some sort of brain aneurism?* It could happen, couldn't it? A sudden, dramatic shift in personality occurring because someone had a tumour pressing against some part of their brain. You read about that sort of thing in trashy magazines – 'Tumour turned my Hubby into Sex Pest', and so on.

Terry's breath is sour and his face is lined – more so than normal, she feels - as though the sickness that has invaded his mind has sapped the elasticity from his flesh as well. His whole body seems to hang, defeated from his shoulders like old cloth and Debbie sends yet another silent prayer up to the heavens above that this is just a temporary blip. As she helps her husband to swing his legs up onto the bed she notes, with not a little alarm, that he is visibly aroused. Dark thoughts tumble across her mind and she wishes, for a moment, that she had some way to lock their bedroom door behind her as she goes to leave the room.

"I...I'm sorry," her husband's voice trails after her and she looks back at him from the doorway.

"Don't worry, love," she manages, raising her voice above the bitter notes of fear and anger that have been echoing across her mind throughout, "Don't worry. You're not well, is all. I'll call the doctor; you just get some rest."

She leaves her husband to his soundless apologies and shuts the door firmly behind her. Her back against the magnolia painted wood, she closes her eyes tightly for a moment and screams silently, her mouth stretched so wide that the skin at the corners hurts and for a moment she pictures the taut flesh splitting, sending warm rivulets of scarlet trickling down her chin and splattering onto the beige landing carpet.

Then, she regains control – as all mothers do. She takes a deep, slow breath or two to calm herself, before making her way downstairs to comfort her daughters. For a moment, woody notes of cigar smoke hang unnoticed in the now-still air of the upstairs landing, before dispersing into nothingness.

***

One day, nine hours, thirty-five minutes and twenty-seven seconds prior to his violent outburst – and seventeen days, twelve hours, forty-six minutes and three seconds before he receives a puzzlingly clean bill of health from his GP – Terry lays in bed while his wife busies herself getting ready for sleep elsewhere in the house. He has a book open in his hands, but struggles to read it, the words seeming to swim before his eyes. He puts the book face down on his lap with a sigh and closes his eyes tightly, pinching the bridge of his nose in frustration.

Debbie enters, oblivious to his discomfort. She holds her fluffy yellow dressing gown closed with one hand, in the other she carries a glass of water.

"I think that milk's gone off in the fridge," she says as she sits on the edge of the bed and kicks off her slippers. "I don't understand, I only got it the other day."

She shakes her head as she slides underneath the duvet cover. Terry winces as she talks. He can sense his own irritation, like a tightly clenched fist in his chest, and tries his best not to show it. After all, he figures, it isn't his wife's fault that his brain feels like sandpaper within his skull.

"I'll have a look at the fridge over the weekend, check the temperature setting," he responds, his eyes still closed against the dim light of the bedside lamp. "Otherwise, we'll have to get someone in to fix it."

"Is a fridge repairman a thing?" Debbie muses, taking a sip of water.

Beside her, Terry shrugs. "We've only had it a couple of weeks, they'll have to do something about it if the bloody thing's not working properly."

Debbie nods in mild agreement and they slip once again into familiar silence, broken only by the sound of Debbie turning pages of her magazine and – from Terry's point of view – the thumping sensation of his blood pounding through his temples.

He turns his head slightly – keeping his movements slow to avoid the pain of the left and right hemispheres of his brain clattering together – and peers at his wife through one half-opened eye.

"Did you have a word with her?" he asks, trying hard to keep the sharpness of annoyance out of his voice.

Debbie sighs and puts down her magazine. Now it is her turn to close her eyes. "I told you; I don't think it's anything to worry about. The messages weren't…rude or anything, you know? Just chatting."

Terry shrugs again. It was his wife who first noticed the text conversations between Lily and an unknown number and brought them to his attention, but since she had 'stumbled upon' them while surreptitiously snooping through her youngest daughter's phone when the girl was sleeping, the idea of introducing the subject into casual conversation was proving tricky.

"Does Hannah know anything about it?"

Debbie shook her head. "I'm not sure they're talking much at the moment, not since the move, you know?" She bites her bottom lip thoughtfully for a moment, in silent contemplation, before continuing brightly: "So, I was thinking forsythia for the back of the garden. Something nice and bright, you know?"

Her husband shifts position in bed and lets out an inadvertent groan as his brain seems to squirm like a moray eel between his temples.

"Is it still bad?" Debbie asks with mild concern, slightly put out that her train of thought was interrupted. It is, after all, just a headache.

Terry rests back against the headboard of the bed.

"I'm sure it'll be fine in the morning," he says, trying to make light of things. "I just need some sleep, that's all."

Seeing that Terry is unlikely to be stricken down by a fatal brain aneurism during the night, I wander away, bored, through the central heating system. As I make my way, I hear him muttering as he rests his weary head on his cotton and polyester blend pillows.

"And the noise of those pipes doesn't help either…"

I smile to myself as I walk towards the other end of the house, where my beloved Hannah slumbers gently.

****

In the early hours of the morning, Terry's unravelling mind finally allows him to drift off to sleep. He dreams.

A young boy walks through open fields beneath a clear blue, summer sky. There are clouds on the horizon which threaten a future cooled by rain, but for now the air is warm and pleasant, not yet touched by darker skies.

The journey across the field is hard going as the grass is badly in need of cutting and the tips of each strand brush against the turned-up hem of his shorts. But still, he wades through the plant life happily, the soil dark and rich beneath the stalks of emerald green. This is a summer's day exploration, with no sense of urgency, and if the journey takes twice or three times as long as planned, the knowledge of this does nothing to darken the boy's mood. The grass itself is filled here and there with wildflowers; bright reds and yellows and blues explode within the lush green grass, lending their dusty fragrance to the warmth of the air.

The gentle breeze is sweet and crisp, birdsong on the edge of hearing and a rhythmic ticking sound sends each individual leaf and petal pulsing in time with the beat of the countryside.

The young boy pauses momentarily and takes a long, slow, deep breath, bringing the *life* around him into his lungs, filling him up to the very tips of his fingers. He smiles, at peace, and looks towards the dark line of trees at the edge of the horizon. With the confidence of those of us who are led by our dreams, he wades off, through the field, towards the beckoning forest.

Though still lengthy enough to brush against the boy's grazed knees, the grass at the edge of the forest grows patchwork, exposing the dark earth beneath. The rich black scent of it fills the air as the boy's journey takes him from field to woodland. A merry little tune rises to his lips and he whistles happily as he makes his way between the trees.

The forest is shaded, but not unpleasantly so. The brightness of the sky above dapples down through wide stretched branches and leaves which flicker in time with the ever-pervading ticking ticking ticking which thrums at the back of the mind, more insistent with every step the young boy takes. The scent of bluebells and night-flowering catchfly hangs in clouds between the broad, dark trunks of the surrounding trees, fragrancing the air with sweet melancholy overtones.

The boy frowns slightly and looks down. His exploration has begun to slow, his movement hindered, and he peers at his feet. Beneath them, the earth has become darker, stickier – clods of it cling each time he raises a foot - twigs and leaves adhere to his shoes and socks, glistening with the thick, black dirt.

The boy... does not seem to mind. The narrative of the dream drives him onward, wading between trees and past lush, overgrown bushes towards a clearing of sorts amongst the greenery. The *tick tick tick* has now become the *schlopp schlopp schlopp* of a heavy dripping liquid, the sound of which reverberates from tree to tree and branch to branch. It matches the thrum of the boy's heartbeat, although he has yet to realise this.

The clearing into which he steps is barely worthy of the name. The surrounding trees thin out, perhaps, the overhanging leaves sparce enough to allow more of the summer's light through, but there is no sense of openness or freedom amongst the woodland. A large, gnarled oak tree – long dead – stands at the centre and within its thick lower branches, the source of the all-pervading *schlopping* sound.

At first, the boy takes it to be merely an extension of the dead tree's warped form – and perhaps at first it is, as dream logic twists and turns the story as it sees fit. But then, its true form is revealed:

A large black dray horse stands, entangled with the tree itself, its large front legs hooked up and over one of the wide branches which runs parallel to the ground as though caught mid-gallop. Its head hangs to one side, its neck twisted and painful-looking. The boy looks on in wonder at the beast and tree so entwined. Deep furrows have been carved out in the ground below, where the horse's powerful-looking hind legs have kicked and skidded, churning the dirt and grass beneath hooves the size of wastepaper baskets.

But now, within this sylvian temple, the dray horse's kicking days are over. The fight within it has dissipated. It hangs, suspended by its front legs from its natural crucifix of ivy-choked oak, steam rising in whorls and curlicues from its lustrous blackbrown flanks. The trees which surround boy and horse stand in respectful silence, the fragrance of the earth beneath them almost rich enough to mask the strange metallic scent which hangs in the air.

From a head which matches the boys own frame in size, a large glossy eyeball stares calmly upward, resigned and broken, and from the horse's broad neck, the slow, steady, *rhythmic* flow of blood from an ugly, jagged wound.

The blood patters down into the dirt beneath the trapped creature, puddles of iron-rich scarlet soaking into ground, turning it a glossy black, enriching the earth about the roots of the tree and beyond - soaking into the forest itself and the grass and wildflowers of the fields.

The boy is drawn towards the horse, and for once, he is nervous. The horse's nostrils flare at the scent of the boy as he reaches out and runs his fingers along the dray horse's muzzle, feeling the warmth of the beast, the softness of its sleek, black hair.

The dray horse's large billiard ball eye swivels around in its socket, staring up at the intruder. Underscored by the gentle, insistent sound of the beast's life blood draining away, the boy stares deep into the dark, glossy surface of the eye. Within its shining surface, madness reigns, and knowledge too. Deep knowledge, a knowledge which fills the boy's mind. He sees terrible things in the darkness, the *pitter patter pitter patter* of blood becoming screams and the pounding of drums in the blackness into which he stares. There are stars there, and something worse, much worse, much darker than the void, that dances behind the stars and between the flickering flames, that dances in time to the pounding of drums within the boy's mind.

Long gone is the forest, the mud and fields beyond. Long gone is life, and innocence. A madness reigns within the world within the eye within the boy's mind, a terrible, wonderful, destructive madness of all things knowable and *unknowable*.

The boy begins to weep.

And in his fitful sleep, so does Terry.

For You

I breathe for you
    With every breath I do not take.

My heart beats for you
With every beat it cannot make.

My soul stirs for you
Uncertain as I am, it lingers still

My hands reach out for you
I long to caress
And try to suppress
My urge to kill
For you

Family strife

I am bored.

It is a little past one in the morning and the house is still. Beneath the ever-present background hum of electricity, only the sounds of gentle slumber fill Hannah's bedroom. I sit on the end of her bed and watch the eiderdown gently rise and fall over her sleeping frame, her eyelids flickering as she dreams sweet nothings.

My fingers twitch as the devil seeks them out and I look about the room to see if there is something with which to occupy them. The tips of each finger skip across her desk, her shelves, each ornament and knickknack a piece of my darling's soul, a piece of *her*, frozen and held aloft in the light and my mind sings at the idea which settles amongst my thoughts like a cuckoo's egg.

Hannah deserves a gift. Oh, selfish girl that I am, content enough to moon about my love and basking in her very presence! I have been blind to see that she might need more from me, more than just dewy-eyed promises, half-whispered in the night. A gift it will be, a piece of me and a piece of her, entwined about her heart – if I get this right. A keepsake of a love she does not yet know or understand.

I set about tearing a strip of silk from the lining of my skirt, scoring a line with the edge of one of my nails. I catch the piece before it can flutter to the ground and hold it up against the moonlight. I cannot lie, there is a sense of giddiness which flutters in my chest at the thought of such fabric wrapped around my darling's wrist.

But it is not enough. It must be an intertwining, a coming together of the two of us. I look over at my love, barely visible beneath her bedcovers, only the spool of dark hair spilling across her pillow giving any indication that she is there with me.

Her beautiful hair, a pool of emptiness in the darkness of the room. A piece of her, a piece of me, what could be more symbolic, more fitting a keepsake?

Her bedsheets do not rumple as I take a seat beside her, but the fine strands of her hair stick to the tips of my fingers as I trace them through her gentle locks. The sensation brings with it a quivering of the heart, a flowering warmth as I twist a collection of the longest of the hairs from the back of her head around my knuckles. When a fine enough collection has been gathered, I *pull.*

She wakes, inevitably, with a gasp. Perhaps the excitement of the moment, as thrilling as it is, also resonates with her somehow? Some unseen electricity of anticipation filling the air. I return to the desk as Hannah sits up in her bed, rubbing her head and staring about the darkened room. I can practically hear her heart pounding in her chest.

She cannot see my work in progress – how foolish I was to gather my resources here in her bedroom, but luckily the back of the chair tucked under the desk masks them from view. I remain unseen before her – both a blessing and a curse.

As I begin to plait the ribbon and hair together, Hannah mutters to herself and slides back down into bed, although the way she tosses and turns suggests that a return to sleep will not come easily. In fact, it is not long before a searching hand turns her bedside lamp on, and she throws the covers off and swings her legs out of bed.

She makes her way to the bathroom.

I decline to follow her - a lady deserves her privacy and besides, there is nothing there to interest me - and so I return to the job at hand, slowly plaiting the bracelet into existence. After a minute or two I hear her feet padding on the landing, before she stops and I hear her speak.

"Lil, are you okay?"

Her sister's bedroom door is slightly ajar and a thin grey light spills from the gap. She pushes the door open further to see Lily sitting up in bed, the light from her phone illuminating her face, her eyes red and sore looking.

"Lil, what's the matter?"

Lily puts her phone face down on the bed guiltily and the room darkens. She sniffles slightly as she looks up at her big sister in some alarm. "N...nothing!"

Hannah frowns. "It doesn't look like nothing, Lilly. What's the matter, why aren't you asleep?"

Lily just shrugs and for a moment Hannah feels like rolling her eyes and walking away, but she manages to stop herself. She sits on the edge of the bed and places an arm around her younger sister.

"You can tell me anything, you know that?"

Lily nods her head slightly. Hannah sighs and hugs her sister closer.

"I know... I know it's really weird at the moment," she says, consolingly. "It's tough starting a new school, isn't it? Making new friends. Mum and dad..."

She trails off, aware that she is balancing on the edge of a precipice of worries that she is not able to think about just yet, let alone talk about with her little sister.

"It'll all sort itself out, I promise." She kisses her little sister on the top of her head. As she does so, she notices the phone – its screen still aglow – face down on the bedcovers.

"Is everything okay at school?"

Lily shrugs.

Hannah hugs her again. "Don't worry, you will make friends."

"I have a friend," Lily mutters quietly, coldly.

"Oh. That's...that's good."

They hold each other in silence for a moment, their eyes adjusting to the gloom. Lily rests her head against her sister's shoulder.

"Do you remember when Nana Janet died?" she asks suddenly.

Hannah frowns, confused. "...Yeah?" She had been twelve at the time, her sister only six. Nana Janet had been their dad's mum – a smiley pixie of a woman who smoked like a chimney. The day after she had found out that Nana Janet had died, Hannah had burst into tears in the middle of her maths lesson and her parents had had to be called to come to her school to pick her up.

"It feels like that," Lily continued.

"What do you mean?"

Lily pauses, and when she speaks again, her voice is thick with sadness. "When she died, and dad was so upset, and he... disappeared. Like, inside his head. And mum was always trying to be happy but you could tell she'd been crying, and no one was saying anything at all, there was just this thick fog of *grey* filling the house and it was so horrible. Don't you remember?"

Yes, she remembered. Although she hadn't realised that her little sister had been so aware at the time. Sure, Lily had been upset at the news, but by the next day or so she'd happily skipped off to school, seemingly without a care in the world. Hannah would have put good money on her sister not even being aware of the oppressive pall that hung around the house during those few months.

"Yeah, I remember," she says, quietly, giving her sister another kiss on the head. "But it didn't last forever, didn't it? Mum and dad are just stressed about the move and everything, don't worry. Everything will be okay in the end."

Nothing more is said, but Hannah does not leave her sister's side. There are tears still to be shed that night, but they are together, Lily safe in her sister's arms.

I am trying so hard not to hate the little brat right now.

I stand in the doorway – even now, I cannot bring myself to enter the back bedroom – and I can feel a cold rage creeping through me. Why does *she* get Hannah and not me? I twist the plaited bracelet in my hands, trying to keep myself calm. The half-finished thing bites into the soft flesh of my palms but I do not care. It feels good, it reminds me that I am here, keeps me grounded.

If I had a stomach, I swear I would vomit across the landing in protest.

Perhaps my Hannah doesn't deserve a keepsake, if she is so willing to abandon me. Why can I not be the one held in her arms, to be comforted by her? Why not *me*?

I make my way back into Hannah's empty bedroom and marvel, not for the first time, the way that a room seems to wither without an occupant. I sit on the edge of the bed and my shoulders sag.

In the thin light of dawn, the bracelet I have made looks like nothing more than a collection of ragged, blood-stained fabric and matted hair. There is no love there, no deeper meaning. It is an embarrassment, nothing more, and I can barely bring myself to look at it. My cheeks flushed, I sweep it into the wastepaper basket before Hannah can see it.

Love makes fools of us all.

For the next two and a half hours, every drop of water in the house turns to blood. However, because the family is asleep, they do not notice.

I am bored.

***

The war brought with it the scent of meat and rusted metal. Sweat-grimed cotton and thick, dark soil. It is the smell of electricity in the air – heavy, like damp sheets hung loosely on a washing line.

War brings with it dark nights spent shivering in a damp tin shelter at the bottom of the garden. Dimly lamp-lit, the walls of the little hut shake in rhythm with the nervous hearts beating within.

During those wartime years, twelve high explosive bombs are dropped upon and around the little town where my family live - where my spiritual form takes root - and the siren song of each one drags my father, mother and sister into far closer a proximity than any desire. Compared with the vast dangers of the wider theatre of warfare, this relatively low number of explosives will be rounded down and rendered to practically nothing in the annals of war, but for my family and others like them, each one will bring them mentally and physically closer to death.

Even from an outsider's point of view such as mine, the weary terror of day-to-day life is palpable.

I do not care to spend time in the shelter with my family. I do not care to feel the tension between my parents, or listen to my sister's quiet tears as she struggles to sleep, blanketed in disquiet and damp sheets. I do not wish to listen to the sullen grunts which pass for conversation between my father and mother, the warmth that once lay between them replaced with a film of cold, grey grit.

Air raid streets are a strange place to be, at once empty and thrumming with life all at the same time. Far above my head, the edges of clouds are painted in soft lines of light as frightened boys do distant battle to protect the dreams of men who live in comfort far below and far away. Out of solemn respect for these desperate pilots, the nighttime streets lie dark and empty: streetlamps dimmed and windows blocked against the enticing call of metal death from above.

Once or twice across the years, destruction falls from on high and the silence of the empty streets is shattered by blood and rubble, where shopkeepers and office workers don tin hats and look for life amongst the dead. A child's hand sticks out between dusty bricks, searching for a loving embrace, for comfort in those last crushing seconds of life.

There is a cold sort of comfort amongst the darkened, shuttered streets when the sirens sound. While families such as mine huddle in fearful protection, empty streets belong to empty hearts, and a perverse calm holds high streets and homes within its peaceful grip. Like a mouse caught and held by still, strong fingers, there is a focused silence that stalks these wartime streets, while watchful hearts beat with fearful pitterpattering.

Even the tears shed for life and lives lost are sobbed in silence when the lights go out.

And it is within this pall of salt-stained cheeks that my mother, father and sister live their days. If the smell of cheap whiskey which hangs about my father was not thick enough besides, the tension which flows like black bile throughout his veins creates a barrier between himself and the world which paints each mood in deep, shadowy darkness. Suspicion of his Germanic name and accent are enough to keep the man from working, his national ties robbing him of pride and purpose as he hides in semi-self-induced isolation from his adopted homeland and their perceived distrust and hatred. He sits and reads and drinks within a numb aura of self-pity and wounded fury at the inequalities and unfairnesses of the world.

His silent rage is no less quietened by the fact that – in a bid to 'do her bit' and provide for her family - my mother begins working in a small arms munitions factory just outside of town, manufacturing empty brass cartridge cases ready for shipping further afield for filling and finishing. She enjoys her work. It brings her a sense of purpose and focus that she has not felt in a while, the feeling of being part of something bigger than herself, something more important.

It also gives her an excuse to be out of the house for the best part of the day, a desire to be away from the sharp-toothed trap of a house within which she would have found herself stuck were it not for the *duty in a time of great need* which called her to the factory floor.

She tries to hide the skip in her step as she leaves each morning to catch the number fifty-three bus which takes her to her place of work and newfound freedom.

But as fulfilling as my mother finds working at the factory, the days are still long and tiring and she often finds herself returning home on an evening with little patience for my father's increasingly irrational and irritable state. It is with a curious mix of fear and weary tiredness that she steps through the door at half past six, hangs up her coat, slips off her shoes and enters back into the family home. She leaves her bag where it falls and drops her keys and purse on the small table in the hall.

On one such day – a Friday like any other – she is particularly tired. A recent fire in the W J Daniels & Co

in the high street has diverted all traffic and added another hour to her commute to and from work, and she practically *shakes* with exhaustion as she steps through the door. Because of this, she takes a small, brown envelope from her coat pocket and leaves it on the hallway table along with the rest of the detritus of everyday life – her poor bones ache and she forgets, for a moment, that it would be far more prudent to keep the thing hidden from view.

However, she does not, and it catches my father's eye as he stands, as usual, in the doorway, watching her return to the family home. Reaching forward and picking the envelope up with fat, pale fingers, he glances down at it. At the same time, he shifts his weight slightly, blocking the doorway and preventing my mother from stepping any further into the house.

"What is this?" he asks accusingly, the brown paper crinkling in his grip.

"This week's wages," my mother replies quietly, not able to meet her husband's eye.

"No," he mutters, simply.

The back of my mother's neck prickles as she senses danger in her husband's tone, and in silent prayer she asks for two things: one, that any scene that might arise from this encounter will be quick, and two, that her daughter will be far away in her room and not be witness to any vileness on the part of her drunken sot of a father.

"No," he mutters again. "This is not your wages. Look," he holds out the envelope before her but even as he speaks, she knows that he is about to say. "This name, on the envelope, it is not you." His words slur ever so slightly as he jabs a thick finger at the name written clearly in ink on the front of the envelope. "This," he continues, "is Mrs Miller's wages."

What can she say in reply? What can she say that her husband does not already know? That she had deliberately supplied her employers with a false name, without which she would not have been hired in the first place? That she was as ashamed of her married name as he was proud, a perverse inversion of feelings brought on by so much more than the international warfare rocking the globe? That this job was yet one more nail in the coffin which contained their once happy marriage? Why would she bother saying any of this – her husband knew it all anyway.

A lie briefly flitters through her thoughts: the whole thing is a mistake, an envelope mistakenly plucked from the pack, the difference in spelling unnoticed, but my mother knows she does not have the skills to pass this fabrication off as truth and this potential balm is too late – her lack of response to her husband's question has already said too much.

Above the heartbeat silence of the small hallway, there is no sound, save the crumpling of brown paper within my father's meaty hand. He stares at his wife with dull, angry eyes.

"*Ich verstehe*," he murmurs, tiredness woven through his words as the tiny flame of – something, hope, perhaps – flickers out beneath this idle betrayal. "I see what it is. Mrs Miller…" he raises his voice. "*Mueller*, you are. *My* wife." He moves towards her, looms over her, and as he begins to shout, copper-coloured flecks of spittle strike the front of my mother's blouse. "You are ashamed of me, is that it? You stupid whore, you think you are better than me? Better than this, our life together?"

Not wishing to engage with her husband – more alcohol and anger than man - my mother tries to move past him, but he pushes her back. A flash of indignant rage passes through her.

"Don't push me!" she cries, frowning at the man before her. He stares her down for a moment, perturbed by the spark of defiance that glitters within her dark eyes. Then, with a lazy grunt, he raises a hand as if to strike and smiles to see that she starts back. He chuckles to see her react to the power over her that they both perceive still exists, albeit in tatters and shreds.

"Yes, my kitten, you can be Mrs Miller at work," my father lowers his hand. "I *allow* it."

He moves aside to let his wife enter the rest of the house. As she walks off into the kitchen to prepare a dinner of sorts, he calls after her: "You come home to *us*, to the bosom of your family, and we will be here waiting every day. Do not forget that! You belong here, my kitten!"

These last words he shouts back at the empty kitchen doorway, before stooping down and plucking the crumpled envelope which contains his wife's wages up from where it fell on the dark parquet flooring. Tearing open the envelope, he counts out each shilling – the sweat from his wife's brow in tarnished silver. With a grunt of mild disapproval, he looks back over his shoulder at the slight form of his wife, before pocketing the coins in his hand. Although my family have no way of knowing it yet, the luxury of relying on my mother's wages will run out long before the dogs of war cease their squabbles.

***

I know very little about the technicalities of being dead. I do not know, for instance, *where* I am. Whether the plane of existence in which I find myself is someplace *other* than the physical world in which my family lives (lived? As I've said before, time works differently here.) Is this an afterlife, of sorts, or just some other life, separate from the living?

In the decades since my death, I have yet to come across another spirit such as myself. Does that mean I am the only one, or are there others nearby who are just as invisible to me as I am to the living souls who haunt my family home? What if there is some *other* other place out there – a place where *other* spirits observe me as I observe the living? If so, I hope they are kinder in their judgements than I am.

I have not, however, remained completely unvisited during these four-and-a-half-score years of spiritual abandonment. The cat hung around for a while – a gingerbrown swirl in the mists of nothingness.

I saw neither hide nor hair of my mother after she died, but then, perhaps that was a punishment of sorts. It was, after all, my fault that she killed herself.

My sister receives a paint set for her eighth birthday – seven different colours in a bright red tin – which she uses day in and day out until every part of the world about her has been captured in watercolour to her satisfaction and each little block of paint has worn down to the bare metal underneath. For her ninth birthday she receives a hard cover copy of Little Women and has a party with six of her friends in the back garden. Jelly and ice cream are served, as well as small triangular ham sandwiches and a cake covered in white icing. There are nine candles on top of the cake and I watch my little sister blow each one out, one after the other.

For her tenth birthday, my sister receives a small metal Singer sewing machine. She has no affinity for sewing, but dutifully tries her best with the machine, like a good girl.

From the age of five, nothing in my home truly belonged to me. I had to share everything – my toys, my books, my parents' love. From the moment of my sister's birth my mother and father had no time for me and me alone, the time had to be carefully divided, sliced down minutely: thin slice by thin slice of seconds and minutes and hours of time equally shared between the two of us.

I never had a small metal Singer sewing machine, is what I am saying.

It seems as though my mother dotes on her one remaining daughter with all the love that she would have lavished on two. I had to share my childhood, my sister does not.

Not that I am *jealous*. I am not *jealous* of the paint set or the small metal Singer sewing machine. I am not *jealous* of the birthday parties. I am not even *jealous* of the tabby kitten that Agatha gets on her eleventh birthday, despite always having been refused a pet of my own. She names the kitten Milly and seems oblivious to the fact that these gifts and the over-the-top shows of affection towards her on the part of my parents are merely a thin layer of whitewash over the crumbling plasterwork of their own relationship; tarnished copper coins to pay the Ferryman of guilt to navigate Agatha through the loss of an older sister.

They walk through life with gossamer fragile skin, their emotions and motivations so painfully obvious to those with the ability to see.

Agatha dotes on the kitten ludicrously – mirroring my mother's attempts at be-ribboning her own hair and singing jolly songs to lighten the mood in her own ministrations to the poor feline. Dissatisfaction and lack of comfort within the marital bed she shares with her husband often leads my mother to creep into her daughter's bedroom through the half-lit moonlit hallways of the house at night – an unhealthy habit that begun soon after my death that has continued long after the young girl has needed comforting in order to reach a state of sleep. My mother spends uneasy nights chasing sleep within the confines of the armchair in my sister's bedroom, or on the floor beneath blankets, or even, on occasion, upon the bed itself, snuggled close to Agatha and the cat.

It is sometimes difficult to tell where cat and girl and woman begin or end.

The cat mewls around the house with feline arrogance, expressing ownership of its adopted home with every last hair on its brown-mottled body. I dislike it enormously, but the wretched thing does not appear to realise or acknowledge this fact. By the time it enters our life I have been dead for a number of years, and in all that time, I have been a phantom – unseen and disregarded by those delicate lives that I have the misfortune to stalk amongst. I am a whisper, a memory, a lost soul, without an atom of physical presence within the mortal realm.

I am a ghost.

So why the *bloody hell* won't this cat leave me alone?

It does not seem to seek comfort or affection from me, but it has a focus in its amber fleck'd eyes which follows me from room to room. I swear I feel those orbs upon me, boring into me, across the house and through the walls. Oh, the cat may snuggle up to my sister and mother alright – they are after all the ones who feed it – but I can seldom be in the same room as the creature without it turning its head this way and that as if to fix me in its inquisitive gaze.

It cannot figure me out, I guess.

During the empty days, when my mother is at work in the factory, my sister at school, and my father slumped in the rage-tinted fugue state in which he spends most of his time, Milly occupies herself by unsuccessfully trying to wind around my feet and between my legs. Or else she sits upon the dresser in the front room and stares at me, little furry head cocked to one side as if trying to figure out what I am. Perhaps she is startled by the mask upon my face, although she shows no emotion, save curiosity.

I am touched, I suppose, to have some link with the living after half a decade of watching from the side-line.

Perhaps I fulfil for the cat the same role that my family plays for me – a mild distraction to chip away at time's vast marble block – but with no real emotional payload on either side. Oftentimes the silent days will pass in this almost empty house: the cat, the motes of dust which sparkle and float through the light which streams through the parlour window, and me; together in silent contemplation of the vagaries of life.

The shopkeeper's shelves are growing emptier by the day in these early days of the war, and my mother sits at the dining table and frets and plans over Agatha's twelfth birthday. As my mother works, my father watches her through heavy-lidded eyes and it is clear that I am not the only one who judges my mother's affections for my sister.

"She will not thank you for what you do," he mutters across the room. "You know that."

My mother shrugs. "She's going to be twelve. What are we supposed to do, give her nothing?"

"Twelve," my father sighs, the word hanging heavy in the air in the silence between them.

"All this," he continues after a moment, sinking back into his armchair, "it will not give you what you want, you know." He closes his eyes, and puffs lightly at his cigar, sending little grey clouds up towards the tarnished ceiling.

The room fills with further silence – a full, *hot* silence - as my mother tries to concentrate on the paperwork before her: incomings and potential outgoings and the continual battle for balance between the two. She makes a mistake, tuts angrily to herself as she crosses out and begins again, before making *another* mistake. She grinds to a halt, placing her pencil on the table slowly.

"And what is it that I want, Herman?" she asks quietly.
"I do not think you need me to say it, my kitten. The way you spoil that girl - what is it, guilt?" He lets out a bitter little chuckle. "Or maybe you think you get it right this time, eh? Maybe you think that twice the affection – twice the money, twice the time – you still get to mother them both." Another long drag at the cigar, an inch of glowing grey ash at the

tip threatening to dislodge at any moment and tumble down onto his shirt.

"One day, who knows? Maybe, she will end up resenting you enough for both of them as well!"

My mother looks up at the father of her children, countless disparate emotions bubbling through her. She understands that his words hurt – she understands his intentions – but she feels very little. It is as though some small part of her, the soul that she used to be, lies within a hollow metal ball within her mind. Protected from the outside world, yet also unable to access it, the emotions and feelings that she is *supposed* to feel – that her husband's words are supposed to foster within her – merely bounce off, reflected by the highly polished surface of her mind.

This empty cannonball in which she resides, she feels, is equal part protection and prison – for what is a prison if not the ultimate guard against the hardships of the outside world? But there is a fragility there, weak spots, perhaps, in the metallic membrane which shields the Used-To-Be from the What-Is, and unbeknownst to her, every targeted insult or degradation sends whisper-thin cracks zigzagging across the surface of her self-imposed protection.

Because my mother knows, of course, that there is truth in her husband's words - although not the whole truth. She spoils Agatha, this she knows, but it is neither some bizarre self-flagellation nor payment-in-kind to her lost child.

It is a strange, unspeakable, unworthy - almost perverse - worm of a thought at the very centre of her mind that drives her actions towards her remaining child. The closer that Agatha gets to the age at which her older sister died, the more my mother feels that she has - in some way - *won.*

As mindworms go, it's not one that my mother could ever admit, even to herself, but it is there, nonetheless. And like a spectator cheering on their team, the more imminent the victory, the more she can practically taste it.

As I watch her wrestle with her emotions and her place within her own mind, a terrible realisation comes upon me. There is a truth in my father's words. As vile and hurtful as he can be, I find my eyes opening and I am shocked by my own stupidity. A word floats around my head, a word for such involved affection towards your one remaining child, a word which perfectly encapsulates what has been going on before my very eyes:

Replacement.

I have been *replaced.*

Of course, Agatha's twelfth birthday would be the final nail in the coffin, but I was blind not to see what was happening in the years since my death. My father and mother had failed to parent me beyond my twelfth year, and so – in my mother's eyes at least – they were building Agatha up as a *replacement* as if to wash away the distaste of my death. A simulacrum for the love they had been unable to lavish on me in the years since I had become worm food.

How embarrassing.

How pathetic.

If I could have placed my hands upon the flesh of the living, I would have wrung that little rat's neck for the sheer *audacity* of thinking she could replace me in my mother's affections.

I wander away from my parents, through the night-darkened rooms of the house, unsure which is the more unsettling feeling, the sensation of being replaced by my sister, by dint of her still being alive and me being dead, or the sensation of being overtaken. My mother's love for her daughter has rendered me a loser in a competition I did not know I was taking part in.

Charming.

The floorboards creak beneath my feet as I step past my old room – untouched after all these years and obviously forgotten by my parents in their desire to raise their one true darling daughter Agatha. Not all family members stick by this rule, however, as the cat has taken to sleeping upon the eiderdown of my bed whenever she thinks she can get away with it.

The wretched thing feels my eyes upon it and it wakes with a stretch, shedding golden-brown fur upon the fabric as it looks up at me with amber flecked eyes and mewls accusingly. *This is my room now*, it purrs.

Even the fucking *cat* is replacing me now!?

With animal insolence, the beast uncurls itself from sleep and in one swift movement leaps from the bed and pads its ways across the bare wooden floor towards me. There is such arrogance contained in each quiet step, each paw upon the ground deliberate and insulting. It wraps itself around my legs, not out of love, but with such a sense of smug ownership of my bedroom, my sister, my family, that I cannot stop myself from reaching down and – with my own feline swiftness – grabbing the damned thing by the back of the neck.

I feel a quiet sense of satisfaction at the shocked expression on the creature's face as I wrench the skin from its back.

The Mask Seller

She walks the streets,
    A smile upon her face so sweet
and still.
Her wares hang about her, carved wood and stone
Blushing porcelain and bone
and metal twined together.

Her eyes are dark and deep; they stare out from behind
her beauty
and watch the curious and indifferent alike.

The Mask Seller walks barefoot, in ragged finery which
hangs in tatters
between the masks which click and clatter
amongst the folds of her cloak.

She walks the streets at dusk,
When truth stands,
With outstretched hands.
half-hidden beneath skies half-lit.

She finds her customers then.
Those that need a mask or two to face the dawning of a new day.
She shies away from those curious few
Who wish to see
What truths lie in the darkness beneath the china doll smile.

So unaware are they that within the darkness
It is masks
All the way down

Best friends and girl friends

Despite Terry's best attempts at horticultural massacre in the front garden, a large wisteria plant infests the front wall of the house from doorstep to guttering. Its thick, twisted trunk stands sentry alongside the front door, while its thinner branches dangle heavy, drooping flowers and leaves twisting along the windowsills and electrical wires that nestle amongst the bricks and mortar of my home.

One such branch passes just outside my darling Hannah's bedroom window, filling the air with its dusty fragrance and darkening the view with limply hanging clumps of purple flowers. Amongst the leaves a small brown chrysalis sits, like a chewed cigar stub. Standing at the window, I watch the gentle thing shiver in the breeze and picture the soup of insect parts within, changing and connecting in ways its previous little caterpillar mind would never have been able to comprehend.

I spend a lot of time in Hannah's bedroom, obviously, and had been afforded the opportunity to watch the caterpillar grow from full-stop-egg into a creeping, crawling stretch of a thing. I had watched it spend its days nibbling delicate curves from the edges of the wisteria leaves in which it lived and hiding from the local blackbirds, completely unaware of the bigger things in life. The caterpillar knew nothing of art or poetry – at least, it never gave any indication that it knew of such things – and yet the simplicity of its life spoke to me of unlikely parallels to my own sad existence.

Strange as it may seem, I had felt a twinge of loneliness when the creature had begun to weave its papery little changing room, knowing as I did that it was the beginning of the end of our little relationship. I was half tempted to throw up the sash and pluck the brown threads from its back, preventing it from changing, from leaving me, and perhaps I would have done so had Hannah not entered her bedroom at that exact moment, chatting in a low voice to her friend Callie, who entered the room behind her.

It is easier to have my back turned when Callie is here. I do not care to see her.

I do not blame my darling Hannah, of course. She does not know it yet, but she pines for me. Our love is so strong it ripples through both our realms, although while I can put a name to the lost love I feel, she cannot. I am nameless in her heart - although the longing is real - and this absence has rendered her vulnerable to the attentions of others. Like bacteria feeding on the corpse of the family cat, this beast called Callie smothers my wonderful girl with her friendship and affection.

I am not jealous. In fact, the perverse spectacle behind me merely makes my heart sing ever sweeter for my Hannah – I cannot help but admire the bravery she shows against the onslaught of facile comments and pathetic attempts at humour tripping from the oozing strips of liver which Callie calls lips.

The chrysalis trembles on the branch before me, wisteria leaves rustling sympathetically in the breeze.

"Wednesday or Thursday?" murmurs Hannah, dumping her bag on her desk and rummaging through it.

Callie sits on the edge of the bed, uninvited, and idly tucks her hair behind her ear. "He said Thursday," she answers. "But I thought I'd get it in on Wednesday if I can, just in case."

"Well, yeah," Hannah's words flutter across the room towards her friend. "You don't want to freak out like last time and hand everything in a day late."

Callie closes her eyes in mock despair. "Oh god, don't remind me."

I watch the chrysalis begin to split – ever so slowly – along a previously hidden seam, and the first hint of a feather-light grey wing begins to show beneath. It almost makes me want to smile.

I am pleased I have something to focus on. There is only so much admiration I can have for my love, having to put up with the rancid wittering of this intruder into our lives. The mind boggles at the obliviousness of people; the gasping, brain-dead way the unwanted manage to inveigle themselves into situations that would be far improved by their absence.

I stare at the birthing of the damp little butterfly before me, pale spots upon its shrivelled wings peeking out between newly formed creases and lines, its twitching, searching proboscis scenting the air of the new world in which it finds itself. Beneath this miracle of life, Callie and Hannah discuss the strictness of college lecturers and the minutia of assignment writing.

It is this that stings the most, I think. My love does not deserve the beige blandness of her friend's conversation; she deserves life and love. To feel safe and warm in the embrace of a loved one. To feel the caress of lips upon her smooth brow, down to the elegant tip of her nose. We would dance cheek to cheek, and I would cease the fluttering of her delicate eyelids with kiss after kiss after kiss.

If it were me, if I found myself here in Hannah's bedroom with nothing but the beckoning air between us, there is nothing on heaven or earth that would prevent me from burying myself within the soft darkness of her hair, breathing in the sweet, beautiful scent of her, losing myself within.

Why, Callie? Why can you not see that my Hannah deserves to be worshipped? I would drink from her, pray to her – she is a rose that blooms from between bramble and thicket.

Your very existence makes me ache, Callie: my chest bleeds for love unfought-for; every utterance from the hole that you call a mouth which does not celebrate the glories of my Hannah cuts across my skin with razor's edge, and I *bleed*.

I dislike you enormously, you fucking pig.

The two of them chatter on behind my back for a while, the tinkling tunefulness of Hannah's voice met each and every time by the thudding dustbin lid clatter of Callie's responses.

Then, as though woken from a deep, dream-filled sleep, Callie asks a question which seems to penetrate my mind, and I find myself turning to watch them for the first time.

"How's your dad? Is he any better?" Callie asks with ill-considered bluntness.

The room seems to darken. Hannah shrugs quietly, staring down at the papers and folders on her desk. "He's okay, I guess. He's taken some time off work and getting some rest but..." she pauses, her eyes dark. "There's something else, this sort of *tension* in the family... in the house. I know it sounds stupid, but I don't think dad would be acting like this if we hadn't moved in here."

"You mean, all the stress of moving?"

"I guess," Hannah murmurs, then she looks up at Callie with such a hollowness behind her eyes that it is all I can do to stop myself scooping her up in my arms and holding her for the rest of our lives. "No, no, it's not the *moving* house. It's the house itself." Her voice drops even lower. "There's something wrong with it."

"What, like it's haunted?" Callie smirks, before looking over at me.

Looking over at me.

I hold my breath and meet her eye.

And then, behind me - a scrabbling crash against the windowpane at my back makes all three of us jump.

The sound of fluttering, ragged wings fills the room for a moment and I turn, half expecting to see the jet-black feathers of some dark angel come to collect my wretched soul sweeping across the glass. Sharp looking claws scrabble against the branch as a calloused beak rips still-trembling shreds of delicate grey wing from the wisteria branch.

The crow or raven – somesuch large black bird – lets out a rasping squawk and flaps heavily away, leaving behind dusty feather prints and bird mess smeared upon the glass and the shredded remains of an empty chrysalis.

"My god, what was that?" Callie asks, a hand on her chest in a show of shock almost as overly dramatic as her eye makeup.

Hannah walks across to the window and peers out, through the filth splattered across the glass. She is practically shoulder-to-shoulder with me, and the sweet scent of her proximity fills my mind.

"A bird," she murmurs, rubbing the side of her arm distractedly. "Must have seen a bug or something in the plants outside."

"Yeah, or a ghost," Callie says, grinning.

"Don't," Hannah says quietly, placing her hand on the aftermath of the bird/window collision and Callie frowns in mute concern. "I don't know what's going on," my love continues and there are tears upon her cheeks, "It's not just dad, there was that thing with Patrick too. I hate it, there's just something *wrong* about the whole house. I don't want to be here."

I want to turn to her, reach for her, want to take her in my arms and feel her heat against me. I wish I could make her understand.

"Come on, let's go out," Hannah says, smiling at Callie after a brief, water-logged pause and I watch them both collect their bags and mobile telephones and other worldly detritus and I long to be a part of them.

And for the first time I sense that I am trapped – and alone – in this spiritual world. Hannah does not live in my house; I fear that I live in hers.

I blame Callie entirely.

She had looked at me – through me – with such cow-like bafflement as the bird had clattered upon the glass behind me that for a moment I had seen myself reflected in her wide, damp eyes. I don't cast a reflection as a rule – unless I want to be seen as a flicker from the corner of the eye – but I had seen myself, horrific and empty, a shell of a person in a cardboard horse mask and a dark blue dress. Maybe it was the shock, though false, of being seen for the first time in decades, but I felt no warmth in my reflection, there was nothing but the harsh truth of my own self.

The last thing I wanted, at that moment, was to be seen.

A poisonous sort of hopelessness seeps between my subtle bones as I stand there, between them both, exposed and yet unseen.

I am nothing if not sensitive to the emotions of others and, sensing that I am un-needed, I leave Hannah and Callie to their own devices.

***

I have found, from experience, that when a light is on in a room that does not need it – or is not common area within the house – it sets people's minds to worrying in a very subtle, low-stakes way. Because of this, I have taken to turning the light on in the upstairs airing cupboard during the day, unseen by anyone until its inevitable discovery in the late afternoon.

It is a minor joy to behold the confusion that flickers across the face of the discoverer – the niggle at the back of the mind: *did I leave this light on?* they wonder. *Did someone else?* they ponder. And more importantly, *does it matter?* Of course not, they conclude, as sheets or towels are removed or stacked within and off they go on their merry way.

Once or twice may cause little impact upon the psyche but do it every day and that little furrow of the brow begins to deepen. *Maybe the light switch is broken,* they think. *I'll have a look at it on the weekend.*

But they never do. Not my parents, nor the old woman before she died. Not Terry or Debbie, not even my darling Hannah - they do not think and they will not think of the airing cupboard lightbulb from one moment to the next during daylight hours. It does not keep them up at night with worry, nor does it send inky undercurrents flowing into conversations between friends or loved ones – it is, after all, simply a lightbulb.

But it is there nonetheless – I see it – sharp and bright within their minds. Its existence brings about a gradual chipping away of their sense of comfort and control. It is a daily annoyance which sits like a pustule within the mind. I am entertained by the thought that one day it will burst within their brains – one more trickle of unpleasantness between the curls and ridges of their meaty cerebra.

The thought brings me great pleasure in times of trouble.

****

The buzzing vibration of a mobile telephone, unseen beneath tattered sheathes of cheap drawing paper, calls the girl from the world of long division homework and she moves from the desk beside her bed to retrieve the device.

Hello

In the darkened bedroom, the underlighting from the telephone's glass screen exaggerates the heavy bags under the girl's eyes. She stares at the message alert, before slowly placing the phone back down. She looks back at her homework but, torn, does not leave the edge of the bed.

We haven't spoken in a while.

How are you?

Her bottom lip bitten nervously, she looks towards her bedroom door and the hallway beyond. She looks down at the screen and her fingers tip tap across the glass almost unprompted.

ok u?

Happier now that I know you are there! I thought you didn't want to be friends anymore! Are you sure everything is all right?

...

...

just a bit tired, u know? lots of homework

Oh, homework is the worst! What subject?

maths

Oh God, maths is so boring! Wouldn't it be great if you didn't have to put up with shit like that anymore!

The swear word – relatively mild as it might be – takes her by surprise and she almost drops the telephone. It takes all her strength of will not to shove the device under her pillow out of sight, as she imagines her parents bursting into the room and demanding to see the contents of her messages.

Don't be ridiculous, she thinks to herself. *I'm almost twelve, I can read swear words if I want to. It's not like anyone is going to know.*

Nevertheless, a hot ball of guilt sits within the girl's chest as her fingers tiptap yet again.

yeah maths is shit isnt it – delete delete delete delete – *maths is stupid isnt it*

How is your dad? Is he still being weird?

...

...

hes okay. he went to the doctor the other day but i dont think there was anything wrong with him really. hes sleeping a lot at the moment

I think you're really brave, putting up with that sort of behaviour. I don't know how you do it. It sounds like your life gets pretty tough sometimes.

...

its ok

Well, I'm just glad that he's not screaming and shouting at you anymore. You don't deserve to have to deal with stuff like that. Some parents can be the worst!

Worse than maths? :P

Much worse!! Wouldn't it be good if we could just get rid of them all?

what like with magic?

Yes! I can use my magic wand! Or a kitchen knife would be good as well!!

...

...

thats so bad! :P

We could be Warrior Queens, fighting against the tyranny of crazy parents everywhere! Death to those who shout and scream and tell us what to do!!!

ur funny ur majesty!

The bedroom is silent. The muffled sound of television floats through the floor, enveloping the quiet space in its own protective bubble. For a moment, the room itself is an island of solitude and light in a sea of unknown dark and a comforting shiver plays down Lily's spine. And then, a voice from downstairs shatters the illusion of privacy, and the girl is called to dinner. She rolls her eyes in unseen rebellion.

i have to go mum is calling

That's fine. Don't leave it so long before talking to me next time, okay? Sometimes I feel like you're the only friend I have!

same! the only person i can talk to anyway. speak to you later

Auf Wiedersehen.

...

can i ask a question?

...

...

whats ur name?

...

Thinking Dust

The idea of dust
    That thinks
Is pretty unsettling, when you think about it.

But when stardust gathers in little balls and clumps
and starts to think deeply about its place in the universe,

We call that humanity
Consciousness
The mind

For that is all we are:

Dust that named itself
Space debris with delusions of grandeur
That tries to distance itself from the void from whence
it came.

But I cannot distance myself, cannot forget my place.

For when I look at you, I see
Only
Stardust
And the infinite possibilities that lie therein.

✳✳✳

Very few people pass by my house - situated as it is halfway along a cul-de-sac with no thoroughfare to the main roads beyond. However, it does not take the few infrequent pedestrians long to adjust their path away from the dangling branch which hangs from the beech tree outside, a victim of last week's storm.

As the people walk, distracted, perhaps or with more purpose in their stride, they take a step to the right to avoid receiving a face-full of slowly browning leaves and twigs. They take a step to the right, off the concrete paving slabs and onto the grass verge which runs alongside the pavement.

And each footstep, bit by bit by bit, wears away the patch of grass that runs alongside the pavement that sits beneath that dangling, broken tree branch.

And as the grass wears away, the soil below becomes exposed to the elements, to the whims and capricious nature of the open skies. The soil, too, wears away, particles and clumps detaching here and there until an empty patch of dirt rests alongside the pavement, the ground now a fraction of an inch lower than it had been before.

***

Other spirits I have not known

The cat is no less irritating dead than it was alive. With the unerring skill that all cats possess when faced with someone who actively dislikes them and all their furry kind, the thing does not leave me alone.

I stand over my mother as she scrubs bloodstains and stringy lengths of tendon from my bedroom rug. While I watch her clean, a smudge of copper-coloured light that is all that remains of the animal weaves its way around my ankles,

Of course, if the wretched thing hadn't made such a fuss in its last few moments, there would have been significantly less for my mother to remove from the walls and floor. As it was, the blasted cat had scarpered from my arms and skidded across my bedroom floor, half its skin flapping in the air behind it like a damp red flag, its claws dragging little curls of wood up from the floorboards in its desperation to get away. With nerve endings screaming in harmony with its panicked yowls, it had careened off the bedroom wall in blind panic, sending gobbets of fur and scarlet splashing across the wallpaper before collapsing in a puddle of its own blood and filth at the foot of my bed.

It was while I was watching the raw, glossy creature bleeding out between strips of its own ragged fur all over my bedroom rug, its now-visible muscles twitching, exposed to the outside world, that I suddenly became aware of footsteps on the stairs behind me. As the cat took its last few tortured breaths on the floor before me, a piercing scream filled the air.

My mother has found the cat.

"Wha…what?!" she mutters nonsensically as her brain tries to take in the charnel house scene before her, and for a moment she stands, reflected back in dead glassy eyes, as still as the animal before her. Then, however, the truth of the scene bursts through.

"Herman! Herman!" she screams at the top of her lungs, backing away until she hits the doorframe.

"What is it?" my father's voice rumbles from downstairs, and I hear the floorboards creak as he makes his way across the house.

"Come here, quickly!" my mother yells again. "But for God's sake make sure Aggie stays down there!"

With more than a little huffing and puffing, my father appears on the landing, loops of grey cigar smoke wreathing his broad shoulders.

"What is all this noise, woman?" he begins, before taking in the scene before him. "*Gott in Himmel,*" he murmurs, as my mother grabs at him and sobs into his shirt. He looks down at her and frowns, before the creak at the foot of the stairs behind him draws his attention.

"Agatha, no," he calls out. "Stay down there, kitten. There is nothing for you up here!" Confident that his young daughter will not stumble upon the bloody scene before him, he turns to his wife.

"What is this?" he asks, ashen faced, looking down at the sad and sorry mess curled up by my bed, before realisation dawns. "The… the cat?"

My mother nods and pulls away from him, almost embarrassed by her emotions. She looks down. "Yes. I guess a dog must have gotten into the house or something…"

Running his hands through his hair in confusion, my father shakes his head. "A dog?" he echoes. "What kind of…" His mind races, trying to fully absorb the scene before him. He sees the pool of blood and shit slowly soaking into the rug, creeping up into the old woollen blanket which hangs from the bedframe. A slow and thoroughly organic desecration of the room in which I took my last breaths.

"*Mein Gott,* we need to clean this up," he mutters, slowly. "Before too much damage is done…."

His words trail away as the animal lets out a low, tortured, twisted growl and a shuddering human-like gasp.

Both my parents jump, and my mother looks up at my father, her eyes wide in horror.

"Oh god, it's still alive?"

They stare down at the red mess in hot silence, but it makes no further sound. Even the flow of blood from its wounds has stopped and it becomes an empty thing before their very eyes.

"Well?" my father says after a moment, glowering at my mother. "You can shed your tears once you've cleared away this filth, eh?" He indicates the walls and floor with the smouldering end of his cigar. "Before the blood has a chance to tarnish our daughter's memory for good? Then you can indulge yourself in selfish misery."

She goes to say something, the words practically crystallising in the air between them, but there is no point. Words would no more soothe the situation than they would bring the family pet back to life, and so instead my mother leaves, silent, to gather cleaning materials in order to cleanse her daughter's bedroom of the scent of death once more.

As my father stands in the doorway of my bedroom, silently worrying at the end of his cigar and desperately trying to come to terms with the violence before him, I am aware of a gentle glow beside me. It has no recognisable shape; however, this fact does not seem to prevent it from to look up at me quizzically.

We stand there for a moment - my father, me and the cat – in silent contemplation of the gleaming mess before us. The scent of blood and animal waste mingles with cigar smoke, and I wonder whether I should feel guilty. I don't, of course, but that's not the point, is it?

I look up at my father and see the heavy-lidded twinkling of tears in his eyes, and I guess, perhaps, that he feels guilt enough for the both of us. He looks down at the blood on his hands and shakes his head once more.

When he leaves, the cat remains – both in spirit and in rapidly cooling body. I hear a clank of wood against metal on the stairs behind me, and my mother appears on the landing, mop and bucket in hand. Resting the cleaning things against the foot of the bed, she kneels before the mess I have made, her hands in her lap in silent contemplation of the task before her.

Death has afforded me the remarkable gift of knowing my family. It is only in solitude – when they believe themselves to be truly alone and unobserved – that the true self is allowed to peer through the mask of everyday interaction. When he is alone, I see beneath my father's hurtful rage to the man who mourns the life he lost, whose insides slowly pickle in guilt and cheap whiskey. I see the smile fall from my sister's face as she leaves my parents' side and makes her way to her bedroom to sob silently into her pillow as her young mind – rife with hormones and dark thoughts – tries to drown out the sounds of anger from the floor below.

But my mother? She just sits there in my bedroom, staring at the corpse of a cat whose disembodied form is even now trying to wrap itself around her to little effect, and she feels…nothing. She starts to clean, mechanically, barely any more of a presence in the room than I am.

Does the desecration of my bedroom mean so little to this woman? Does this vile act not reach into her chest and threaten to crush her heart in its grip?

She picks the animal up by the tail and under its forelegs, feel the weight of it as she places it in an old cloth bag which immediately begins to darken a sticky red colour. My mother watches the butterfly-wing-spread of blood through cloth for a moment, before reaching across and placing the heel of her palm on the fabric, roughly where she judges the animal's neck to be.

My mother does not know if the thing is still alive or not – it's not, of course, the ball of light between us that has started to vibrate in some otherworldly replica of purring is confirmation of the cat's passing – but she leans forward anyway, placing all her weight upon her palm until she hears the gentle crunching snap of delicate feline vertebrae.

She does not wince, she barely blinks, no flush of upset rises in her cheeks as she begins to work at the thickening pool of murky-looking blood with a damp cloth.

I feel no guilt at all – my heart is as emotionless as hers appears to be – and yet, I do not wish to stay and watch her. I do not wish to be with her as she cleans the carpet.

I do not wish to be with any of them.

***

The cat stays with me for two weeks exactly. Over those fourteen days, it is my constant companion. Despite having no real form, it does not appear to have let its feline nature behind and is often to be found hovering within the warming shafts of morning light which stream through the parlour windows or running skittishly from room to room between feet which it can no longer trip.

I cannot help but wonder, two weeks later when I first realise the cat is nowhere to be found, if perhaps that is the length of time it takes for the cat's soul to be judged. Perhaps that's all this phantom realm is - God's waiting room. Our sprits walk these tormented halls while the Choir Invisible carries out an elaborate system of tallies and checks and judges the quality of our souls.

Is fourteen days the right length of time to check a cat's soul? Perhaps it was a very good cat, and fourteen days is an express route to the feline Great Beyond. Perhaps that little beast's soul weighed heavy upon the scales and that two weeks' deliberation was merely the warm up act before an eternity of fire and brimstone for a cat with darkness in its mind.

It's best not to consider what that means in regard to *my* apparently endless stay in this spirit realm.

My sister cries for her pet cat, of course, but then she should have ensured it kept out of my bedroom. My father searches – briefly and half-heartedly - for evidence that a dog or some other feral creature got into the house somehow, until the alcoholic clouds descend upon his brow once more and he slumps into his armchair, indifferent to his daughter's sobbing.

My mother… goes to work. She comes home. She cleans, she cooks, she comforts her daughter. She haunts these rooms as surely as I do, but less convincingly. If she speaks to her husband at all, I do not hear.

Three days after the discovery and subsequent clean-up of the dead cat, she buys a tin of aspirin from the local chemists on her way home from work. There are twelve pills in the tin – white and round, each one the size of a child's tooth – which she hides within the folds of a lacy handkerchief slipped into the back of her bedside table. The empty tin she places at the back of her undergarment draw, certain that her husband will not stumble upon it there.

The number twelve circulates around her head for the next few days. She wakes up to see it etched upon the ceiling, she hears it in over-heard conversations on the bus to work. Taking this as a sign – and not wanting to arouse suspicion in Mr Timmins who owns the local chemists - she alights the bus two stops early on her way to work the following day and purchases another tin from a store close to the munitions factory.

The number twenty-four does not seem to haunt her so, in fact she feels a lightness upon her shoulders as she works on the factory line. After the event, those who care to recall note how much happier she seemed on those last few days. If not smiling, exactly, then *peaceful*, they will say.

A little over a week after I killed the cat, my mother stays up late, sewing a patch over the frayed elbow of one of my sister's cardigans. She fusses over the fabric choice, having nothing in maroon to match the colour of the wool, and settles instead of a section of old pillowcase which is decorated with little pink and white flowers. Once the repair is finished, she sews a matching patch upon the other elbow of the cardigan, both for aesthetic reasons and to prevent future wear and tear. She knows full well that it will be a while before repairs like this are carried out again.

After setting aside the remaining scraps of fabric and tidying away her sewing box, she screws her eyes up tight and turns off the lamp.

Opening her eyes, she looks around the darkened parlour – afforded some form of night-time vision through the judicious avoidance of the sudden '*click!*' between lamplight and darkness – and takes some comfort in the familiar room lit only by the silver of the moon. She listens to the familiar creaking of the floorboards beneath her feet as she walks, feels the gentle nudge of the bedside table against her thigh as she leaves the room and closes the door gently behind her.

She makes her way up the stairs and is tempted to do so with her eyes shut, knowing that the memory of the journey lives within her muscles. But she does not; as confident of a successful ascent as she is, she would not want her sleeping family awoken by the sound of her stumbling on the stairs.

My mother places the folded cardigan upon the end of my sister's bed gently but turns away from its sleeping occupant with barely a moment's hesitation. A sentimentalist might suppose a glisten upon her cheek as she leaves her daughter's bedroom, but there are none there to witness my mother's last night on earth.

She walks past my bedroom door without so much as a second glance.

And so. She reaches her own bedroom, already rattling under the stentorian onslaught of my father's drunken snores. The cacophony does not reach her now, however, and she opens her bedside table, taking out the handkerchief now bulging with its collection of pills.

The night sky is my mother's accomplice – it shines bright upon the room, illuminating each little pill as she lays them out neatly, side by side, all twenty-four of them upon her bedside table.

Underscored by the heavy breathing of her husband, she takes the first pill and then the second, taking a small gulp of water after each one. She does not take the whole two dozen – in fact, she muses to herself as she lays back on the eiderdown, she needn't have bought the second tin at all. But the family finances are no longer her concern, and it is always good to buy in bulk when possible.

She closes her eyes. Her stomach hurts, but it is one hundred miles away and one hundred miles below and belongs to someone else now. It is no longer her concern.

The cat stays with me a further four days after my mother's passing, but I believe this to be a coincidence, rather than being indicative of some wider connection. When the animal is finally gone, I find myself more alone than I have ever been before.

There is not so much as a suggestion of a glow that might hint at my mother's presence here with me.

Not that I look for her. Not that I care.

I just find it interesting, that is all.

My sister discovers my mother's corpse, my father in too-deep-a-drunken stupor to be roused by a mere dead body cooling rapidly on the bedcovers beside him.

His daughter's screams, however, certainly *do* wake the man and he grumbles sourly towards consciousness, before turning his rheumy eyes upon his child.

"What is it, Aggie?" he rumbles. "What has upset you, my kitten?"

"There's something wrong with Mama," she manages to say through panic-streaked tears.

***

By the time the doctor arrives, tall and sombre looking (in the years since he last stepped over the threshold to examine a corpse within this house he has developed a grumbling liver and an ulcerated stomach lining) the few remaining untouched pills upon my mother's bedside table have found their way down the lavatory pan, flushed onwards to medicate the little fishes in the English Channel.

My father watches the man of medicine nervously, as he sits at my mother's dressing table mapping out the details of her final moments in his interminable scrawl. His beard still glistening with tears, my father bites the soft flesh of his thumb and stares through thick, tired eyebrows at the doctor's tweed-covered back.

"Headaches, you say?" the doctor murmurs.

My father nods mutely, before realising that the doctor's focus is on his paperwork, not the newly-minted widower and so he clears his throat in muttered confirmation. "Headaches, yes. Ever since she started working at the factory. I think, maybe, the noise does not sit well with her. *Did* not."

"And so, she was self-medicating with aspirin?"

"Yes."

Misadventure, the doctor's notes will read. Whether or not he believes this in his heart of hearts, it will be a matter of public record. My mother will not be denied a Christian burial, nor will the family be mired in shame – although no official paperwork on earth could stop the wagging of tongues and the gossiping of fishwives.

My mother's legacy will be written in miscounted pills and muddled dosages and untruths and black ink.

The doctor arranges for the removal of the body and says goodbye to my father with half-spoken words and empty handshakes. The temperature of the house cools significantly as my father closes the front door and makes his way to the parlour, where my sister sits curled into a ball, nestled in the armchair that her mother had favoured for an evening. She holds a cushion to her face, soaking the embroidered fabric with her misery.

"My kitten…" my father begins, standing over her, the words drying in his mouth. He has no words to sooth his child, this is not the role he would have ever chosen in life. His daughter's sadness eclipses his own, and he opens his arms to her.

Her reluctance to find comfort within his embrace does not go unnoticed by my father, but she does not see the frown that clouds his face – she is too preoccupied in her own grief. However, the young girl has lost her mother, the black despair in which she finds herself demands the warmth of others and she finds herself enveloped in those big strong arms, her cheek against her father's broad chest.

He strokes her hair comfortingly, filled with love for his daughter. He plants a kiss upon the top of her head, and looks up towards the ceiling, imagining he can see through the wooden boards to his wife's dead body. A weight that he had not realised was there lifts from his shoulders, the black fog of guilt releases his soul from within its grasp.

The score was settled now, it seemed, the scales balanced. There is a lightness in my father that almost makes him smile, and he is glad his daughter's devastation prevents her from seeing his face.

He had made a mistake in the past, yes. Many mistakes, perhaps. Mistakes that had damaged the very foundations of their family. But his wife could no longer hold that over him, could she? He may have sent some cracks zigzagging through the foundations, but the selfishness of her suicide had truly torn the walls down on top of them. He wonders if, in her dying moments, she had realised that she was now just as tarnished as he was.

There is a knock at the door, it will be the gentlemen from the funeral home come to take his wife to her final resting spot and my father nods to himself. Yes, it is done, a line drawn under the events of the past.

"It is just you and me now, kitten," he murmurs lovingly, pressing his lips against the soft brown hair at the top of his daughter's head once more, and to his mind this comforts her.

But it is not comfort that dries Aggie's tears, but dread. A yoke of it weighs down upon her, dampening her emotions like bonfire embers in the morning dew.

The tears she cries for our mother's passing - even now drying on her father's rumpled shirt - are the last she will ever shed, from now until the day she dies, several decades later.

Pulse

Your blood

Speeds through
Badump
Badump
Day in
And out
It beats
Away
You do
Not know
Or feel
But so

Badump
Badump
I hear
It go.
My heart
Is still
No scar-
let flow
Within
My veins
Is there
To show

Badump
Badump
A swoon
Or blush
For love's
Sweet brush
Against
my cheek

But if
Perhaps
When fear
Draws near
A sweet
Increase
Of speed
And pace
Of beat-
Ing heart
Badump
Badump
You'll beat
For two
Badump
Badump
For me
And you.

Together

What is sex? I don't really understand the need, the importance, the high regard with which it seems to be held by the wider world.

It comes as no great shock to know that I was a virgin when I died – I was only twelve after all. My knowledge of the opposite gender was limited to catching a glimpse of my father getting out of the bath and half-whispered secrets between girlfriends – discussions of older sisters walking out with various unsuitable young men, much to the chagrin of parents who had been guilty of similar misdeeds in their own youth. There were rumours of sweaty assignations and implausible suggestions for how babies were made even before my monthlies began and my mother's muttered assurances of the burdens of my budding womanhood.

Who is the dreamer? Father, daughter? Sister, mother? Wife, husband, lover?
Slumbering eyelids flicker, heads heavy against too-warm pillows, and thin moonlight paces room by room looking for entertainment in those late-night

minutes and early hours. Fear creeps in through sleeping skin and shared minds dream darkly:

A line of rust-tainted water drips from behind a bathroom mirror, leaving in its wake a stain the colour of blood clots which seeps into the white painted plasterwork. Slowly, the copper-hued water pools on the clean white porcelain, traces around the bottom of the polished taps and trickles into the bowl of the sink itself.

After my death, no supernatural curiosity in this realm or any other would have drawn me to my parents' bedroom on those few occurrences of marriage duties being performed. They were, I'm glad to say, infrequent, although not without their contamination of the house-ly ether. My mother would be more closed off than usual the morning after their eiderdown shenanigans, followed by stormclouds all of her own, while my father prowled about the house like a feral animal bathed in the glow of his own musk and filth.

The dark redbrown stain on the wall stands out amongst the greys and whites of the cold, bleak bathroom, a jagged line which splits the wall in two; a line of darkly glistening viscera, seemingly a glimpse beneath the pale flesh of the house itself. As the water slowly trickles down the wall, it seems to pulsate with life.

Other moments of red-raw darkness occurred in later years, the stench of which never fully lifted from the paintwork even after my father passed away. Tears enough to wash the walls may have been shed in those moments, but all the oceans of the world could not have scoured this house clean.

The water collects around the infinite dark of the plughole, gathering about a smudge of red which stands out jarringly against the gleaming white surface of the sink. The smudge itself blurs and mingles, the bright red smearing to pink and then fading completely as the tainted water slowly reaches the lip of the plughole, holds itself for a moment against the curve in a meniscus, which bulges then breaks, sending the water down into the dark.

Empty bedsheets grew yellow with age during the decades that this house was occupied by the old lady who would, eventually, die within these walls. She had been a spinster in life and death, unless the Reaper took pity on her rotting form and showed her a love unknown in her last moments - all ragged shroud, ivory loins and dust-dry caresses.

She certainly *was* smiling, but that was probably just the curve of her jawbone showing through the desiccation of skin and muscle.

The drain gurgles loudly. An echoing sound which reverberates around the room as the trickle of water from the unknown source behind the mirror blossoms into a flow which cascades down into the darkness of the drain like sweet port wine.

The dreamer, unseen, never peeks behind the mirror to find the reason for the flowing water. Even in the dreamscape, self-preservation runs deep, and there is terror there, behind that circle of reflective silver, that threatens to satiate the curious in the most terminal way possible.

So, aside from a few snatched glimpses of writhing bodies on the television late at night, the activities of Terry and Debbie are my first real insight into the frenetic bedroom habits of other people.

The lights are dim - walls and ceiling and skin bathed in the pink-hued glow of one solitary bedside lamp standing sentry over the scene playing out between bedcovers. Fingers explore, they squeeze and pinch at flesh hidden beneath thin cotton. Lips caress, tasting perfume, soap and sweat in equal measure – soft plump pinkness against rough stubble or powdered cheeks.

Beneath the mirror, and despite the open plughole, the sink has begun to fill up. Slowly at first – a change in the pitch of the tinny gurgling sounds from the empty-looking drain suggest a clot of hair or something more unspeakable blocking the pipes – but soon

there is too much murky water for the plughole to hold and so it spills out into the bowl itself. It laps against the curved white porcelain, leaving traces of itself behind with every wax and wane. The flowing water fills, splashing into the sink now, dark red splattering up the walls and over the rest of the countertop and before long, miniature tides slap against the very edge of the sink, in rhythmic crests and falls.

Kisses come, tender and fierce, hungry. Tongues dart flirtatiously, pushing against each other, entwining as if to merge as one from two.

Multi-tasking hands explore while busy lips work, feeling the heat, the otherness of bodies curled around each other. Thighs and bottoms squeezed and held, lightly smacked or roughly gripped. Each new caress elicits sighs and groans and giggles and lustful grunts as fingertips trail from the public to the private.

The first drip splatters almost imperceptibly onto the bleached wooden floor of the bathroom, the tiniest dribble down the outside of the sink and the lightest of splashes heralding the trouble to come. And then another drip, and another, they pitter patter in pairs like a heartbeat on the bathroom floor.

The year is 1945. The war in Europe has been over for three months now, the Allies victorious. Well-spoken men on the wireless talk of 'moral leadership' and 'the eyes of the world' – the weight of all things lies heavy on shoulders of the Western world. In the back garden of my childhood home a large bonfire flickers away, lapping at the lower hanging branches of nearby trees and sending billowing clouds of black, acrid smoke up into a cloud filled sky. My father stares on, grim-faced, a cigar clamped between his lips, as he watches the floral fabric of my mother's armchair catch the flames and begin to smoulder.

"A new beginning, eh, kitten?" he mutters over his shoulder to my sister, who stares on in mute horror, but he does expect a reply. He is lost in his own world now, his mind shattered by too much, too soon.

"A new beginning," he says again.

His lips leave hers behind - needy and not-yet-fulfilled - with gentle bird-like kisses trailing down her chin and down her alabaster neck, the taste of warm perfume on the tongue. Those searching lips reach the swell of her breast, cupped in his hot and eager palm.

Hearts beat hard and nipples harden, rising to the lover's mouth and down within the dark, under covers, underwear, inner thighs – so warm and almost-slick – receive attention. Hot places, forbidden places open up anew to urgent inquiries as old as time itself.

Once again, the cascade of water builds until a murky waterfall flows from the sink, tumbling onto the floor and staining the tiles. The water pours at such a rate – far above, the wall behind the bathroom mirror bulges outwards with the forces of the flow

from the still-unseen source. Where the floor should be flooding, however, it seems instead to be giving way beneath the onslaught. The bathroom tiles are gossamer soft, are woodland mist, beneath the water and the small room resounds with the sound of water crashing into the space below.

Fingertips slide over soft hair and thrumming flesh and with lover's strength and lover's purpose he rests his hand over her sex. Gentle caresses between her thighs, between and across her, in harmony – or close enough as makes little difference – with the eager way he kisses and nibbles at her breasts, her neck, her chin, her own eager mouth.

And so, that is where the dreamer goes next. Through strangely familiar hallways and down too-steep stairs, the dreamer pads on silent feet, following the sounds of crashing water. The walls of the house stretch high above, disconcertingly high, and in the shadows that form there, strange things flutter their wings and keen to the sound of footsteps below.

As they kiss, as his fingers stroke, she sets out on her own exploration. He is already hard for her, mirroring her own liquid arousal, and so she wraps her hand around him through the thin cotton of his pyjamas, feeling his pulse beat for her as blissfully as if she might feel the beating of his heart while resting her head against his broad chest in some moment of quiet comfort.

The natural state of water is to flow, to rush and splutter full of life. It sustains us, as it did our ancestors and the animals we once were. It is curious, therefore, that the sound of rushing water is in itself a wholly *unnatural* sound to the modern ear. The pulse quickens and in the darkness of these hallways – where the shadows twitch and unfamiliar portraits leer through fly-specked frames – the roar and rush of water overwhelms all other sounds. The sound of creeping things and heavy footsteps which match your own, step by step by step, of whispers on the edge of hearing and susurrations of winged things, all masked by the ceaseless crash of water which rings alien between these twisted walls.

She strokes, he groans. His kisses quicken, his fingertips deepen. His wife opens beneath his touch, hot and salty-slick, hairy and obscene and knuckle deep he looks into her eyes. They are connected, top to toe, and deep within the gleam of her eyes he sees infinity, he hears the pounding drums of instincts millions of years old driving them both forward. Hormones course through iron-rich blood, pushing them both onwards in glorious inevitability.

At last, our dreamer finds the flow, a wall of water pouring from ceiling to floor in an empty room hung with curtains grown dark with mildew. Despite the rushing water the air feels warm and unholy, the only

illumination coming from yellowed lampshades hanging from the ceiling, swaying slightly in the splatter and splash of the waterfall. Invisible cobwebs caress the face, clinging to the skin in shuddering threads shed from the damp fabric of the surrounding curtains.

His lips begin their journey down her body once more – the smoothness of her throat, the softness of her heavy breasts, her stomach. He breathes her in, tasting her with each tender brush of his lips against her skin. She whimpers with mock-petulance as he shifts on the bed, his manhood leaving her grasping fingers as he positions himself over her, disappearing before her underneath the covers.

Keen hands pull back damp cotton underwear and push apart warm bare thighs. She shivers tremulously as searching lips journey down through sweat-salted curls of perfumed hair towards the pull of soft, swollen love.

There are no windows, no doors. In fact, were the dreamer not solely focused on the crashing water before them, and turned in retreat, they would no longer find the door through which they entered.

He tastes her, devours her. In turn tender and with driving force, he laps away at his lover. The mother of his children bites her lips as her husband worships the lushness between her legs, his tongue invading her. A wave rushes over her, her legs clamp about his ears and for a moment there is no hint of light or air between the two of them. But still he licks and laps and sups from her with lustful energy, craven onwards by his fleshy entrapment.

There is a familiarity to the room, despite the rust-tinged waterfall rushing through its centre and the curtains hung around the walls in tangled, rot-sloughed curls. Beneath the dreamer's bare feet (Were they always walking barefoot through the house? In the bathroom? On the stairs?) the carpet feels rough and gritty, speckled here and there with blooms of black mould as though nature was slowly claiming the room for herself.

The year is 1946. The home in which my father and sister inhabit is a quiet one. Whole sections given over to a state of preservation more akin to a museum diorama than a family home. My bedroom – long since scrubbed clean of cat blood and bowel contents – stands untouched as ever, the dust upon the eiderdown serving as an additional layer of insulation for any potential spirit that might be in need of rest and had little reservation in snuggling between a dead girl's bedsheets.

In my parent's bedroom, my mother's side of the room lays empty and untouched. Not so much of a shrine, this. My father had removed my mother's belongings from the room less than a month after her interment in the local cemetery, burning those that could not be given away.

One evening, shortly after my sister has finished her bedtime ablutions and climbed into bed, my father puts down the newspaper he has been distractedly reading, and stares mutely up at the cracks in the ceiling. Turning off the lamp, he makes his way upstairs, his footsteps heavy on the bare wood floorboards.

He stands on the landing, lost in thought for a moment, until – like a man travelling a dark, predetermined path – he enters my sister's bedroom.

By the time he leaves, night has well and truly fallen. The house sits in darkness.

As he works away, he throbs to attention, swollen, bouncing against his stomach as he gropes blindly at the elastic of his pyjama trousers, tugging them down over his thighs, exposing himself obscenely in the darkened room.

The dreamer is pulled closer to the water, watching it crash down onto the carpet which soaks it up hungrily, like woodland moss.

They drop to their hands and knees, and with great urgency begin to scrabble at the fabric of the carpet. Beneath the dreamer's fingernails the carpet comes away, disintegrating into slime at each touch. Driven by madness, the dreamer pulls and pulls and huge swathes of carpet come away to reveal, beneath the surface, damp, grey sand.

They are entwined, conjoined, grasping and gasping in crashing sensuality. One hand slides up, and gropes blindly at her breasts – needing to feel their warmth, their heaviness against the softness of his own palm. The other hand grips tightly at her bare thigh, pulling her legs open further, granting his tongue deeper privilege.

The sand is the colour of seaweed-slicked low tides and sandbanks that skirt the edge of inner-city rivers. As the waterfall babbles and ripples through it, disturbing the surface grains, it brings forth the scent of decay, of long-rotted marine creatures. Having torn away the foetid carpet from the floor, the dreamer's eager search continues. The sand is icy cold to the touch, but nevertheless the dreamer digs in, scooping out handfuls of foul-smelling sand from beneath the rushing water and throwing it madly to the side.

She rocks and grinds against her husband, letting the rhythmic swelling pleasure build within her base, wanting each sweet moment to last for ever. She feels his hot breath upon her, the roughness of his cheek upon the smoothness of her own bare inner thighs, and reaches down, taking handfuls of hair in her grip and holding him in place, desperate to take as much from him as she can before the inevitable.

Again and again, in a desperate race against the tumbling sand which is constantly dislodged by the cascading water, the dreamer digs. Glass-sharp grains lodge beneath fingernails which break and tear at each

plunge of the fingers into the murky sand and scour little lines in patterns upon the dreamer's skin, sending curlicues of red out across the damp surface of the sand. All is pain and cold and grit and panic.

Until.

Fingers scrape against something hard beneath the sand, something buried deep. Searching fingertips seek out each edge, clear and crisp despite the muck with which it is covered, and with considerable effort the object itself is cleared from its burial chamber.

For they have crossed a line, the two of them. An unspoken step, hand-in-hand, which comes from a lifetime of togetherness. Each plays their part unprompted – his lips begin their journey back up her body, her knees part further, feet lifting from the softness of the now damp bedcovers.

Without a word she takes him within her hand and guides him, welcoming him in. So matched are they in rhythm, so perfect their timing, that his lips meet hers at the precise moment that he enters her. Sensitive flesh, slick and ready, becomes one in that moment and eyes widen with a lust and joy un-dampened by years or familiarity.

It is a house. A child's toy. Wooden and solid, a replica of the larger house within whose foundations it was found. The surface of the house is cracked and weathered as befits a treasure buried beneath damp sand, the once-bright blue front door now faded a funereal mauve. Each little window holds no glass, but plain, solid looking wood, inviting no casual examination of the interior of the strange miniature. Set into the front, a heavy looking latch, securing the two halves of the front of the wooden toy.

Her heat holds him, takes him further and further, deeper and deeper. He adjusts his hands, shifts his position above her to take his weight more easily, a delicate balance – a battle between lust and physics. He masks each shift with a flurry of kisses about her cheeks, her neck, her breasts, and she smiles in acknowledgement of the movements above her – each one sending ripples of heat through her thighs and stomach.

And there is a sound. It is faint, barely audible above the crash of the nearby waterfall, but nonetheless, it is there. The sounds of a party, raucous and musical. Voices travel in the dark, laughter and singing and the hubbub of pleasant conversation. All emanating from inside the doll's house.

And so – deep within – a race begins and a battle fought between base, biological urges and the desire to satisfy another. Which will win? The act itself is pleasure given form, in all its sounds and scents and sensations, but pleasure for whom? For both, is the goal, but the ending is in sight and written before the first move was made and with each thrust buttock and internal tightening that ending creeps closer.

With the same external forces as before willing the dreamer on, the latch at the front of the house is opened, the face of the thing split sharply in two as doors open widely on silent hinges and the rooms of the doll house exposed.

The sounds of revelry stop.

The house is dressed plainly. There is little colour, few pieces of furniture. A wardrobe here, a table there. Unloved, unlived in, the dreamer almost imagines they can hear the sound of tiny footsteps echoing around each sallow, miniature room. Three bedrooms and a bathroom make up the top floor (the latter stained a murky brown colour which may – once upon a time – have been red) and downstairs consists of a kitchen, living room and parlour.

The year is 1949. My father works as a day-labourer for a local building firm. The days are long and tiring, but he does not resent the blisters and bruises. Each injury acts as payment in kind for past or future transgressions.

In order to find employment in the first place, my father has had to soften his accent. He keeps his head down and speaks as little as possible. With an acidic twist in his gut, he changes his surname. He briefly wonders if his wife is looking down at him, judging him, but he does not spend too long in anguished self-reflection – after all, burying disquieting thoughts has become second nature by now.

When he is at home, he drinks too much.

My father's income is not enough to sustain the family home, however, and so my sister has found employment as well, behind the perfume counter in British Home Stores. She smiles at the customers and laughs at the stock-boy's jokes. The store manager thinks she has potential. The long sleeve blouse she has to wear as part of the uniform is useful in covering up the deep pink scars which she has etched into the pale skin of her forearms.

At night, she cries herself to sleep.

The lovers wish pleasure for each other, that much is true, but there is a selfishness in sex – the need itself brings it forth and so there comes a point where each deeper thrust brings with it a counterweight of calculations regarding the satiating of one's own driving lusts and the providing of pleasure for another. Too fast, too slow, too deep, too shallow, a rhythm lost, an angle shifted. Sometimes the right word at the wrong time or a hint of moonlight cast across a delicate cheek and picking out true beauty can be enough to start the urgent surge within, a quickening of pace as the winner of this romantic skirmish becomes clear to all involved.

The drabness of the empty house brings with it a heavy sort of dread, a pit-of-the-stomach ache. The doll's house draws the eye and fills the mind.

Suddenly, like an extinguished flame and for no discernible reason, one of the bedrooms darkens.

Debbie looks up at her husband through a haze of passion and love. She wants the sensation to last forever, but equally cannot stop herself from pushing back against him, feeling the thrumming in her thighs and belly as his weight pushes down upon her.

There is something hidden in that dark little room, the dreamer is certain, something unclean and unspeakable and dangerous. There is a desperate urge to get away, to strike the house, tear it into splinters and flee the darkness but the dreamer cannot. The house holds them still.

A lightning bolt of doubt flashes momentarily blue and harsh across her mind. She knows her husband of twenty years' body better than she knows her own, has intimate knowledge of her lover's form etched within her subconscious. But for a split second something is wrong. His body is too big between her thighs, too heavy. He is a different person. She opens her eyes, momentarily panicked, only to see her husband before her, above her, inside her, and the fear fades away like waves upon the shore.

And then, another room plunges into shadow – the parlour this time. With these two rooms in darkness the dreamer knows, _knows_, with a survival instinct as real as any other, that this is a countdown, with the waterfall an ersatz ticking clock in the background.

Two of the seven. Two of the seven, no three – the discoloured bathroom falls to gloom – and the unknowable horror that lurks within the doll's house now has three rooms in which to hide.

In their final moments together, they need each other deeper than could ever be possible. Fingers dig into soft flesh, kisses too hungry for the pretence of lovemaking. They claw and scratch at each other, they grunt and grasp. The air hangs heavy with the scent of their bodies as they writhe together, clinging onto each other for dear life within a tempest of hormones and lust. And in that moment, they crest upon those waves together, and breathing stops and heartbeats slow and in that moment, it seems like the world exists for them, and them alone.

Four rooms. Over half the house is dark now, and the dreamer tries to get away again, tries to move, but fear and sick intrigue root them to the spot. With over half the doll's house now hidden unseen, a gentle sobbing fills the air. The dreamer's tears? Perhaps these tears are shed for loss and despair – the gentle murmuring of wind through dry grass, a plaintive heavy, heaving sob which builds and builds.

They hold each other as the waves of passion dissipate. Short beats tease within them, and they look at each other anew, returning to each other from places unknown – animalistic dreamworlds within their own bodies and souls.

Even after all these years, a blush rises to the cheek in gleeful acknowledgement of the act committed.

He rolls away, although never out of contact, and together their lungs refill and hearts do their best to regulate once more. Blood pumps to more prosaic body parts and thoughts beyond the bedroom slowly form in their minds once more.

Five rooms now, the last of the bedrooms – the smallest in fact – has darkened. Something glistens behind the shadows now, something wretched. The dreamer can see it, glinting in the half light cast by the swaying electric lights in the ceiling above. It is all they can do, however, to keep their hands from their ears, the quiet sobs have now become the howls of terror. No more are they tears shed in mourning for moments lost, but in terror for moments yet to come.

Beneath the covers they hold hands like teenagers.

But at the back of Debbie's mind, tarnishing her thoughts like a cheap silver ring, sits the knowledge that – for the briefest of moments – she had been making love with someone other than her husband.

Six rooms. No. The house is too dark now, it does not belong to us, to the dreamer. Whoever buried this toy house beneath the sand and carpet did so with good reason. Close the latch, the dreamer tells themselves, shut the doors and say no more of the filth that plays

within the shadow laden rooms. Shut the doors, drop the latch and bury it deep, before the seventh room darkens.

Before the seventh room.

Darkens.

The year is 1951. My sister stands in the middle of the parlour, looking down at my father as he lies bleeding onto the rug. Little red bubbles of blood gather and burst at the wound at his temple, and my sister imagines each one letting out a little cloud of black smoke – the slow release of his polluted soul into the ether.

Interestingly, he takes longer to die than either my mother or I did, and in all that time my sister does nothing. She even gives up watching him after the first half an hour and retires to the kitchen to make herself a cup of tea.

The stain my father leaves behind on the rug remains there for the next fifty years, until its removal – along with most of my sister's possessions – by council workers upon her death. By that time, of course, the stain has long since faded to a murky brown colour, hardly noticeable among the loops of flowers which make up the busy design of the rug, which is then unceremoniously dumped into a skip at the municipal waste and recycling centre.

It will eventually be burned on a rubbish dump in some third-world country whose government is more than happy to turn a blind eye to skies turned black with the smoke of decades-old refuse and the last few embers of a malicious and abusive man.

Write Your Name

Write your name upon your palm
    Lest it be forgotten.
Not the back of your hand, mind,
For who knows what or who might peek.
And if they know your name -
They feed.
Do not say you were not warned.

Take care, stay calm and cool your brow.
Fretting brings not succour
But sweaty hands and pounding heart
And say you reach the clearing up ahead
And finding only cobwebs in your mind
You open up your palm and read
The inky creases of your skin

Your name has run
Away
And you are lost.

***

The night is unseasonably warm, the moon unusually bright. The sound of music floats through the too-still air.

Terry cannot sleep. He tosses and turns, unable to find escape from the feverish atmosphere of the night.

The music – oh, the music! He can feel its vibrations through the mattress beneath his body, through the pillows on which he rests his head. They pulse in the fillings of his gritted teeth and clang in the tangles of his mind.

People are so inconsiderate, he rages as he switches once more to the cold side of the pillow, *don't they know what time it is?*

But what time *is* it? Terry can feel a panicked degradation creeping at the edges of his thoughts. He tries to centre himself - to calm himself - but still the music *violates* him, shattering his thoughts and dreams into multicoloured shards.

He kicks the bedcovers off and lays there in his pyjamas for a moment, before swinging his legs over the edge of the bed and climbing heavily out. Half-asleep, Debbie mutters to him from the other side of the mattress, but the music fills his mind and body to such an extent that he does not hear her. Squinting against the rhythmic thudding in his brain, Terry steps into the hallway.

The landing *thumps* in time to the beat and Terry lets out a low growl. *The nerve of some people.* He presses his face against the cool glass of the landing window and peers this way and that in the darkness, searching unsuccessfully for lights and people and any sign which might point him in the direction of the inconsiderate *bastards* throwing a party so late at night. The neighbouring houses are still and silent, however.

Tearing himself away from the window, he glares accusingly about him. Panic begins to rise in his chest.

A creeping suspicion begins to take hold as he makes his way downstairs. No, not a suspicion, not yet. The merest tendril-tip of a thought, perhaps, a dream-logic understanding of the world and by the time he reaches the bottom of the stairs, he knows exactly where the music is coming from.

In the downstairs hallway, everything dances. The squeal of a trumpet sets the hinges and door handles spinning, the rapid *tssk tssk tssk* of a snare drum ripples through the fibres of the hallway rug. The jazzy piping of a clarinet sends waves running through the very brickwork of the house and

Terry stands amongst it all, unmoving, a shipwreck jutting from an ocean of sound. He stares, unblinking at the parlour door, his eyes burning acid-like though the paintwork and he *seethes*.

A smoky yellow light shines out from beneath the door. It flickers slightly, as though momentarily blocked by someone passing on the opposite side.

Fists clenched in anger, Terry stares at the painted wood. The music is louder than ever now, and he squeezes his eyes tightly against the onslaught. Beneath the instruments he can hear the sounds of laughter and conversation echoing as though coming from some distance away. The scent of alcohol and cigarette smoke drifts through the air.

Raising his fist slowly, Terry begins to hammer against the woodwork.

"Keep the noise down!" he attempts to yell, but the words seem to catch in his throat, embarrassing him. He hammers again and this time, louder:

"Keep the fucking noise down!"

For a moment he fancies that there is a lull in the music, although whether this is just wishful thinking or not it is difficult to say. The sound of a lone trumpet rises above the rest of the band – an indignant *BLAART* of a sound; an auditory two-finger salute – and Terry growls again. Het sets about hammering with both fists, pounding hard enough to a cause a *crunch* in the bones of his hand.

"Let me in, you fuckers!" he yells, desperately trying to make himself heard over the sounds of making-merry. "This is my house! You can't have a fucking party without me! Let me in!"

"Terry?"

He looks up to see Debbie staring down at him from the top of the stairs. Hannah stands behind her, her hair in a sleep-induced halo, a puzzled look on her face.

"Terry, what are you doing love? It's three in the morning."

He wipes his face with the back of his hand and looks up at his wife and daughter in despair. "They won't…stop!" he cries out.

Debbie takes a step or two towards him, warily, holding her hand back behind her to prevent Hannah from following. "Who won't stop, Terry?"

A frown breaks across his brow like cobwebs at dawn as the question fills the hallway. *Who?* The musicians, of course. *What musicians?* The ones playing the music. *What music?*

What music?

What music?

"What music?" he mutters to himself, suddenly cold in his sweat-damp pyjamas.

The night is dark and empty.

***

Fingers *tippytap* away under bedcovers.

dads getting weird again

...

...

Really? What's he doing now?

just like freaking out my mum and sister

My dad was the same. Always arguing and shouting. Although, to be fair, the shouting wasn't the worst part...
People like us, they have to stick together, Lily. I've told you, me and you against the world! If I could, I would make anyone suffer who would cause you harm, my darling girl!

u r so weird! :P

What can I say? I feel things deeply – and I've never had anyone in my life like you before. I can't wait to meet up!

i thought u said we couldnt meet?

Oh, didn't I tell you? I've got a plan, its going to be brilliant! We are DEFINITELY going to be together!

yay!!!

We're just going to have to sort a few things out first...

Invaders

In those moments when I am able to bring myself to look in the bathroom mirror, I do not recognise the face staring back at me. It seems to move as I do - I tilt my head slightly and it does the same. I tilt to the other side; its mimicry continues likewise. I lift my right hand; my reflection similarly lifts its left. Beneath my mask, my teeth bite down onto the edge of my tongue with a gristle crunch so hard that blood flows, sending little rubies scattering from my lips and down my chin, dripping onto the front of my dress. The girl in the mirror bleeds in much the same way – if there are any differences I have not the patience to search them out.

Since Hannah and her family moved in, I have grown unaccustomed to being alone. From decades spent with only the previous owner for company – a quiet, desiccated old spinster for many years even before she passed away – to a house filled with *people* and all their comings and goings and dramas and disagreements and voices and heartbeats and heaven knows what. It is little wonder that, when I do get a moment of peaceful and solitary contemplation, I no longer recognise within myself how to handle such luxury.

And of course, it is not just this family with whom I have to spend my time. Even the fact that Terry currently spends more time at home under doctor's order would have been palatable were it not for the fact that this family's determination to remove all traces of the previous owner continues unabated. I frequently find myself forced to wander amongst workmen during the day – finding unfamiliar face after unfamiliar face in all manner of crevices and nooks about the house. Sometimes I feel that if it were not for the calming presence of my Hannah, I would wrench the flesh from my bones in utter frustration.

I used to love playing in the garden when I was younger. My sister and I would create fairylands amongst the flowers, populated by beautiful princesses with daisy-chain crowns who sat upon snail-shell thrones and dashing heroes who would scale the dark, foreboding rockery to the North to best any challengers for the fair maiden's hand.

A statue stands in the corner of the garden – a stern but understanding guardian to supervise these young storytellers at play.

After I died, I did not care for the garden as much. First and foremost, it was the way the war encroached in such an ugly way – the lawn dug up to make way for the metal airraid shelter at the back of the garden, the flowers pulled up to make way for a vegetable patch. A fairyland torn asunder by the uncaring, humdrum malice of war, without so much as an acknowledgement of this sacrilege on the part of my father.

But even without the constant reminder that my childhood memories no longer had a home amongst my family members, I found it difficult to be in the garden. Maybe there was something beyond my understanding that pulled my spirit back inside, perhaps I could not stray too far from my bedroom, and the location of my final moments on earth. Perhaps the natural place for lost souls is to be trapped between four walls and not beneath an open sky. For whatever reason, while in no way *prevented* from wandering in the garden, I cannot do so for longer than a few moments before I find myself irresistibly drawn back inside.

She walks around the garden in sensible shoes and a sensible haircut, muttering into the mobile telephone gripped in her sensibly manicured hand, while juggling with a clipboard in the other, making notes. She examines the cherry laurel and the dog rose, the dilapidated rockery and the *dianthus caryophyllus.* She pokes at the large mound of lawn that rises in one corner – the last vestige of a long-forgotten compost heap I suppose - with one distracted sensible toe and glares thoughtfully at the weathered statue.

The statue matches her gaze impassively, dignified and calm as always. I wish I had her control – as it is, I can barely stop myself from plunging my hands through the kitchen windows in protest at this sensible woman and her rational, sensible judgement of my garden.

She brings the cold air in with her as she enters the house once more, slipping off her shoes and walking in stockinged feet behind Terry and Debbie into the dining room. The table already covered in shiny catalogues bursting with images of unfeasibly beautiful gardens of such vibrancy and brilliance that they must surely have been the result of an artist's brush, rather than the chilly hands of Mother Nature.

"So, Debbie, Terry," she says with unearned informality, "I think there's a lot we can do with your back garden."

Her name is Jill, because of course it is. She lives in a neat little house on the outskirts of London and enjoys embroidery and calendars featuring cats in amusing outfits. She is currently going through a divorce which is sad in its amicability. *We just drifted apart,* she tells friends and family when they inquire after her wellbeing, although deep down she knows her marriage ended when she finally announced to her husband that she had performed an intimate act upon a male coworker in the back of her Ford Fiesta in a layby off the M4 the previous summer.

This is not the most interesting thing about Jill, however.

There is darkness in her veins, a darkness which flows across her skin like ink in water. She has no knowledge of the fact, but she is descended from the High Priest of an obscure and murderous Anglo-Saxon religious sect.

Under dark skies they would gather on clifftops, whispering prayers of supplication and beatification to ancient, eldritch gods. Shit smeared, naked, their eyes spun wild as they inhaled the scented fumes of powerful hallucinogenic herbs and roots.

Lust and madness were their business, the desecration of the body, the rape of the mind before their twisted deities.

And none so evil, so driven, as their High-Priest. Under his orders, babes were dragged from their mother's arms and torn apart like rags, still warm blood lapped from the stones by the hungry tongues of the unholy congregation. The young and the old, living or dead, animal or human – all were used by the desperate members of the sect to satiate their fevered lusts and call forth the blessings of their cold, obsidian spirit lords.

But good things cannot last forever, and when the end came for the sect, it came like a blade to the throat – swift and messy. In fact it was the towns and villages nearby who first noticed something wrong: the lightening of the morning dawn, no longer permanently darkened by heavy, thunderous clouds, the calming of storm-tossed seas. Those townsfolk who had been unlucky enough to trade with sect members spoke of deals unfulfilled and goods uncollected. The blasted heaths and wraith-haunted woodlands that had once echoed with unholy chanting in ancient tongues lay abandoned – empty save claw marks in the disturbed earth.

It is a truth in every cult or religious faction that somewhere, at some level in the hierarchy of priests and preachers, there is some layer that understands the untruth of it all.

Regardless of motive, be it greed or power or sheer just-for-the-hell-of-it-ness, someone knows it is all a big joke and therefore *worships all the harder for it.*

In the death cult, it was Jill the sensible garden lady's High Priest ancestor who knew exactly how empty his congregation's chanting was, how unlikely to bring forth any dark gods from the beyond. He knew just how foolish bathing in the blood of the innocents was and revelled in the nonsensical ideas of murder and sexual corruption as a path to the One Truth Above Truths.

So, it was he who received the biggest shock of all, when, during one particularly tumultuous, bacchanalian midnight, the very fabric of the earth beneath them was torn asunder, and the Unholy Ones rose in dark silhouette against wine-red skies, bringing forth waves of cold-hearted madness and violence crashing across the very heart and soul of the filth-splattered cultists.

The High Priest found himself being violated mentally, spiritually and physically by a dozen chitinous, ichor-coated tentacles belonging to the very eldritch beings to whom his people had been praying all along. The irony wasn't lost on him.

In the last few seconds before his mind lost the ability for rational thought and his bloodline corrupted for generations to come, he thought only of his mother, and wept.

Jill knows none of this, of course. She does not know why her skin itches around the baptised or the sight of blood subconsciously arouses her. She cannot name the sense of sadness that runs through her being like a seam of coal. She does not know that – like each generation of her family before her – she will face the infinite torment of a fiery, otherworldly hell upon her demise, every atom of her lost soul consumed a million times over by the be-tentacled elder gods called forth upon this realm by her ancestor all those centuries before.

Jill knows none of this.

Perhaps if she did, she would not talk at such length about lawn depths and soil quality and the unsuitability of leylandii in urban garden clusters. My ears bleed slightly.

Discussion turns to the practicalities of digging up the lawn and making it level, which seems to me like a disturbing level of invasion on the part of this woman and her team of brawny workmen, but Terry and Debbie do not seem to care for the originality of a sloping lawn – why am I not surprised? For a moment, a shadow of distress flickers over me. Distress at the utter dismissal of - not only my childhood garden - but also the effort put into it by the old lady who lived here before this wretched and destructive family.

In her younger years, of course. I doubt she even knew she had a garden in the last decade of her life.

Above their heads, the living room light flickers on and off momentarily, and the garden lady looks up apprehensively.

Debbie smiles. "Oh, this house!" she says, nudging her husband who stares blankly at her for a moment through red rimmed eyes, lost in his own thoughts.

"Hmm?"

"The lights flickered again, Terry."

We watch as Terry's mind seems to defrost in front of us. "Yes," he manages, smiling weakly, his lips cracked and sore. "The house is pretty old."

"That's the trouble with moving into an old house, isn't it?" Debbie continues. "You inherit the fifty-year-old wiring as well!"

Jill smiles patronizingly, and makes a mental adjustment to the list of costs she is tallying in her head. A household that can't even keep the lights on probably isn't going to stretch to the premium package, she thinks.

"Well, I think that's everything," she says, closing her notepad with a decisive sweep of her hand. "I'll get some plans drawn up and sent over to you, and then maybe give you a call in the week. What do you think?"

"That sounds great. Really great."

They leave the room on a flowing stream of platitude, unaware that they are planning the surgical removal of yet another part of my childhood, another part of the life I left behind all those decades ago. Am I destined to haunt an unfamiliar land for the rest of my days as the wolves of progress tear through the remnants of my past? Perhaps, when the last familiar mote of dust has been removed, the last strip of paper painted over, the last root from the last plant has been torn from this place, the anchor which holds my spirit here will be taken with it, and I will drift apart into tendrils of stardust and memories, a drop of ink spread wide within the waters of a vast, cold ocean.

I sit in the middle of the dining room table, my shoes scuffing the varnished surface. As I weep for the loses I have faced, the room is filled with the scent of the earth after a rainstorm.

Later that afternoon I curdle the milk in the fridge and the resulting sense of restored balance in the world soothes my soul.

***

The rough and brawny labourers employed to violate the garden have, at the very least, the decency to stay outside as is right and proper. If I try hard enough, I can avoid sight of them for days on end.

That is not the case for all the indignities through which I have cause to suffer.

The worst thing is, I may have brought this one upon myself.

Now that is not a claim I make lightly, nor is it a particularly palatable idea. I suppose that moments of self-reflection are inevitable in my decades-long entrapment within these four walls, however I do not envision making a habit out of them.

But perhaps some of the blame *does* lay at my feet. If I had not delighted in travelling through the central heating systems at night, the family would not have felt the need to hire a plumber to carry out an exploratory investigation into the pipework in the walls.

His name is Charlie, and he may very well be my nemesis.

Charlie is plump and bald. The end of his nose and the apples of his cheek bear the ruddy pinkness of too much sun and alcohol and the greying stubble on his chin gives him the appearance of having fallen face first into an ashen hearth. He has four children of his own, nine grandchildren and one great-grandchild. On more than one occasion he has donned a fake beard to appear as Father Christmas at a local school. In one weeks' time he will kill himself.

He will lie to his wife about his plans for the day, before taking his work van, driving to the nearest town centre and buying two packets of painkillers in each pharmacy and chemist that he sees. In the last one that he visits, he will also buy a packet of razor blades and a large bottle of orange juice.

Charlie will then get into his van and drive across London to a small patch of woodland close to his childhood home. Parking his van, he walks familiar paths through brambles and undergrowth until he is well and truly beneath the hornbeam and birch of the woods. As he walks, he drinks orange juice and swallows painkillers.

The sun that filters through the leaves above is warm on Charlie's face, and his mind is filled with the smells of his younger years – soft leaf-litter scents and the musk of nature taking its first steps into autumnal slumber. He smiles for the first time in three days as he closes his eyes in peaceful contemplation.

He does not keep them closed for too long, however. Charlie does not like the dark, not now. Behind his eyelids, it is not the unknowns, the what-might-hide-in-the-darks that terrifies him, that haunt his mind and clot his thoughts. It is what he has seen, it is the *confirmation* of horrors beyond which torment his mind and bring him here.

The bottle of orange juice is empty, the pills mostly gone. Conscientious, even in his last few moments, he tidily folds up the carrier bag containing the leftovers and stuffs it into his jacket pocket. *It will be here;* he thinks to himself.

The remains of a tree trunk lie on the ground before him – a lightning-storm victim from years past long given over to rot and woodlice – and Charlie pauses and takes off his jacket. He lays it over the dead leaves and twigs of the woodland floor like a picnic blanket and then awkwardly lowers himself down, resting against the fallen tree to keep his balance. Even through the fabric of his jacket, the dirt beneath him is cold, and he guesses that it may not take too long before the dampness of the earth begins to soak through. Putting this uncomfortable thought out of his mind, he lifts his face to seek the sun instead and focuses upon the firmness of the tree trunk against his back. *We never should have left the trees,* he thinks to himself as he searches in his pocket for the packet of razors.

One selected, he slides his sleeves up, revealing the fish-belly-pale skin of his forearms, and in one motion draws a jagged scarlet line through the soft flesh.

Whether in contentment of a job well done or a result of the chemicals floating through his bloodstream, Charlie smiles at the sight of red trickling from his self-inflicted wound. He goes to pass the blade from hand to hand but finds he cannot grip with blood-slicked fingers and fumbles the razor, dropping it. A cursory glance at his side merely confirms it lost amongst the dried leaves and tangled weeds at the tree trunk's base, and so Charlie lets his arms fall by his side, unwilling to search further.

His arm throbs and a sickness swells in his stomach, but Charlie's legs are as lead, and he sits rooted to the spot as firmly as any of the trees that loom overhead. *There are worse places to be,* he thinks; the sun on his face, the scent of nature filling his senses, the soil beneath him (blood-sticky now). As grey mist curls about his vision he strives to take it all in, to fill his last few moments with the beauty of his surroundings.

It is, alas, not to be. As his lifeblood soaks away, a heavy tiredness grips his eyelids. Charlie struggles against their closing but he fights in vain and false slumber takes him. The last seconds of his life, therefore, are spent in hateful, nightmare-haunted darkness.

His body will be found, three days later, by a mother and daughter out collecting wildflowers for a school science project. Scavenging woodland animals will have eaten his face, and one of his hands.

But this is yet to be. For the moment, trauma has yet to take this man and leave him three-days-dead in a woodland on the other side of London. For the moment, he is in my house.

I do not like him being in my house.

The only thing in this world for which I feel even a fraction of the love that I feel for my darling Hannah is the sweet sound of the silence of empty days. Hannah, her mother, and her sister fill the house with life which echoes from wall to wall when they are here, but during the day, when they leave for their places of employment or education, I savour the peace and quiet of an empty home.

Terry does not disturb me. On doctors' orders, he rests in bed for most of the day, a feverish shadow with little impact on my day-to-day life.

But Charlie the plumber *does* disturb me. He *does* impact my life. Because Charlie listens to the radio. Charlie whistles. Charlie hums. Charlie mutters to himself under his breath.

All day.

From the moment he sets foot on the hallway carpet in the morning, to the moment his van leaves the driveway in the evening, Charlie is a living, breathing burden, brought here – it seems – with the sole purpose of torturing the very flesh from my spectral bones.

If there was an end in sight for his one-man infestation of my house things would, perhaps, not seem so awful. However, since the only fault within the pipework of this house is my doing alone, it is a problem both un-findable and un-fixable and therefore – although he does not know it – there is no solution to this wretched man's work and no conclusion to come to and therefore *no reason to ever leave this house.*

Every morning, he lets himself in with a borrowed set of keys. The hallway is cold and empty. The *house itself* is cold and empty - which is strange because Charlie has been told that the man of the house is unwell and asleep in the bedroom upstairs. He has little proof of this, save for the occasional sounds of movement from above.

Sometimes he fancies he hears footsteps on the stairs, or the creak of a floorboard behind him, and turns to greet the source of the sound, only to find himself alone in the room after all. "Don't be daft," he mutters to himself, rubbing the back of his neck. After all, there are workmen toing and fro-ing through the back gate into the garden all day, so it's not so unlikely he would hear noises hereabouts. After all, it is not like he is alone.

He is definitely *not* alone.

These rational thoughts are not quite enough, however, to alleviate his feelings of unease. He chuckles to himself:

"You're goin' simple in your old age, Charlie," he mutters to himself. But still, he cannot shift the sense of *something* weighing on him. On more than one occasion, he catches a glimpse of blue or the darkness of an empty eye socket. In the large mirror overhanging the fireplace in the parlour he sees – fleetingly – a figure standing behind him, merely to find on turning that the folds of the coats hanging in the hallway give form where there is none.

He tries to tell himself that it is all nonsense, but slowly Charlie finds his usual positive approach to life failing him. The stillness of the house unsettles him, even the dust motes that float in the air cause unease. More than once he enters a room and just stands there - his mind blank, all purpose forgotten.

Today he works on the boiler, which is nestled amongst the discarded memories and cardboard boxes in the loft. The space is warm and dark, with cobwebbed corners hidden in gloom cast by rolls of badly fitted insulation. Here and there, slates are visible through holes torn in the thin lining of the roof, through which float the gentle sounds of the outside world.

Far above in the rafters, two bare bulbs shine a dusty yellow light down onto the space below, but even so Charlie positions a camping light next to the boiler in order to illuminate the job properly. As if in protest at this intrusion on their territory, the lights above flicker occasionally, sending jagged shadows scurrying between the beams.

Over the years, Charlie has become accustomed to the trials and tribulations of working in older houses, and he's been in some far worse conditions than this. Even so, with every momentary surge of darkness overhead, he frowns and rubs the back of his neck distractedly.

Resting on his toolbox by his feet, Charlie's portable radio plays classic rock to fill the gloom. The sounds of aging rockers float quietly about the empty space like smoke, and provide his idle ears something to focus on, rather than the empty ticks and creaks of a silent house.

Still I run out of time or it's hard to get through, Till the bird on the wire flies me back to you.... The radio trills out between crackles, the words wavering beneath the sounds of static.

Charlie shakes his head and reaches over, giving the radio a sharp tap. It is an old thing, covered in paint and plaster splatters, and prone to losing stations. As he turns the thing off and on again the music swim back. He smiles a grim smile, and draws his arm back, perhaps quicker than he needed to. For a moment, he feels vulnerable, exposed, although there is no one in the loft with him.

He tries to ignore the prickling of his skin as he takes his wrench and works away, and – when the music disappears with a crackle once again - he is tempted to leave it be.

But the sounds of the house crash into the silence – the ticking of a hallway clock, the murmur of floorboards warming in the morning sun, the swell of rhythmic breathing – and after a split second of internal debate between the animal and the rational, Charlie shakes his head. Convincing no one, he rolls his eyes in mock annoyance.

"Blasted thing," he mutters, frowning and picking the radio up, prying open the battery compartment and checking for leakage, before setting it back down again, just in time for it to start playing once again with another burst of static.

He briefly considers turning it off completely if the darn thing is going to play silly buggers, but the idea of working in silence – in *this* house – is not one that he wants to give weight to.

He shifts slightly and the beams creak underneath him.

A few minutes pass and the static returns - crackling quietly for a moment, before the radio turns off altogether. Charlie stares into the middle distance, his eyes glazed, not wanting to look back at the silent radio, trying to ignore the racing of his pulse. For a man convinced he is alone, he works *awfully* hard to hide his true emotions.

The feeling of terror that only grips in the middle of the night, when you wake up – bedcovers tossed aside – and the icy dread that fills your mind as you wrestle with the knowledge that you *have* to pull them back over yourself as protection from demons unseen, *while at the same time* being too terrified to move because of those self-same horrors, is the feeling that grips Charlie for an impossibly long time. He does not want the silence. He wants his radio to work. He does *not* want to move.

After an irrationally long time, the chemicals of fear dissipate enough for him to slowly reach out his hand. But, as his fingers brush against the surface of the radio, it bursts into life once more, louder than ever, a blast of trumpet and saxophone, the sounds of wild partying.

Charlie jumps up in alarm, an unwise move beneath the pitched roof, and smacks the back of his head sharply against a beam. Debris and dust clatters down around him as, swearing under his breath, Charlie scrabbles about on the floor for the radio.

Once the wretched thing is retrieved and thumbed into silence, and with the cacophony of jazz music still ringing in his ears, Charlie stands in mute contemplation. His heart thumps within his chest at such an alarming rate that he wonders briefly if he is having a heart attack. No attack is forthcoming, however, nor is there any sound from the loft hatch to suggest the incident has been noticed by anyone downstairs. Gingerly, Charlie reaches up to feel his scalp, wincing as he does so. When he withdraws his hand, there is a smear of blood on his fingertips.

"Nothin' serious," he mutters quietly to himself. "Bit of a bump, that's all."

As he moves to put the radio back down, his foot hits something metal. A square tin, with a chocolate-box scene of flowers and Georgian carriages on the lid. He picks the thing up, his fingers leaving marks in the patina of dust and cobwebs on its surface. He looks up into the gloom above him, looking to see where the tin might have fallen from, but no obvious hiding place is forthcoming.

There is always an element of trust, an unspoken agreement between a workman and the family in whose home he spends his time, and in the decades of plumbing behind him, Charlie has never broken this trust. Never peeked inside a jewellery box or peered into an open underwear drawer. If in the course of his work he finds loose change, he carefully deposits it in a neat little pile on the kitchen counter before leaving for the day.

But this tin…draws him in. The paint is chipped here and there, but beneath the layer of grime, it seems pretty untouched. As he examines it, he feels something shift inside, something light sliding across the metal interior.

A beam overhead creaks gently; the cobwebs that hang from the bare lightbulbs above bounce slightly, caught in an unfamiliar breeze.

Ignoring the dull ache at the back of his head, Charlie pulls the lid from the tin. It opens with a gasp, a scrape of metal upon metal, and he looks at the folds of paper which fill the tin to the brim.

A wave of motion passes over some of the black bags of old clothes stored about the hatch, as a draught from some unpatched hole in the slates somewhere drifts through the loft.

He wonders if the owners even know that the tin and its contents are here. Curious, he plucks one of the pieces of paper from the tin. He takes it to be a letter at first, perhaps from a wartime love, but as a few lines catch his eye, he realises they are, in fact, pieces of poetry.

My love's embrace is gentle, midnight warm
The darkness of the night breathes in her soul

Charlie reads silently, his lips moving slightly as his eyes scan each line. He nods to himself, then takes another from the box.

I am
The figure at the corner of your eye
The unseen fingers brushing against your hand as you reach for
something in the dark

He shivers slightly as he reads, his skin registering the cooling temperature of the loft in a way that his mind does not. Tracks of dust dance about his feet.

My soul stirs for you
Uncertain as to if it lingers still.

Above him, the storage boxes and bags of old clothes vibrate and dance to strange and unsettling music, but Charlie does not hear. He does not notice.

He holds the paper up to his face to read it better, before realising that the difficulty he is having is caused by the shadows of the lights swinging overhead. He cannot look up at the lights, however. His attention is drawn to the figure that stands by the loft hatch.

Charlie cannot move; his breath catches in his chest.

The light from below and the flickering of bulbs overhead cast the figure in semi-silhouette, but he can see that she – he presumes it is a she - looks like she has stepped from one of the images in his mother's photograph album. Photographs of her and his aunties as young women during the Second World War. Greys and blues, pleats and buttons. An outfit from a museum.

In the gloom, he cannot see her face, but what he can see seems wrong. Distorted, elongated, with dark holes for eyes. The head of an animal in a dark midnight blue.

"You. Have. No. Right."

Whispered though they are, the words seem to fill the dark space of the loft. The figure stands in eyeless contemplation of Charlie, still and unmoving, specks of dust and loft insulation floating down around her.

Red hot waves of anger wash out from the motionless figure, the two dark pits in its face burning him with a rage made all the more terrible by their emptiness. Nervously, he shifts his grip of the metal tin in his hands and looks down at it guiltily.

"I'm sorr-," he begins, but as he looks back up the figure has crossed the space between them with impossible speed and stands before him.

Ice cold hands sweep up and grip his face, ragged blood-stained fingernails digging into his skin. *"You. Have. No. Right!"* The figure screams in a voice like tortured metal. There is no breath, no warmth, no weight of being, but the force of emotion is enough to send him reeling like a pipe wrench to the face.

Charlie lets out a low, guttural sound, a whimper of disbelief from the back of his throat, his eyes wide and white. The terror soaking through his brain sends his body juddering in shock, his heels banging against the beams beneath him as he tries to back away. The metal tin drops from his hands, scraps of poetry falling like confetti about his feet.

Above his head, a lightbulb bursts, taking with it the last remaining fragments of the plumber's sanity. Tiny shards of glass bloom into the air, one hundred horse-faced ghouls raining down on Charlie's bare head and neck. He cries out, instinctively reaching up to protect himself, and in the darkness realises he is alone once again.

He bleeds, wide eyed and dry-mouthed. As his heart beats its staccato rhythm inside his chest, he manages to force himself to turn his head and look about him at the loft space. He takes in the silent black bags, the cardboard boxes that surround him, and wipes the sweat and blood from his eyes. He looks down – the prettily-decorated metal tin and folds of paper are nowhere to be seen.

Charlie does not know how long he stands there; he does not count the seconds, minutes, hours that pass as his fractured reality knits together into something new, something different. He makes his way unsteadily towards the loft hatch, leaving his tools behind, and tentatively climbs down into the living space below. No questioning eyes are there to greet him, no inquiring bodies investigating the noises above. He is alone.

He leaves the house, gets into his van, and drives all the way home in silence.

***

There are times when I wonder if the problem is with her, and not me. That my darling Hannah is unreceptive to my love - not through any fault of mine - but perhaps because she is incapable of love. I realise this seems indescribably petty, mean spirited even, but when one is in the throes of true love, one's heart looks for reason and tales as yet untold in every passing glance or motion.

I know I am fooling myself, of course. Deep down, I know that my darling does not possess frost-bitten fruit in place of a heart, but there are times – in my weakness – that I am comforted by the possibility. I am not at fault in this relationship, she is. Perhaps she suffers from some disorder of the blood or brain, some misshaped tumour pressing against a nerve cluster which prevents her from feeling the way I feel.

My own, uncorrupted heart sings at the thought that, perhaps, some disease of the soul ravages my love and withers away her ability to feel as she *must* feel, towards me.

But I pay no nevermind – I have love enough for both of us. A joyful exuberance of love and lust and hope for Hannah – a love that makes me want to wrench apart her ribcage and settle cosily within her still-warm frame, kept safe and comforted by the sinews of her form. Such desire have I - to reach inside her, fill her limbs with mine, *wear* her if I could, my sweet angel's skin a cloak of love about my shoulders.

But suddenly, something happens which proves me wrong. Hopelessly, pitifully, ashamedly *wrong* about the whole wretched situation.

Hannah *is* capable of showing love. Just not to me.

Yet.

His name is Patrick.

Imagine a snail shell, beneath a damp rock, at the discarded end of an overgrown garden made humid in the afternoon sun. A garden where the scent of life is overpowered by that of rot and decay, of composting plants and rancid, unwholesome things.

The snail shell is occupied. It is filled with life that squirms and writhes in this dark, warm place. The original owner of the shell is long dead – eaten away from the inside by maggots hatched from fly eggs deep in the invertebrate's stomach. The maggots glisten whitely within the scraps of slimy flesh which still cling to the curved interior of the shell. If you listen hard enough, you can hear the mewling of the creatures as they blindly crawl over each other's bloated, unspeakable bodies.

Now imagine, these despicable things, satiated as they are on the decaying flesh of this most lowly of creatures, each begin to excrete. In their rat-king knot of filth within the snail shell, each maggot's waste smears onto the bodies of its siblings, mingling with their own natural mucous. A hateful ball of maggot-filth-coated vileness sweating in the darkness, in the heat of the afternoon.

This is Patrick.

He imposes altogether too much on my darling Hannah and though they seem to spend an inordinate amount of time out of the house, when they *do* deign to return home, I am forced to suffer the indignity of looking at his gormless face. It is not even as if being in another room soothes my rage – his ridiculousness burns through brick and mortar and etches itself on my innocent soul from across the house. How my darling Hannah copes with it all, I do not know.

That's not quite true. I *wish* I did not know.

There is a flush that rises in Hannah's cheeks when she sees him, a territorial way she holds his gaze for a beat too long. Something *animal* changes within her every time he enters the room and I am heartsick and I am betrayed.

Since Patrick's arrival into my home, I have little taste for life. Nothing amuses me. I begin the simplest of tasks, only to find my attention wandering like never before. Cobwebs sit ungathered and rest, untouched, in the corners of the room. A small vase of pale pink cornflowers sits on the dresser in the parlour, untouched by blite or blister. The central heating leaves me cold.

I find even the poetry within me has dried up. It seems indulgent to allow myself such luxuries at a time like this, but even when I manage to put pen to paper, I fear the muse has left me. My latest effort died upon the page before it even had time to take flight – an aborted foetus of a poem:

Patrick

Patrick, you are a shit.

I hate you.

The words do not sing in my heart nor cry from my lips. The boy is nothing more than a stutter in the rhythm of my life.

Patrick fell in love (or whatever placeholder emotion serves the same purpose within the troglodytic workings of his soul) within seven seconds of seeing Hannah across the crowded lunch hall of the college which they both attend. Arriving several weeks after the beginning of term, my darling Hannah had found herself having to traverse the tricky terrain of well-worn cliques and friendships which were so established they had grown smooth and lumpen over time. Her natural warmth allowed her to carve a path for herself during lessons, but in the social strata of lunchtime she found herself lost.

With Hannah lost, and at her most vulnerable, the weasel Patrick spied her. Serenaded by the sounds of clattering cutlery and chattering teenagers, he swells with a dreary kind of lust, and in his mind, she is his.

He finally plucked up the courage to speak to her amongst the damp scents of old paper and nervous sweat of the college library. The sun shone through windows badly in need of a clean, illuminating the scene in the sickly yellow light it deserved. A washed-out urine-stain light for a washed-out urine-stain of a boy who approached Hannah while she was studying.

"Anyone sitting here?"

Her eyes, as dark as well water, alight from the pages of her geography textbook and rest briefly on the empty chair in front of her, before flicking up towards Patrick, and then finally across to the tables that surround them. The library isn't empty, but there are plenty of unvacated tables dotted around the place. He didn't need to approach her. He didn't need to sit with her.

She smiles lightly and shakes her head. "Nope."

"Do you mind if I sit?"

She nods and then looks surprised when his expression changes slightly.

"Oh, you *do* mind, sorry," he begins, and Hannah smiles.

"No, that's… that's not what I meant. Of course you can sit there," she laughs and watches him as he sits down in the empty seat, a relieved blush pinking his cheeks. She waits for him to pull his books and his laptop out of his bag and settle down.

"You're new here, aren't you?" he asks.

"No," she smiles. "I've been sat here for at least half an hour. You're the new one."

A confused frown passes across his face, giving him the appearance – momentarily – of an inbred pug, before breaking into a broad grin.

"No, I meant here at school."

"I know what you meant!" she says. "Yeah, we moved here a few months ago."

He wants to tell her that he has fallen in love with her, but he settles for:

"I'm Patrick."

"Hannah."

They talk about college and music and films, and they talk and they talk and friendship blooms like rot within an over-ripe plum. Together with Callie they spend time away from the house and I do not understand why. At first, I feel it was only charity – pity, perhaps, towards the ridiculous boy – but soon it becomes clear that they are stepping out together and I hate him so much.

I hate *her* too, and this is his most unforgivable sin.

The greatest injustice, however, is how little my darling Hannah seems to expect from this relationship. There is so little wooing, so little chase to their partnering. If I had it within me to weep, I would.

He stands on her doorstep, a gormless smile upon his face – the face of a simpleton – waiting for Hannah to open the door. He fidgets nervously, not an ounce of poise or confidence about him anywhere. How my love does not turn him away at the very sight of him I do not know, instead she opens the door and offers him a smile that could be described, at best, as charitable.

"Alright?" he says on seeing her.

Alright? I ask you, how is that for poetry?
She deserves so much more.

I follow the two of them down the hallway, wishing I could declare my love for Hannah in a manner which spoke of its strength, its severity - if only to teach the boy that there is a correct way that these things should be done! I would speak of her exquisiteness, the music in her soul, the sweet decay within. But I know the gossamer threads of my words would leave no trace upon either of them and so the two of them remain uneducated and unaware of the adoration my Hannah so richly deserves.

I try to leave them to their own devices, I truly do. I pace up and down the hall. I sit upon the kitchen floor, the deep cold and damp of the ground below the house seeping uncomfortably through the terracotta tiles. In the parlour, I try to occupy my mind with literature, but the selection of books on offer is significantly drearier than when my parents were alive, and since I have no desire to expand my mind towards the inner workings of either motor vehicles or minor celebrities, I was not tempted by the contents of the so-called magazine rack.

They fill the house, the two of them. Just as the beating of a heart travels through every vein and capillary to be felt in the tips of the fingers or the thin flesh of the temples, so their emotions seem to seek me out no matter where I hide.

As I make my way upstairs, I wonder if I worry too much. After all, Hannah and Patrick are neither star-cross'd lovers nor soulmates. The steps creak beneath my feet - the swollen wood in argument with decades-old joins and part-rusted nails - and each familiar sound calls to me to calm my brow. *One day, he will be dead,* they attempt to console, and this much is true. In a little over seventeen years' time, Patrick is found hanging from the back of the bedroom door by his new wife, the result of pressure on the carotid sinus in his neck during an auto-erotic asphyxiation self-pleasure session gone badly wrong. Before calling for an ambulance – and after recovering from her initial shock – she will do her best to pull his trousers back up in order to afford her husband of two weeks some dignity, although this will be difficult as he will have defecated over his own ankles in death. The air is filled with the scent of human faeces and festive pine air freshener. It is three days after Christmas.

The thought acts as a cooling balm, somewhat, to my troubled mind. This dalliance, whatever it is, is nothing compared the wider plans and paths of the universe and the silken thread which my beloved Hannah weaves through the cosmos to her own pattern, her own design. Patrick is merely a tangle to unpick - he will never be able to claim her as his own.

But.

Unable to stay away, I am drawn to them, and I enter Hannah's bedroom to find them both sat on her bed. They are talking, but anticipation hangs in the air like perfume.

"Can we go out to see a film, then?" he asks.

"I've got to be here to let the workmen in, you know that." She looks back at him as he slumps in mock disappointment onto her bed. "Don't be such a brat!" she laughs.

He props himself up on his elbows and looks up at her petulantly. "Your dad's here, isn't he?"

She pauses for a second. "He's not feeling well, it wouldn't be fair."

He senses her tone and doesn't say anymore, but part of him thinks it's just an excuse. He looks back towards the bedroom door as if imagining the walls and woodwork were glass, affording him a view into Hannah's father's bedroom and the chance to assess for himself just how *unwell* the man is. He knows there is truth to her words, but still, he cannot help but feel hard done by.

"Well," he says, not looking at her, "I bet we can think of something to occupy ourselves while we wait."

She smiles. "Oh really?"

I feel my gorge rise. If I could, I would vomit.

What are you doing, Hannah?

She sits on the edge of the bed next to Patrick, and I take pains to turn away, but like a fairground hall of mirrors, the two of them are everywhere, and they surround me.

"You're so beautiful."

"Shut up!"

Just shut up!!

They lean into each other to kiss, his eyes closed, hers open. She looks at him in this intimate moment, her gaze caressing his features, and I see nothing short of naïve *adoration* in her eyes. Her physicality responds to him and their lips brush, with such weight of meaning and lightness of touch.

I am not angry, just disappointed, and almost by its own volition my hand reaches out and grips the back of Patrick's head. There is no real force – he might perhaps have felt something had he not been otherwise occupied.

With no plan, guided only by the emotions in *my* heart, I push my fingertips through the back of his skull.

It's not an unpleasant sensation, with resistance much like pushing one's fingers into warm, wet sand. I don't understand the practicalities of things on a spiritual level – it's not as if his skin is torn or bones broken by the introduction of my fingers into his head. I feel a warmth inside, but that could be more of an impression, rather than the actual temperature of Patrick's brain matter registering on my skin. A wave of serenity washes over me.

The effect is immediate. Mistaking Patrick's groans as the sounds of euphoria at first, Hannah soon draws back at the taste of copper on her tongue. She looks in horror at the blood that streams from Patrick's nose and from between his lips as several veins within his head rupture. At first, thinking the film of blood that covers Hannah's lips and chin as hers, Patrick does not register the gushing from his own face. It is only when he finds himself unable to speak, and a spluttering, bubbling sound leaves his throat, that he realises that something is terribly wrong. Uncomprehending, the last thing he sees before his eyes roll back into his head and he passes out from shock is the sight of Hannah's face, grey and dripping with his own blood, as she begins to scream.

***

A generalised onset seizure, the men at the hospital call it, and keep Patrick in for any number of tests and assessments. I think of it more as *the trials of love*. Regardless, having been gifted a mouthful of his mucus and blood, Hannah no longer seems romantically interested in Patrick. I have saved her from so much – he would never have made her happy.

Not like I can.

My Love's Embrace is Gentle, Midnight Warm

My love's embrace is gentle, midnight warm
    The darkness of the night breathes in her soul
And supping deep, the stars begin their swarm
While moonlight up above fulfils its roll.
Doubt not, my love, decay will hold you strong
Within its arms, a life alive beats soft
Death-sweet, its kisses sing their tender song
As spores of tenderness on zephyrs waft
To grow anew in chambers mildew-webbed
Hearts pounding heavy under dust and rime
For when that saintly moon – its phosph'rescence ebbed
And darkness o'er about descends, I find
Fresh humour in my veins when she is near
Always, my love, I lay with you in fear.

Buried

"What do you mean, there's something under the lawn?"

I stand, framed by the back door, watching Terry and two workmen looking for all the world like three garden gnomes placed haphazardly about the grass. One of them scratches the top of his head in cartoonish confusion.

In the lawn in front of them, where the grass rises at a gentle incline to a height three or four feet above the garden proper, a glimmer of darkness looms through the greenery.

"There's something under there, mate," the elder of the two workman says, "Nearly mucked up the digger blade, didn't it?" This is a statement, not a question, and he looks at Hannah's dad not expecting a response, but merely to check that he understood the severity of a cracked digger blade, and the financial penalties an incident like that would have entailed.

"What d'you think it is?" The younger workman muses to himself.

"It'll be some brickwork or something, you mark my words," the elder workman muses. "I bet someone's tried to do a two-level thing back here, but it's not been maintained." He looks at Terry again, the potential peril that the digger blade had been in still weighing heavily on his mind. "You gotta maintain these things, see? Or the weight of the soil's gonna push against the bricks and whatnot and take it back over." He traces a finger through the air along the rise of the lawn. "Yeah, there'll be a wall of some sort all along there." He nodded to himself. "Did the previous owner not mention anything about the garden before you moved in?"

Terry shakes his head. He does not like being with these workmen. He feels exposed in front of them, out in the light, and briefly imagines that they can see inside his mind, see the oil slick sickness behind his eyes which he tries desperately to keep hidden. He can feel the younger of the two workmen staring at him.

"No, we... we never met the owner. She died before we moved in."

The elder workman tuts, as if to indicate that while he had every sympathy in the world for the owners of houses whose previous owners had died before passing on vitally important information regarding hidden things within their garden, this situation was entirely Terry's fault, and that a man who does not have an in-depth knowledge of the quality of soil in his garden – and the mysteries contained therein – was, in the elder workman's view, not a real man at all.

Somewhere a wood pigeon coos, and the scent of late blooming clematis floats on the breeze. Terry kneels down to get a closer look at the object jutting from the half-dug soil. He sees the edge of something metal, grown dark with rust and mud, which would have been about three or four feet tall if the garden didn't slope so much down to the back door. He is intrigued by it; it is a mystery to take him out of himself and calm the troubled seas of his mind.

"There's something metal here," he mutters. "It's not bricks, see?"

He reaches out to touch the murky looking surface.

"Metal, is it?" the elder of the workmen muttered before turning to his workmate. The two of them began to chatter behind him:

"Water tank, do you think?"

"Maybe. Or some kinda greenhouse frame. Whatever it is, I wouldn't touch it until we know what it is."

The workman's voice seems muffled, but Terry withdraws his hand anyway. He is aware of further conversations going on behind him, but they do not seem relevant to the now that is this strange object buried beneath his garden. His eyes trace along the chipped, mud-caked edge of metal, and he sees within its form the weight of past lives and stories the telling of which have long since died on the tongue. He feels his mind clearing and finds himself falling forward, into the darkness visible just underneath the rusted edge, where clumps of soil have begun to fall away.

"Mate?"

"Oi, mate, you're gonna have to move."

Slowly, Terry feels the hot, thundery headache returning and he looks up at the workmen by his side. For a moment they appear as formless silhouettes, the light in the garden colder and brighter than before, like an over-exposed photograph.

The two men look down at him. The older one speaks slowly, as to a child.

"You're going to have to move, mate." He points at the object protruding from the soil. "So's we can get this shifted."

"Yeah, sorry," Terry replies as he gets unsteadily to his feet. "So, what's the plan?"

The older workman takes a deep breath. "Well, I don't really know, depends on what we're looking at here. We'll have a bit of a dig around with the shovels, see what we can see. Could be just a large box or something, an old compost bin or something, in which case we can get it shifted. Could be something larger and deeper – foundations for an old shed, that sort of thing. That'll definitely take a bit of shifting – we'll have to contact head office to sort that out." He pauses for a moment, and looks Terry up and down. He's not sure quite what's going on, but part of him wishes he hadn't taken on this job. There's something unhealthy about the man before him, a strange nervous energy, despite the heavy bags under his eyes. He looks back up at the house and fancies that – for the briefest of seconds – they are being watched.

"Look, whatever it is," he continues, turning back to Terry, "it's gonna cost a bit more and take a bit longer. Unless you want us to cover it over, and leave it like it was?"

"No!" Terry says, louder than he meant to. The workmen look at him sharply. "No, thank you. I want to find out what it is." He nods his head thoughtfully. "It doesn't matter how much it costs or how long it takes, keep... keep digging." He smiles at both of them, his eyes too bright. "Let's get the garden finished, yes?"

The younger of the two workmen looks over at his workmate as Terry walks back to the house, but the older man merely shrugs. "Carry on digging, I'll get on the phone to Jill to tell her what's going on."

He looks back at the house, and without realising it, looks directly at me. He shivers, despite the warmth of the day.

****

Her room is gloomy, a grey pall paints the air, unaffected by the fairy lights which dangle in loops from the bookcase. She sits propped up on the pillows of her bed, her bare feet pushed beneath the cool cotton bedding. A maths book lies open on the bed next to her, homework half-completed, half-forgotten.

Her face is pale in the bright illumination of her phone, the harsh white light casting ghoul-like shadows across her cheeks and picking out the delicate spiderwebs of veins in her tired eyes. The girl radiates such excitement it is surprising she doesn't hover several inches above her bed.

The phone in her hand buzzes.

So?

no I was too nervous

I thought we were both going to do it?

did you do it

Well, yes. But I've done it many times before. It's not special unless we do it together!

The girl feels sick to her stomach as she reads, a nervous flutter at her chest. She stands on the edge of a cliff, staring down into waters heavy with expectation as her thumb hovers over her phone.

does it hurt

It's not about it hurting, is it? It's about being in control. I thought that was what you wanted in your life? I know you feel different from the rest of your family, they just don't understand how awesome you are. Let us take this next step together, my princess!

...

...

Im scared

I thought you were ready, that's all. Don't worry about it if you're not. Some animals become so used to the trap, they forget that they should be fighting to escape. If you don't want to share this with me, I understand.

i DO want to share this with you

...

ur my only friend

I know. You're my best friend, Lily, I would never force you to do anything you didn't want to. I want you to be in control of your own life! But don't worry, if you're too frightened to go through with it, I still respect you.

Lily's mind is filled with white noise, her thoughts skittering away as though repelled by magnets. Even with her eyes closed the insidious glow of her phone finds her, lighting up the inside of her head, impossible to escape.

where should i do it?

Her fingers type of their own volition, making their own decisions in the conversation. Taking control, that's what her friend said, so why did she feel like she was being led head first? But equally, why did she feel so exhilarated? Her eyes dart to the bedroom door, to her bedside table, back to her phone. She types an urgent "?" and then deletes it immediately after.

Why is there no reply? Was a careful response being considered, mulled over? Each word being considered carefully in order to create the perfect impact upon her heart? Or perhaps the conversation has been discarded, ignored...

Upper arm, I think. Or maybe on your upper thigh? No one in your family is going to look there.

...

No one in your family looks there, do they?!

ew no!

Well then, my Warrior Queen, you know what to do. Our families torture us with their rules, their madness, how else will be seize control of ourselves? It is only through the extreme, by walking paths they are not brave enough to tread themselves, that we can separate ourselves from the herd. I would love for us to have this, so why not let yourself sing for me?

Lily's heartbeat is a call to arms, battlefield drums through the mists. She looks again at the small pink jewellery box on her bedside table, a smiling unicorn emblazoned on its plastic lid.

Within a moment or two, the lid is off – though she is unable to tell whether she removed it herself or some force unknown is to blame.

Between the cheap clip-on earrings and plastic beaded necklaces lies a razor blade, gleaming dully – wrenched from a disposable razor stolen from her mother.

The phone in her hand buzzes, and she looks down at the message.

Auf Wiedersehen

The two words, heavy with confidence, glow before her. For once, she feels calm.

***

Terry stares out of the kitchen window while Debbie bustles behind him. Sonar-like, the sound of clattering crockery outlines unspoken things in the space between them.

"It's just incredible, isn't?" Terry mutters.

"Hmm," Debbie replies with a non-committal grunt, transferring small cakes from fridge to plate and arranging miniature sandwiches in delicate patterns of cheese and ham.

A large tarpaulin shape looms at the back of the garden, guy ropes hammered tightly into the sod and soil, pulling the dark green fabric tight over the large boxy shape beneath. Terry stares in wonderment at the darkness of the object within. A doorway to another world, a dark and mystic portal to the beyond. Beneath the warm scent of baking, the tang of cool earth fills his nose and mouth, bitter on his tongue.

"Are you just going to stand there?"

Pools of icy water glisten dark and still upon hard, cold stone, soaking into too thin fabric, while all around the tarpaulin thiwp-thwips in the autumn breeze.

"Terry?"

He turns to look at his wife. "What?"

He looks down at the proffered plates of party food then up at her, perplexed.

Debbie sighs internally. She bites her tongue, knowing that even being downstairs, being dressed, is an enormous achievement for her husband at the moment. She appreciates the fact that he has managed to pull himself free of the sucking tentacles of depression, no matter how briefly.

And so, for the good of her family and her marriage, she does not comment on his pallid appearance, or his tendency to drift off and stare into distant space at a moment's notice. She holds out two plates of sandwiches and raises her eyebrows in gentle encouragement.

"Take these into the other room and put them on the table, love."

After a beat too long, he takes the plates from her and walks quietly into the other room.

****

It is certainly unlike any party I attended in my short life. The family gatherings of my youth were loud and dangerous affairs, the sound of laughter and music filling the air as thick as cigar smoke.

There were rules to these parties, of course. As a child you had the option to remain in the same room as the adults - and open yourself up to condescension, cigarette ash in your hair and the occasional sip of stolen sherry - or you could retire to one of the safe havens around the house, enclaves of offspring huddled in gossiping, giggling corners, playing cards or jacks. The older boys and girls would glower at the young ones, lost as they were in the limbo of embarrassment and hormones which precluded them from taking part in any form of merriment with either their parents or their younger siblings.

This party, however, is so dreary as to be almost comical. The sound of people chattering forms a glaze over the room. Occasionally a laugh pops through the gentle hubbub like a bursting bubble, but even this seems subdued somehow, as though I'm viewing the whole world through a veil of cotton gauze. I try to resist the urge to pluck out their dull lifeless eyes as a way to ease my boredom.

The birthday girl herself looks most forlorn. She sits upon the sofa, plate of food on her lap, and smiles and makes muted conversation with her relatives. Her new school is nice, she says. The other pupils are friendly, she says. The idea of being a teenager now was exciting, she says. No, she isn't sure what she wants to be when she is older, she says. Beside her, Hannah reaches down to gently squeeze her sister's hand in support.

Exhausted by the lack of activity, I sit at the dining table and softly rearrange flakes of puff pastry on the tray before me into declarations of love for my Hannah. It is not an easy task.

Hannah's Uncle Charlie has hair plugs and once drunkenly groped his boss at a work party. He will die of a brain tumour in ten years' time – I can smell it on him. He stops by the table and plucks the last of the cocktail sausages off a plate and into his mouth in one swift movement, before wiping the grease from his fingers onto his jacket and heading over to one of the small groups of adults chatting quietly.

I watch as they talk about the weather, about new cars and old jokes and their banality makes my head ache. I see them all, every thought, every path ahead of them. I see the ones with sins they wish to keep hidden and crimes left unpunished. I see every petty little indiscretion that sits upon the paths they tread like a steaming pile of freshly grunted dogs' mess.

Hannah's grandmother worked as a secretary at a local mechanics for forty years before she retired. She was good with numbers and fiddled the books for decades, using her ill-gotten gains to fund a holiday to the beaches of Southern France every Summer. Through some strange twist of fate, she will outlive both her daughters – Hannah's mother and aunt – and end her days alone and forgotten in a nursing home just outside South Ruislip, dreaming of stolen banknotes and sun-bronzed bodies. One of Hannah's older cousins is having an affair with her next-door neighbour and will die due to complications during a routine operation on her knee. Another uncle, this time on her father's side, watched his best friend drown at the age of ten and refused to find help. At the time he had been jealous of his friend over some petty childhood disagreement – now long faded into irrelevance - and had watched the young boy struggle to keep his head above water while swimming in a river which ran through a local park that had been a regular hangout for children after school. He had watched, cheeks burning with anger and shame, as his friend had struggled and gasped, each second dragging him further down, each mouthful of air bringing with it more and more water, until, eventually, the thrashing and the struggling and the bubbles just...stopped. The uncle himself will die of a heart attack during a holiday to Mykonos in thirteen years' time. He will die face down in a puddle, so there is some irony there, I suppose.

Oh god, I hate them all.

Terry looks at the person next to him.

"What?" he asks.

The older man – his father, Hannah's grandfather – raises an eyebrow. "Are you alright, Tel?"

"Yeah, why?"

"I don't know. You seem sort of… distracted?" his father replies gently.

Terry looks at the older man, then at the two other members of their small group, and realises that he has no idea how long he has been zoned out for, no idea how much of the conversation he has missed. He smiles, nervously.

"Yeah, sorry. Just tired, you know."

Sara, Terry's younger sister, groans. "Tired? Tell me about it. I was up all night with this little man." She jiggles the bundle of chubby limbs and large blue eyes which she holds at her side. Her father reaches across and chucks the little one under one of his chins.

"Oh, that reminds me of someone else at this age," he chuckles, looking up at Sara.

"I know, I know – I was a terrible baby, dad!", she laughs, rolling her eyes.

Her father grins. "Not like this one, of course," he says, placing a hand on Terry's arm. "This one slept the whole time!"

His sister says something in reply, but Terry doesn't hear. He looks down at his father's liver-spotted hand as if it was something alien, something confusing. He frowns again and looks about him, looking for all the world like a watchful cat. He watches his wife gently scold the birthday girl for staring at her phone rather than talking to people, he watches the mouths and the eyes of the members of his family and other guests who stand around the room chatting and eating. He swears, beneath it all, there is music. Harsh, jagged, jazzy.

Abruptly, he leaves the conversation with his father and sister and makes his way across the room, leaving them staring at his retreating back in concern. Making his way past the small groups of partygoers, Terry reaches the small radio on the windowsill and turns it on. Music plays, loud and electric, its volume making everyone jump. Merry tunes fill the air and Terry smiles to himself – any other music that may have been playing on the edge of hearing all drowned out by the songs on the radio.

Debbie bobs across the room, nervous and slightly irritated. "Terry, love, what are you doing?"

Her husband lets out a short, bark of a laugh. "It's a party!" he explains, his eyes shining glassily.

She purses her lips and reaches past him to turn the music down. "It's a bit loud though."

Terry winces as the soft golden sounds of swing music return, the scent of damp stone filling the air. Sweat beads across his broad pink forehead and he stares wildly at his wife. "It has to be loud, my darling!" he cries as her turns the dial up again.

He looks at the other guests, some watching with mild concern, others desperately trying not to appear as though they are listening. He seeks out reassurance in their blank stares but finds none. The room is dark, too dark to be comfortable, and in the shadows dark things breathe and squirm and sing to him. He feels smothered by the cold darkness and scrabbles to break the surface, to break free.

"Lily!" he shouts suddenly, his voice filled with a manic sort of glee, and the birthday girl starts. She looks up at her father from her place on the sofa.

"Come dance with me!"

She grips a plate of half-eaten party food before her like a protective talisman as a blush rises up her throat and cheeks.

"W-what?"

"Terry love," Debbie hisses. "Don't be silly, Lily doesn't want to dance with you."

"Why not? Why shouldn't she dance with her father?"

"She doesn't want to, dad," Hannah mutters from where she sits, beside Lily on the sofa.

A standoff ensues. The heaviest thirty seconds of silence this house has ever known, which is saying something, considering I once bore witness to my own dead body cooling in a bedroom upstairs.

And then, Lily's phone buzzes.

Her hand quickly snakes down to her side and Terry's eyes narrow. He waves a finger towards her.

"You see," he whispers icily, addressing the room. "You see, this is why she won't dance with her father, why she ignores her family."

"Stop, love," Debbie mutters.

Terry goes to speak again, to admonish his wife for interfering, when the sharp rattle of gravel against metal rings out across the room and he jumps. "What was that?"

Debbie puts her hand on his arm. "What, love?" she asks, more than a hint of frustration in her voice.

Terry stares at his wife, confused and unfocused for a moment. "Nothing," he murmurs blankly, although the rattling sound still echoes in his mind. He nods to himself as if in agreement with some great truth, before turning back to his daughters. There is a wary anger in my Hannah's eyes, although her sister sits next to her with all the fire and colour of a wet rag.

"Who is it, eh?" he spits. "Who calls you away from your family? Some friend? Some boy?" He casts a sneering glance around the room, at the faces of the partygoers who watch him, horrified. "Don't you see what she's doing? How she's spoiling the party?"

"Terry, lad, I think that's enough now," his father says sternly, walking across the room towards his son.

"Yeah, leave her alone dad," Hannah manages to say, although Debbie shoots her a worried glance. Don't get yourself involved.

The family stands about Terry now, he has made a circus act of himself. The dullness of the afternoon ripped asunder, revealing glossy darkness beneath. Like some sort of wild animal, Terry snorts and grunts, his mind baying at the crowd. He looks about him, listening out for the sounds that torment him, sounds only he can hear.

"Terry, love, I think you need to go back to bed." Debbie manages to say, trying to pull her husband away. "You've exhausted yourself, that's all."

"Yeah, lad. Do what Debbie says, eh? Get some rest." Terry's father looks at him, his gentle eyes crinkled with concern.

But Terry bats away their attempts to calm him down. "You want me to go, is that it? You," and here he juts a finger out towards Debbie, "are ashamed of me? Ha!" he laughs. "I'm ashamed of you! All of you!"

He pushes past his wife and his father and storms across the room. As he reaches the door, however, he stops and turns.

"Darkness," he exclaims. "That's what brings you here, that's what binds you together. But I am in the darkness, I am of the darkness. I see that now, and I see all of you. All. Of. You!"

These last three words are spat with such force, such venom, that the muscles in his neck stand out like vines, flecks of foamy spittle spattering from his lips.

"Jesus, should we call the police?" someone mutters as Terry finally disappears upstairs, but Debbie shakes her head.

"No, no, he's just tired," she manages to say. "I knew today would be too much for him." She turns to the others – her family, and Terry's too - and smiles a smile that convinces no one. "I'll make another appointment with the doctor, don't worry."

I watch my love as she comforts her sister, as well-meaning but ultimately pointless adults gather closer to offer words of reassurance. Someone even mutters "there, there" which only goes to show no one ever really knows what to do with an upset child.

Neither my father nor my mother liked to see tears. They made my mother nervous. She would pass comment to us, one eyebrow arched in judgement, if we saw a parent trying to console a wailing child at the park or out in town. She saw it as a weakness, of sorts. I had been a quiet baby, apparently, and my mother would frequently mention this fact as a source of some pride. My sister had been a significantly less agreeable infant – a fact that my mother would not hesitate to bring up during any conversation of our early childhood, something which irritated Aggie immensely.

My father's response to tears would simply be to laugh, or try to tell a joke. It was not until many years later, after much unnoticed observation, that I realised that he was afraid of gentle emotions such as sadness. His brash exterior, the booming laughs and explosive anger, were merely shields against the softer aspects of life and emotion which ultimately filled him with fear. Perhaps in those quieter moments, in the glisten of tears, he felt the damaging pull of introspection.

"Don't worry," Hannah whispers to her younger sister, her arm around her, her cheek against the top of her head. "Don't worry, he didn't mean it. He'll get better, I promise." Her words ring hollow, but they seem to sooth, and by the time Debbie has gathered the emotional fortitude to bring forth Lily's birthday cake, the bland haze of normalcy has more-or-less returned. They even manage to sing a passable rendition of *Happy Birthday* as the cake is carried in, candles ablaze.

As Debbie sings, as she places the cake upon the table and looks at her youngest child, this strange, pale girl making her way shyly across the room to blow out her candles, she considers the fact that her little girl is drifting away from her. Memories of childhood fading into the ether, the celebration of her twelfth year on the planet opens up a greater world of unknowns, of fears. Debbie shivers in frightened anticipation of the years to come, the inevitability of her children growing up and moving on.

"Make a wish!" she says with a smile, as Lily extinguishes the candles in one breath and proceeds to scrunch up her face in mock concentration, just on the off chance that – this time – the magic works for real.

Debbie leans forward and places a kiss on the top of her daughter's head, breathing in the scent of her, her warmth for a moment. Lily looks up at her mum and smiles.

"So, who wants a slice?" Debbie calls out as she pushes the tip of the knife through the white icing that covers the top of the cake.

But something is wrong. Even before the first cry of shock fills the room, she knows that something is wrong. The knife slips in too easily, the cake collapses in on itself as she pushes down, white icing crumbling away.

A filthy, impossible, redness oozes from the inside of the cake, out across the tablecloth. Debbie drops the knife in shock, and it splatters down into the glossy red liquid pooling out from where there should only have been sponge and buttercream.

As the mess spreads out across the tabletop, it brings with it a wave of anger, of disgust, of disbelief that rolls over the guests in their hurry to get away, to flee the unbelievable sight before them. Chairs tumble; glasses are dropped. Paper plates and party food are trodden into the carpet.

And at the centre of them all, still sat at the head of the table, Lily stares at the nightmare before her. Her eyes are wide and innocent and fearful. She does not hear the heaving sounds, the cries of her family around her. The only sound that reaches her is the *schlopp schlopp schlopp* of thick scarlet dripping from the edge of the table, onto her lap.

***

The room is dark, illuminated only by the harsh white light from a laptop screen. Debbie stares at it, the light catching in the stray strands which stand out from the rest of her hair, giving her the appearance of being mildly electrocuted. Tired eyes stare at the screen, and tired fingers tap away at the keys.

"Mum?"

She looks up at her oldest daughter, standing in the doorway. In the darkness, Debbie hadn't noticed her. She manages a weak smile in way of greeting.

Hannah stares at her mother and takes a seat at the table next to her. She can practically see the fear and worry pouring from her mother like cemetery mist, as she bites at her thumbnail anxiously.

"Mum, what the fuck is going on?" she manages to say after a moment.

Debbie sighs and closes her eyes, her eyelids weighed down with emotion. She shakes her head. "I don't know," she mutters.

Hannah slumps back in her chair. "But what was that today? First dad going off on one, and then that…cake. Jesus."

"Is your sister asleep?"

My darling girl nods. "Yeah, just about. She's in my bedroom; it was the only way she was going to get any sleep." She chuckles to herself mirthlessly as the day's events run through her mind. "I mean, Jesus. It was fucking mental."

"Hannah, sweetheart, stop."

She goes to open her mouth, she wants to scream in fear and confusion, to shake her mother and demand protection from a world becoming rapidly more unfathomable.

"Mum, I'm just scared," she manages after a moment.

Debbie looks at her daughter over the top of the laptop screen. "I know, love." She sighs. "I've made another appointment with the doctor."

"A doctor?" Hannah speaks quietly, trying hard to keep her voice measured and controlled. "Mum, you and Nana Meg spent the afternoon cleaning up blood and…and…and shit out of the dining room carpet. We don't need a doctor, we need an exorcist!"

Debbie leans forward and frowns. "What?" She shakes her head. "No, Hannah I don't need nonsense like that from you, please." For a moment her eyes shine in the gloom. "I need you to keep it together for me, okay? Whatever happened to the cake, it wasn't ghosts, was it?" Her shoulders sag heavily. "It was more likely…" She trails off.

"More likely what, mum?"

After a beat, Debbie pushes her chair back and reaches for the sideboard behind her. She pulls open the bottom drawer and retrieves a handful of papers.

"I'm worried it was your sister, playing some sort of sick joke."

She hands Hannah the papers. They are drawings, all of them. Dark lines in swooping, scribbled loops giving shape to dark images, eyes and teeth and open wounds. Red seems to cascade from the page, stark and sticky. Each image seems to be a battle for control – careful images of faces, animals, buildings, ably drawn by a youthful hand, become warped and misshapen by scribbles so deep that ridges are torn through the paper. A mind at war with itself.

Hannah cannot take her eyes off the dark, twisted images. Her mouth is dry. "Where did you…?"

"Your sister's bedroom. Hidden amongst her art books and things."

"I mean, I knew she wasn't feeling particularly happy at school since the move, but this is on another level."

"You're telling me."

Hannah shivers gently and drops the papers. After a moment, she turns them face down, although that doesn't seem to make them any less disturbing – she swears the images are burning their way through to the other side of the paper in a desperate need to be seen. She looks up and reaches across for her mother's hand; the compassion and love of that girl knowing no bounds. "Don't worry mum, we'll look after both of them."

Debbie squeezes her daughter's hand tightly as she quietly begins to sob.

***

I am ecstatic. Overjoyed. The words she spoke, they hang heavy with such meaning, such promise. She believes in ghosts. She believes that there is something more to this world than the physical, that there is a spiritual realm which can reach out and touch the world of the living.

True, she sees it as an enemy to be removed – an obstacle perhaps - but still I see it as a positive inroad.

And, also true, she still does not seem to sense me, my tenderness, the way I stroke the soft warm skin of her cheek as she sleeps, the love I have for her which could fill an ocean and half.

But this is just the gentle unfurling of the damp and shivering wings of a young moth after chewing its way out of its cocoon – there is so much potential in this moment, so much future.

I am so happy I can barely contain myself. Black mould spreads beneath the parquet tiles in the dining room and I joyfully drag my fingers through it, revelling in the sensation of the filth under my ragged nails and I howl in the moonlight for my love.

We will be together.

Today has been the most wonderful of days.

This I Will Remember

It can be hard to remember things,
   When you remember *every* thing.
When a lifetime's reminiscences sit at your fingertips,
rife for the rummaging at any given moment.
One single thread of conversation unpicked from the
tangle of voices at a party,
One particular scent of one particular spice pulled from
a busy, fragrant market,
One mote of colour spied in a gallery of fine art,
But this,
This I will remember.

∗∗∗

He does not sleep and so he does not dream. In his mind, clouds of warm, rust-coloured dust blossom outwards and fill the air.

Except it is not air, not anymore. Once, perhaps, but time and nature have sought to fill the void. The earth thrums with life and whispers its secrets to him, its breath at his ear cold and sweet with decay.

The darkness surrounds him, ageless and absolute. It is a hard darkness – of desolate caves and vast moonscapes. It holds him in its cold, damp arms and loves him, in its own way. Eventually the coldness of the dark fills him, leeching the warmth from his flesh and gifting him a chilly eternity.

You know the strange way your eyes seek out light in the dark. The sudden plunge into pitch black at the flick of a light switch, the panicked blindness and nothingness ahead, and then slowly, slowly, the edges of furniture and features begin to pick themselves out of the darkness. Silvery grey-blue edges of a world made of night bloom about you, until the sideboard is *there* and the armchair is *over there* and a million electrical lights twinkle their own little constellations, illuminating the darkness to such an extent that you wonder how you could ever have been afraid of the dark?

Well, this darkness is *not* that.

This darkness is absolute and infinite and gloriously, horribly inevitable - the dark inside a coffin buried six feet beneath the turf, it is; the darkness of the deepest ocean trench.

And trickle by trickle, it begins to fill. It begins to close. Seeping water and shifting earth bring forth soil and silt, cloying and smothering. As the sands in an hourglass flow, so do clumps of earth and motes of dirt into crevices and cracks. A mouth, twisted open in never-ending rage, finds itself filled with dirt that coats the tongue and clogs the throat and brings with it the mixed blessing of lungs no longer able to choke. As years go by, one eye socket, cracked and empty, is further blinded by layers of leaf litter and London clay, while the other stares blankly out into the abyss.

And in the darkness, there is nothing. A nothing which makes stalactites of time.

In fact, the dark renders time so unfathomable that a passing sightless creature burrowing by amounts to barely a ripple in the emptiness. Questing roots from nearby trees seeking nourishment from the decomposed flesh that has leeched into the soil hereabouts are naught but teardrops in a vast, uncaring ocean of time.

Once, perhaps, beneath the soil, the song of the old gods would have held him in its embrace. Gods of the hunt, of the night sky, gods of the heart beneath the soil, would have reached for him and he would not have been alone. His spirit would have joined and conjoined with the goat-horned ones, the swift and watchful ones, those that howl and those that laugh and those whose silence chills the blood.

But ageless gods from a time before have no place beneath the gardens of polite society, and so – for decades – he finds himself alone, with only crawling things for company.

And then, slowly, his world seems to wake up. He will never understand the whys and wherefores of it, but the Information Age sprays its electronic seed indiscriminately, tainting all it touches. The world above his dirtbed slumber wakes and connects in ways incomprehensible to those that came before and wires beneath the ground start to throb with knowledge, leaking into the soil like toxic waste, coating everything in its path with an invisible, caustic, unique sort of *life*.

It calls out to him in its strange unworldly voice. He had no knowledge of the old gods and therefore was not hurt by their absence in the dark, but the buzz of the new world pulls at him through the soil in ways he never even imagined. An urgency speaks to him, in its pounding, inescapable bass, and maddens him – a terrible waterboarding of the *now*. And like a fossil forming over billions of years, bone eroding and replaced by the slow drip, drip, drip of minerals until what was once alive is only stone, so the life that once there was becomes a sort of hardened, crystalized *longing*.

And then one day, accompanied by the crumble of soil and the sharpdull blade of a shovel, a light opens above him.

***

Houses

When houses are empty
    And alone and unobserved
They sing to themselves.

Homes with basements sing
In rich baritone. Foundations rattle,
And hot water pipes ring,
With melodies underscored by creeping things
In dark places.

Homes with attic space have voices
High and sweet,
With hollow woodwind notes through dusty rafters.
Feather light, these voices drift upon the breeze.

They whisper gentle ballads
Of the love they hold inside,
Or held,
In days gone by.

Listen now, stay still,
See if you can sit, unnoticed,
And you may chance to hear
The symphonies that fill each room.

Perhaps one day, your house
Will sing for you?
Voiceless words will echo out,
Floorboards creaking,
Concrete groaning – intangible words
Of love for one who made a house
A home.

The carriage clock

My mind slips back aways.

Hannah and her family have lived in my home for six months, two weeks, four days, seven hours, one minute and seventeen seconds. Her younger sister has yet to have her twelfth birthday. The garden is still on their 'To Do' list.

Terry and Debbie have redecorated most of the rooms in the house at this point, removing or painting over floral wallpaper in a wide range of colours with exciting names such as *polished stone* or *cotton mist*. Some days I feel as if I have fallen headfirst into a bowl of porridge.

Only my Hannah shows a hint of decorative flair. Fairy lights above her bed contrast strikingly with black and white pictures of moody looking musicians cut from magazines and bold prints of posters advertising films I have never heard of. She has such eclectic tastes, my Hannah, and I could sit cross legged on her bed and listen to her talk about the things which interest her for the rest of her life. Of course, I always have to share these moments with other people, but sometimes, that is almost bearable.

When it is not bearable, I find comfort in sitting in the loft space above Hannah's room. I like to close my eyes and lay amongst the dust and cobwebs and imagine the warmth of her, the scent of her, floating up through her bedroom ceiling and filling the space above. In those moments of deep stress, I find the fact that the loft has been left practically untouched by Hannah's family a real comfort. It is the place I keep my heart, away from prying eyes, in a tin hidden in the rafters.

The lights in the loft are dim and prone to flickering, and though the roof space is large and echoing, neither Terry nor Debbie have felt the desire to venture further than the few feet of storage space that fan out from the hatch which is the only way in or out if you are not dead.

The rest of the loft is given over to poorly laid insulation – rolls of yellowing glasswool occupy the space, preventing access to the darkest corners under the eaves of the house. Which is why, in the shadows, remnants of previous lives lay hidden, untouched and unseen.

There is a box of neatly folded fabric – remnants of a rainy-day sewing project still waiting for its rainy day; two blank photo albums, pages grown yellow with age; a glass fruit bowl wrapped in pages of newspaper from 1987; and a brass carriage clock in a paper bag.

The carriage clock used to stand on the mantelpiece in the parlour. It chimed softly at quarter past and to and played a tinny little tune at half past and on the hour. It had been a wedding present to my parents from my grandparents, many years before I was born.

Now it sits in the darkness, in a brown paper tomb. All logic would dictate that its clockwork would have run down years before, and the things itself should have ticked its last tock long before Hannah and her family took up residence in the house below.

But logic would be wrong. Ever-so-faintly, the clock still chimes the quarter hours, still plays a tune on the hour and half hour, still keeps the time - albeit only for the dust mites and the spiders and me.

Its hand travels well-worn paths about the clockface despite the degradations and intrusions of the passage of time, despite the cobwebs and dust, despite the bloodstains.

***

My sister is eighteen years old. She works on the perfume counter in the British Home Stores in town. Mrs Burnley – in charge of Perfumes, Cosmetics and Ladies' Sundries - rates her highly: my sister is punctual and polite, if a little quiet, and does not indulge in idle chatter or gossip the way that some of the other shopgirls do. There are no unpleasant suitors to greet her at the staff entrance at the end of the working day, bringing with them the oily scent of potential scandal and disruption. Her uniform is smart, her hair and makeup enhance her natural prettiness in such a way as to entice customers - no woman wishes to be served by a girl with pimples or greasy hair, says Mrs Burnley.

My sister does not socialise with the other girls outside of work, and if they see her as perhaps standoffish or cold in this respect, she is calm and gentle enough a soul that they do not judge her too harshly.

She works hard, my sister, not to draw attention to herself. If the ragged cuts that tiger-stripe her arms have bled in the night, she carefully wraps them in cotton pads and bandages, so no tell-tale spots of blood soak through the fabric of the sleeves of her uniform. If the bruises collected at her collarbone start to gather in clusters further and further up her slender neck, then she sets her alarm clock half an hour early so that she has the time to apply a mask of foundation over the fingertip-sized marks before she leaves for work.

The thought of spending her lunchtimes in the large store cupboard laughably labelled '*Staffroom*' sets her teeth on edge – the idea of having to spend what little free time she had being forced to make small talk while eating egg salad sandwiches and drinking weak tea was enough to make her want to cry. Instead, she ate her lunches on bench in the park during summer, feeding the ducks in the duck pond scraps of crust. In the winter, she would decamp to a nearby tearoom, take a seat at one of the small tables overlooking the high street, and dream of being anyone but her. On Fridays, she would buy herself a currant bun as a treat.

One rainy Tuesday lunchtime, sometime in late January, this is where she sits. She stares blankly out of the window, not watching the passers-by scurrying for shelter, but tracing the paths of raindrops as they hit the glass, collect and gather and run together, before trickling down to splash into little puddles on the windowsill. Her cup of tea cools in her hand.

The low sound of somebody clearing their throat cuts through her reverie, and she looks away from the window and up at the figure casting a shadow over her.

"It's…erm… Miss Mueller, isn't it?" the figure asks, quietly.

Agatha blushes lightly and nods. "Yes, sir," she murmurs. Standing beside her table is the assistant manager of Men's Attire, Mr Bullen.

Bertie Bullen is a slim, serious looking man a decade and a half her senior. He is a widower of five years, and a kind, if quiet, soul. He is currently dripping wet, and his glasses are slowly steaming up as he stands before the young shopgirl sitting before him. He clears his throat again.

"Erm, is there any chance…?" he indicates the empty chair opposite her, and for a moment she looks from him to it in confusion. Then slowly she notices the hubbub of voices around her and realises that the tearoom has slowly filled with shoppers sheltering from the rain. Something clicks in her brain, and she blushes brighter.

"Oh! Oh, yes. Of course." She smiles at Mr Bullen as he takes the seat gratefully and places his lunch down on the table.

"Thank you, Miss Mueller," he smiles. "Erm, I guess a lot of other people had the same idea."

"The same idea?" Agatha looks at him, confused.

Mr Bullen chuckles lightly at the strangeness of the girl before him. "Erm, about getting in out of the rain, I mean."

"Oh, yes," she places her cup down, but it clatters slightly too loudly in her saucer and she looks away, over at the other people now filling seats and steaming slightly through their conversations.

Her eyes flit from person to person as she tries to think of something to say.

"Beastly weather, isn't it?" she manages after a moment.

"Yes. Although... although good for the garden, I suppose."

"Ducks!"

Now it is Mr Bullen's turn to look confused.

"I beg your pardon?"

"Ducks. Isn't that what they always say?" Agatha takes a sip of tea. "Lovely weather for ducks... when it's raining."

"Do they?" Mr Bullen looks up from his sandwich and glances out of the window, staring down into the empty street. "I'm not sure there are many ducks in town today."

He laughs nervously and Agatha smiles at him.

Bertie Bullen does not realise it yet, but he has fallen in love with her.

A week passes before the two of them speak again. The weather is fine, and there is no need for them to share a table. And yet, when Mr Bullen sees Agatha sitting alone, he makes his way over to her. She looks up and smiles as he approaches and nods when he asks to join her.

"It's good to see you again, Miss Mueller," he says, as he sits down.

"It's good to see you too, Mr Bullen."

Rays of late winter sunshine dance across her face as she sips her tea and for a moment they sit in silence. Neither of them realises it, but they are comforted by each other's company. When they sit together, the sun is warmer, the chatter of their fellow customers reduced to a gentle music.

"I hope I didn't interrupt you?" he says gently, pointing at the book that rests on the table by her elbow.

"Oh no, don't worry. It's always nice to have someone to talk to."

Mr Bullen takes a sip of tea to hide his smile before continuing. "May I ask what you're reading?"

Agatha turns the book over to show him the front cover: *Taken at the Flood* by Agatha Christie.

"A murder mystery? How exciting!"

"It's silly, I know, but there is something comforting about books like this, you know? In their familiarity, their structure."

"And the villain always gets caught in the end."

Agatha's innocent eyes flicker. "Yes, I suppose they do. Most of the time."

Mr Bullen smiles blandly and takes a bite of his cheese sandwich. He chews in slow contemplation of the young women before him.

"She comes up with such terrible crimes, time and time again," he continues, having swallowed his mouthful. "It makes one wonder what she must make of her fellow man."

"I don't follow."

"Whether she sees evil in all of us, you know? That we all have within us this propensity for darkness."

"Well, don't we?"

Mr Bullen is startled by the young lady's reply and thinks carefully before replying. He straightens his plate, his teacup and saucer absentmindedly.

"No," he says, slowly. "I don't think people do, as a rule. Oh, there are a few bounders here and there I suppose but…" he looks at her for a beat too long before glancing back down at his plate, blushing. "I think there's plenty that's wonderful. You just have to look for it."

Mr Bullen dabs idly at the crumbs on his plate with the tip of his finger, unaware that they map out a perfect copy of the constellation Andromeda. In quick succession he removes the stars Alpheraz, Mirach and Titawin before gently pushing the plate away.

"And do you look for the wonderful in life, Mr Bullen?" she asks.

"I try to yes, Miss Mueller," he replies, quickly. "Some days it is easier to find than others, but on the whole, it is there."

He finds it difficult to sit still, Agatha notices, as he speaks of wonderful things. *His hands, his feet, his shoulders, constantly in motion.* She watches as he tears the edge from a clean white paper serviette and rolls it between the pink tips of his fingers. *But he doesn't move out of nerves or anxiety, but as though he is filled with...*

He presents her with a small, rolled, paper rose.

"...music."

"I beg your pardon?"

She cradles the paper flower in her palm before she realises that she has spoken aloud. "I mean to say, thank you. It's very sweet," she manages.

"May you find your wonderful today, Miss Mueller," Mr Bullen says with a smile, before getting up from the table and leaving to run some errands before going back to work.

Agatha plucks the crudely made flower from her hand and looks at it thoughtfully. *It is a nothing, a scrap of curled paper, nothing more* she says to herself.

Nonetheless, she places it carefully in her purse before she returns to work.

In fits and starts, a friendship blossoms. In arid soil, untended and bereft of light, the roots of something greater than the two of them begin to grow. Tentative tendrils in the dark crawling upward, seeking a chance to grow, to live. For these two lost souls, a connection is made that neither would have thought possible.

And so, as the other girls in Ladies' Beauty notice a ready smile upon Agatha's lips and Bertie's colleagues in Men's Attire comment wryly upon the newfound spring in his step, the tearoom becomes a holy pilgrimage, and both hearts beat anew.

***

The room is dark, a man declares love for the woman in his life. Fifteen feet high, in flickering greys and blacks, he looks at her earnestly, hoping that she trusts him, that she believes the things he says.

The room is dark, a killer strikes. Once, then twice. He is quick, and brutal, a man of shadows. His lust for violence satiated, he fades back into the darkness.

The room is dark, an alleyway illuminated by harsh lamplight. A body lays in a silent, crumpled heap, silhouetted against the pale cobblestones.

The room is dark, nervous hands find each other, hold each other tightly. Two pairs of eyes stare up at the silver screen like stars twinkling in the night sky. A bubble of togetherness separates the couple from the others in the room, a strange kind of privacy in the midst of the Friday matinee crowd.

Five months of tea shops visits had passed by in a blur and a variable winter had slowly turned to spring before blossoming into summer. The idea had been broached – by whom it is unclear – that the warmer weather might bring with it opportunities to meet outside the restraints of the working day. The Elysian Picture House was the chosen destination, its darkness and anonymity soothing any potential concerns about being seen together outside work – not that there was even a hint between Agatha and Bertie of anything other than friendship. Certainly, any suggestion of stepping out together or – God forbid – courting would have shocked them both. They were as baby deer, tremulous and shaking with each staggering step in the strange new world they found themselves in. Still shining with the blood and mucous of the past, they were making their way unsteadily into the light, no thought in their heads save the delicate placement of each wobbling footstep.

The room is dark, smoky light flickers and an innocent man's life unravels on screen before them. Agatha and Bertie share a bag of shop-bought bonbons as they sit and watch and, although neither of them could possibly know it, their hearts beat in time with each other. They are happy.

This happiness will be short-lived.

***

Leaving the picture house, the skies seem clearer, the birdsong sweeter in the trees. They stroll together, side by side, as Bertie walks Agatha to her bus stop.

"What did you think of the film?" he asks.

"Oh, marvellous, really marvellous," she replies. "Although the ending was a little disappointing."

"I agree. It left you wanting more, I felt. Why describe the dénouement rather than show it? Perhaps they ran out of money while making the film."

"Can that happen?"

"I suppose so."

"Well, anyway, I thought Rex Harrison was terribly good."

"Yes, he has such a presence on the screen, doesn't he? I thought he was rather good in The Ghost and Mrs Muir as well. Have you seen it?"

Agatha shakes her head. "No, I'm afraid I don't go out very often."

"Well, we shall have to make it a regular thing then, won't we?" Bertie smiles at her.

"Yes, that would be lovely!"

She smiles up at him, and then a frown crosses her face. Bertie looks up to see that they have arrived at the bus stop. It is empty – perhaps they have just missed the bus, perhaps their time together will continue for that little bit longer - but they both know that this moment of theirs is drawing to a close.

He takes her hands in his, feeling the warmth, the softness of her.

"Agatha, I have enjoyed this afternoon immensely, and I do hope that there will be others."

"Oh, Bertie, yes." She says, her smile returning, her face brighter than the day. "There will be others, I'm certain there will be."

And then.

And then.

He leans forward, almost imperceptibly. His lips tighten ever so slightly, and Agatha looks on as a confident blush rises in his cheeks.

She feels her pulse fluttering in her chest as Bertie closes in to kiss her, feels pins and needles prickling her fingertips. At this closeness, she can smell the soap upon his skin, the gentle undertone of aftershave and it is…too much.

Entirely subconsciously – and completely at odds with her feelings for the man before her – she feels panicked, sick to her stomach. She wants him to kiss her, but at the same time the idea horrifies her. Images of writhing bodies fill her mind, pale pink flesh and dark, sweat-slicked hairs in clammy embrace, inescapable heat and weight pressing down on her. She thinks of pain, of blood, of stained sheets and shame and fear and a hate which fills her very soul to the exclusion of all other emotions.

She places a gentle hand upon Bertie's chest and holds him back.

"My… my bus is here," she manages to say, barely managing to keep the panic from her voice.

Bertie, ever the gentleman, accepts her mild, unspoken rejection. The blush deepens at his cheeks, and he wishes the ground would open up and save him from the cloud of embarrassment which he now finds himself in, but makes no comment. Instead, he looks up at the red double decker which draws up beside them.

"Ah, yes. Of course." He smiles at Agatha, although he cannot hide the hurt in his eyes. "Thank you for a lovely afternoon, Miss Mueller. I look forward to seeing you at work on Monday."

Agatha nods but says nothing. She climbs aboard the bus and does not look back. The conductor watches her as she takes her seat before looking down towards Bertie, standing forlornly on the pavement.

"You getting on, sir?" the conductor asks.

"No, thank you."

The conductor gives a nod and rolls his eyes good-humouredly, attempting to convey his shared confusion in the ways of the fairer sex. As the bell rings, Bertie smiles sadly and walks away. He does not even wait to watch the bus drive off, which is perhaps for the best, as Agatha doesn't look back once.

***

By the time Agatha returns home, the warmth of the afternoon has become a heavy, humid evening. Yellowgrey clouds fill the sky, bringing with them a strange light which washes out the streets, making them seem flat and lifeless.

She makes her way up the garden path and opens her front door.

Stepping across the threshold brings no relief from the heat of the outside world and Agatha feels beads of sweat begin to prickle beneath her blouse.

Despite this, Agatha opens no windows nor attempts to lower the temperature in any way. Instead, she heads straight to her room, closes the door behind her and lets her handbag slip to the floor. She sits upon the edge of her bed, her thoughts skittering and skidding about.

She tries to calm her mind, centre herself, tries to picture Bertie, tries to imagine spending time with him again, but finds the idea far too… difficult. The thoughts and emotions that crowd her mind render it incapable of such a task.

A familiar numbness holds her in its grip as Agatha looks across at her bedside table and at the small metal aspirin tin which sits amongst the pots of face cream and bottles of sleeping tablets. A tin which used to sit on her mother's bed-side table and which has been empty of aspirin for almost a decade.

Agatha rolls up the sleeves of her blouse, revealing the pale skin of her forearms, criss-crossed with raised pink scars and fresh, angry-looking lines of scabbed blood. With-out thinking – her mind is too full to actively participate in any decision making – she reaches across to the aspirin tin and takes from it a razor blade, dull grey in the half-light of the bedroom.

As though summoned into being by the fresh line of ruby red, the sound of the front door slamming open reverberates from down below and Agatha's eyes widen. Light and sound rush back into the room and – as the sound of her father's footsteps echo up towards her - she looks down at the cut on her arm.

"Where are you, my kitten?" her father's voice rumbles through the house.

The grey numbness of her mind dissipates like early morning fog and Agatha finds a hardness in her chest – a ball of scar tissue in place of her heart. She rises from her bed and pulls her sleeve down, a trail of blood trickling stickily down her wrist and thumb.

Placing the stained razor blade carefully back in its tin, she makes her way downstairs.

Her father sits in his armchair, peering at the local newspaper. As his daughter enters the room, he glances at her, his eyes travelling over her, taking in the care with which she has dressed, the touch of makeup at her cheek, the curls in her hair. He makes no mention of any of them.

"There you are, my kitten. I was beginning to wonder where you were."

"Sorry Papa, I didn't hear you," she replies.

"Do not lie to me, my darling," he says quietly, returning his attention back to his newspaper. There is a strange tone to his voice, almost hurt. "I deserve better than that."

Not knowing what to say in return, not knowing if her father even expects a reply, Agatha stands there, mute. She stares at her father, and sees, in the heat, the sweat beading out across his red, mottled forehead. She sees the glistening skin beneath the stubble upon his chin and cheeks, and the stains at the armpits of his work shirt. The scent of the man seems to fill the room – the decay within him leaking from his pores in dark waves. She wants to run from the room, leave this house, this place, this *thing* that calls itself her father, leave it all forever.

But she knows now, after her date with Bertie, that there is no other life for her. Whatever the sickness within this man that sits before her, it has tainted her as well.

"Why do you stand there, my kitten?" he asks, his voice breaking through her train of thought. "Go. Go make me a cup of tea. Some of us have spent the day hard at work, putting food on the table. The least I can ask for is a cup of tea, do you not think?"

"Yes, Papa," Agatha replies, and she turns from the man and heads for the kitchen. She does not see him look up and watch her thoughtfully as she goes.

The kettle boils, the teapot warms, and Agatha takes a breath. She closes her eyes and feels centred.

And slowly, she allows herself to *hate* him. Instead of dismissing these dark thoughts – tamping them down to fuzzy nothingness – she allows the hatred to stew. The emotion begins to spread, to fill her mind like the brewing tea before her. Her mind steeped in deep, liquid anger, until every lobe and cortex is stained with loathing for the man in the other room.

And she makes a cup of tea.

As Agatha spoons a large teaspoon of sugar into the cup and begins to stir, the soft sounds of Benny Goodman and his swing orchestra begin to float through the house and she feels an acid sting in the pit of her stomach. She walks through the too-warm house back to the parlour and finds her father standing by the mantelpiece. He has his broad back to her, and at first she thinks he is swaying in time with the music, but as she gets closer, placing the cup she is carrying down on the sideboard, she realises that he is crying.

"Papa?"

He turns to her, and Agatha sees he is holding a photograph from the mantle in his hand. Two figures smile out from the frame, a man and woman on their wedding day. The black and white of the photograph hides the brilliance of the flowers held in the woman's hand, and bright blue of the summer sky above their heads, but it cannot hide their joy and excitement, captured on film so many years before. A happiness so dazzling, it is nothing less than cruelty when compared to the shattered, crumpled shadow that the groom would one day become.

"She was... so beautiful. Your mother... I loved her so very much, you know?" He stares at the photograph with eyes red rimmed with melancholy. "You remind me so much of her."

"We were happy once, you know," he continues. "It may be difficult to believe after everything – the way things were at the end – but she was my life, the music of my mornings and the reason for my very existence. My heart beat for her. I didn't mean for the way that things…" he trails off, tears running down his cheeks, and places the photograph back on the mantle. "Every day it hurts, my kitten. Here," he slapped a large, hairy-knuckled hand against his chest, "I bleed for your mother, the way she was wrenched from me."

He turns to Agatha now. She looks at him with a mixture of curiosity and disgust. Her father may be standing before her in the parlour, she realises, but his mind, his consciousness, speaks to her from the same inky void in which he dwells in those moments of dark nighttime sin. For a moment, she imagines that she can see a glossy black tentacle coiled inside of his mouth instead of a tongue, although from where I stand, I see nothing but the truth of a tragic, evil man.

"You, my kitten, you I will *not* lose."

"Papa, I don't understand what you- "Agatha interjects, but her father once again dismisses her with a wave of his hand.

"You think I have not noticed? The light that shines from you? The smile – not for me but for who? Look at you, such a beautiful girl." He begins to raise his voice now, commanding the room in the same way he used to do when he and mother would host parties that lasted the whole night long. "*My* beautiful girl. You think I do not know that other men want you, my kitten? I see the desires that lie in their heart, but you will never belong to anyone but me!"

He lunges out and grabs Agatha by the wrist, his thick fingers digging into her pale skin. "Come dance with me, my kitten. You never dance with me anymore."

Taken off guard, she finds herself pulled towards the man. She tries to jerk her arm away but, in the moment, he spins them both, moving discordantly out of time with the gentle swing music playing on the record player. The dance is perverse and heavy, and Agatha struggles in her father's grip. She pushes back at him but is unable to get away.

"You see," he says as she struggles in his arms, "she will not dance with her father. She will not – oh!"

With his fingers still wrapped around her wrist, he lifts her hand and notices, for the first time, the trail of blood running from beneath the sleeve of her blouse. Semi-dry, it glistens darkly against her skin.

"My kitten, what is this that you do? You hurt yourself?" he shakes his head, horrified. "No, you cannot leave me this way, not you. There is so much more dancing to be done!"

With a smile, he brings Agatha's hand to his mouth and darts his tongue out, licking along her blood-streaked fingers. She cries out and tries to recoil from him but her back presses against the mantelpiece, preventing her escape. Ornaments clatter to the floor as she tries to get away; a vase falls, our parents' wedding photograph smashes onto the corner of the hearth and Agatha brings her free arm around in one wide swing.

In her hand she holds a smart brass carriage clock which she brings down onto the side of her father's head. The sharp metal corner lands against the soft flesh of his temple with a dull thud. With a spluttering cry of alarm, he collapses to the floor.

The man looks up at his daughter with wide, dumb eyes, blood already oozing from the ragged wound at the side of his head. Agatha does not hesitate, does not speak, but with a blankness behind her eyes, she brings the clock down once again. This time she strikes him squarely in the centre of his forehead, leaving a plum-coloured V-shaped dent.

Blood starts gushing from her father's nose now, his eyes rolling wildly in their sockets.

"Stop! Wha' are you doin'?" he manages to splutter, although he barely has time to raise his hands in an act of self-preservation as she hits him again and again and again, and soon all he can do is make quiet bubbling sounds from within a widening puddle that stains the rub a deep red.

She stands over him, the sleeves of her blouse sticky with blood, speckles of it across her chest and face. Scarlet-slick, the carriage clock slips from her fingers and hits her father's legs with a tinny little chime. He does not react, although the shallow rise and fall of his chest indicates that there is still some life within him. For now.

I am gripped by the grey-formed outline of an emotion – fear. What if, after all the deaths that have happened under this roof, it is my *father* whose spirit chooses to linger on beside me? Am I to spend the rest of eternity in the company of this abusive, drunken pervert? I am filled with a silent scream of horror and ricochet from wall to wall at the thought. It is too hideous to contemplate.

There was a time when I would have given anything for companionship, but this would be too cruel a joke on the part of whatever bastard god lies beyond. My mind becomes nothing but darkness and the clanging of brilliant iron stars and when I finally pull myself together, Agatha is sitting in father's armchair staring down at his body which is now completely still.

Thankfully, I remain unaccompanied upon this spectral plane. Whether my father's spirit has passed on or not, it appears not to be something I need to concern myself with.

By this point, my sister has evidently bathed and changed her clothing for there is not a trace of blood upon her – neither our father's nor her own. As she stares at the man's lifeless body, a sense of calm has fallen on her. Her breathing is measured, her mind at some sort of peace, the white noise of emotions within her fading to a gentle, restful grey. She contemplates a life without her father. Eventually, night falls.

***

Bertie Bullen, hurt and confused by Agatha's reaction to his attempts at wooing her, makes no attempt to speak to her again. He avoids the tea room completely and within one month of the fateful visit to the pictures he requests a transfer to a branch of British Home Stores two towns over. He never sees Agatha Mueller again.

Two years and two days after his transfer, Bertie takes a shortcut home from work and finds himself mugged by a seventeen-year-old Teddy Boy with a switchblade and a nervous twitch. As he attempts to hand over his wallet, the youth stumbles and accidentally plunges his blade into Bertie's stomach. Shocked at the shuddering gout of blood that pours from his victim, the youth makes a run for it, leaving Bertie to bleed out on the cold stone of the alleyway.

The coroner's cursory examination of the dead body dis-covers nothing of any particular interest – a middle-aged male in reasonable health; death by penetrating abdominal trauma – although he makes two notes against his records. One, that the victim wore pink lace camiknickers beneath his suit, and two, that the wallet found discarded next to his dead body had been empty, apart from a pair of cinema ticket stubs dated two years prior.

***

Father had always been a large man, stocky and broad shouldered, and if anything, in death he seems even larger. Certainly, his lifeless body takes up most of the floor of the parlour. Agatha, on the other hand, has a frame that barely even registers as slight and it takes her most of the evening to manoeuvre our father's body onto an old bedsheet from the back of the airing cupboard, before dragging it out into the garden under cover of darkness.

The night air is cool – gone is the closeness of the afternoon – and under different circumstances spending time in the garden under the stars might have set Agatha's fevered mind at ease. As it is, she merely stands in the gloom considering the practicalities of digging a grave in the centre of the yellowing lawn. Her muscles ache and the small of her back cries out at the thought of such labours, when suddenly a patch of darkness calls to her from the back of the garden.

Half hidden beneath curling weeds and shifting turf, the old Anderson shelter stares blankly back at Agatha. She grips the twist of cotton sheeting tightly in her hand and sizes up the yawning doorway of the shelter, calculating the width of the corpse's shoulders. *Yes*, she thinks to herself, *it will do*. A final resting place as good as any. A few bags of soil from one of the local builder's merchants to seal up the doorway afterwards, and there would be no chance of foxes or stray cats unearthing anything incriminating. Buried in the decades-old dirt and detritus at the bottom of the shelter, there would be no chance of our father's bones ever seeing the light of day again.

Bones Beneath the Soil

I will sing for you, when you are bones-beneath-the-soil,
  A never-ending lament for long lost and distant love,
  And hold you as in the sweetness of a dream,
  Or the gentle dewdrop of the softest petals of a summer
rose.
  Sleep now, my love, wrapped within a blanket of dark,
  And whisper to me, secrets lost to fear.

  I will dance for you, beneath a moon which shines upon
our love.
  Dance to sweet and perfumed melodies plucked from
midnight's dream,
  When you are buried far beneath the ever-entwining
roses,
  And all I have left of you are the memories and the fear
  Of a life amongst others who do not know their way in
the dark.
  Will you miss me too, or will you be at peace beneath the
soil?

I will weep for you, every morning, on waking from my dreams,
And envy you, safe and warm in the unknowable dark.
Your long-dried lifeblood enriching the soil,
The way you used to enrich my soul with the humors of your love.
The joy and laughter that filled the world when every morning *you* arose
To face the day with a heart that drove back fear.

I will search for you, through thick and cloying fear,
Through the thorns and vines which, on your leaving, rose,
From what was once the richest and most habitable soil,
Blocking out the light of unknowing and bringing down the peaceful dark
Of powerful and blissful love,
Although on waking it was found to be a most bitter dream.

I will think of you, your petals and your thorns, my rose.
The darkness of your eyes, that sung of deep, unending fear.
The warmth of your embrace, bones-beneath-the-soil.
The beauty of your laughter lighting up the dark,
The way you shaped the world about us with your love,
Feasting on the wayward souls entangled in the web of your
dreams.

I will live for you, although the path ahead lies dark,
The way will be made clear by the flickering candle-flame-glow of your love.
Although I could never hide from the dread that stalked your dreams,
Your love will allow me to rise above it like the blooming of a rose,
And though I long to swim once more in the waters of your fear,
I know that I must live for you, bones-beneath-the-soil.

I clip the rose, its blooded petals drifting gently to the fertile soil,
And wonder, do I fear that every moment spent with you was but a storm-toss'd dream,
And standing in the dark, doubt that there was ever love at all?

Paradise

When I was younger, I used to wonder what heaven would be like.

While not a particularly religious family, my grandmother had gifted me a book of children's Bible stories for my seventh birthday.

The stories themselves were of little interest to my younger self, but the illustrations drew me in with their bright colours and details picked out in gold ink which glittered and shone in the light. The Tree of Knowledge from the Garden of Eden, the newly minted rainbow over Noah's Ark, the dazzling colours of Joseph's coat. All of them picked out in fine golds and reds and blacks and blues.

This then was heaven, I had thought. A world of stark colours and brilliant golds, the lifeblood of the landscape shining with precious riches as far as the mind could see.

One illustration stood out in particular – the building of the Tower of Babel. The artist had endeavoured to draw a cast of thousands working away on this mighty tower by the sea – this monument to the tenacity of man and the ultimate affront to God. But while all these tiny figures in the picture worked away, sawing wood and laying bricks, there was one that stood apart from the rest, standing alone on the little sandy seafront beneath the clifftops where the tower was being constructed.

Perhaps it was just an error on the part of the artist, a stray pen stroke or an attempt at filling the page with background characters, but this person seemed so separate, staring off into a red and black seascape fringed with tints of gold.

And I could imagine the cold, damp sand between my toes, the scent of seaweed on the breeze. I had no point of reference for the beach that had been so carefully illustrated in my Bible - couldn't imagine the scents and sounds experienced by the lonely little ink figure on that distant bygone shore - but I *could* imagine looking out at the vastness of the greygreen English Channel, stretching off into an infinity which seemed endlessly explorable, sunlight glinting on the crest of each rolling wave.

This sense-memory comes from the only time I visit the sea in my childhood - a daytrip with my parents and my sister to the South coast. My mother and father are in a jovial mood - this is a good few years before my death and my world is mostly laughter and music, with only the occasional dark cloud.

The day has been long and tiring, an English summer cooled to grey skies and a sandy breeze which prickles my skin. I shiver in my bathing suit, the pink wool cold and heavy against my goosebump'd skin as the sounds of life behind me drift away - as T.S. Eliot wrote – nothing to nothing.

Above and about me, seagulls drift and dip among the beachgoers, fighting over discarded sandwich wrappers, searching out crumbs. I squeeze my eyes tightly closed for a moment and feel myself a sponge – absorbing the wonderful noise of *others* around me, disconnected and adrift from my family and other beachgoers. I wriggle my toes again, ground myself in the now of the beach. When I open my eyes again the colours of the world flash in bright, saturated lines and shapes - reds and blacks and golds reign supreme for the moment of two it takes for my vision to adjust to the light.

There is ice cream in my stomach and on my tongue, and suntan lotion on my nose, coconut scented and ironwhite and for a moment my skin feels transparent and unfocused and open to the English seaside for the rest of eternity.

And in that moment, I know that this is heaven.

And even now, although I have spent the years since my death within a world that is so far removed from heavenly as to be laughable, I hope that little girl, that younger me, has truth on her side. Perhaps there *is* a heaven. Perhaps there is a place of ceaseless calm where the heart knows nothing but peace.

Who knows, perhaps I will find myself there one day. Perhaps even with my darling Hannah by my side.

Is it wrong for a ghost to hope there might be life after death?

***

Agatha lives alone for seventy years after the death of her father. She never marries, never even courts particularly. After the ill-fated Bertie Bullen, the idea of a romantic liaison makes her feel sick to her stomach. And so, she returns every evening after work to an empty house, as the decades slowly pass. She is satisfied by this, to a certain extent.

-CLICK- ... man's best friend, isn't that right, Dr Marcus? Well, yes, actually Jen. Studies have shown that petting your dog or cat can have a significant, positive impact on... -CLICK-

She continues to keep her head down at work, but she is organised and thoughtful and good with customers, and after a few years finds herself promoted, first to weekend manager and then to Head of Department (Ladies' Perfume).

Management suits Agatha's solitary disposition. She is firm but fair with staff and customers and the natural hierarchy of the shopfloor distances her from the other girls who work the perfume counter – and her gender is a natural barrier between herself and the other heads of department across the store – so that she never has to worry about the minutia of making friends. She finds that she needs not indulge in anything above polite small talk to keep the days ticking by. Friendships are not forthcoming, and thus she does not need to go to the effort of nurturing them.

-CLICK- ...it's a glorious sunny day here in Walton-Upon-Thames and our antiques experts are ready to find some bargains. But will Tom finally sniff out success with this silver Victorian snuffbox? Or will Georgina speed ahead with this... - CLICK-

Every summer she rents a holiday cottage in Dorset. In 1985 she travels for over twenty-four hours via Singapore to Australia, to stay with a cousin who had been a Ten Pound Pom shortly after the war. She gets mildly sunburnt beneath the Australian sun and visits Ayers Rock and the Sidney Opera House. She buys a picture of a kangaroo painted in vivid coloured dots and swirls from a gift shop in Adelaide Airport on the way home. She hangs the painting in the hallway of her house, where it contemplates the gloom of England with one stark white, red-rimmed eye. It stays there – the kangaroo, not just its eye – for many years after the holiday memories have faded until – one morning in an early year of the new millennium - Agatha stares with mild despair at the painting, as she realises that a previously un-regarded branch of eucalyptus on which the kangaroo perches is in fact a cartoonishly large and angrily tumescent penis. Blushing pinkly at the thought of her hallway being decorated with animalian erotic art for the previous two decades, Agatha removes the painting and replaces it with a macramé wall hanging from a local church bazaar.

-CLICK- ...by one of the most audacious forgers? We're here in London this week, north of the river, with the Mackenzie family, and a piece of art which has been in the family for generations... -CLICK-

Bit by bit she saves her pennies. It takes a good few years but eventually she manages to pay off the mortgage on the house and own it outright. She is thrifty but not miserly – darning stockings if necessary, but treating herself to the occasional cream cake on the way home from work after a particularly busy or challenging day. She finds comfort in simplicity and routine and, on the odd occasion when things feel off or get on top of her, well – there is a razor blade in a tin on her bedside table which helps her regulate her emotions. Old habits are hard to shift.

-CLICK- ...is known the world over for its gold and silver-wares, and what better than this, a sparkling new library, to put the city on the map. It's a city rich in culture and colour, with a history steeped in jewellery design, but will any sparkling treasures grace our experts' tables today? Only... -CLICK-

And so slowly, moment by quiet moment, the years go by. Wallpaper fades, paint flakes away, ornaments gather dust and houseplants die and one day Agatha finds herself retired and alone without the organisation and structure and strange companionship of the working day to give her life shape.

And everything begins to fade.

-CLICK- ... so marvellous for you to invite me to New York like this. Well, gee whizz, it's been so long since I've seen you, Aunt Jess. And besides, you've always been so supportive of me, I had to invite you to opening night. Oh, I knew you'd be on Broadway one of these days. Well, it's not exactly Broadway, Aunt Jess, but the theatre... -CLICK-

It is a tragedy, Agatha would muse from time to time, that films and television programmes make such a big deal of the concept of 'fading to black' to signify the end of a story or the closure of a scene. Even theatre performances descend into the darkness when all is said and done. There is a comfort in a fade to black, a sense of completion. The lives of the players, the characters, are no longer our concern, some director behind the scenes has declared it so. You want to know more? Tough luck. That is not knowledge that you are privy to – the fade to black has seen to that.

-CLICK- ...got three new contestants lined up today to see if they can beat the buzzer. Let's find out who they are. Hello, I'm

Liam, I'm an IT consultant from Aberystwyth. Hi, my name's Sharon and I'm a... -CLICK

Infinitely more heart-breaking, more depressing, is a 'fade to beige', and it was in this murky nothingness that Agatha found herself existing. A fade to beige, she felt, was a cloudy emptiness that you could *feel in your very bones*. A ceaseless grind without reward or even a tangible impact on the wider world. Never the antagonist, even in her own story, Agatha felt herself being pushed into the background even more once the world of work was no longer one she had any part to play in. The world in which she now existed was soft and beige and endless.

-CLICK- ...careful! Just stay still, it's a deep wound.... There, hold that in place.... What were you thinking, she could have killed you! I wasn't thinking, doc. Yeah, well, that's your problem, isn't it? You never... -CLICK-

Acquaintances and distant relatives pass by and pass on and gradually the number of Christmas cards she feels obliged to write each December dwindles down to next to nothing and those she receives in return number fewer still.

-CLICK- ...So what have we got here, Gareth? Well, it appears to be an image of a seated woman, beautifully drawn. You can see the light pencil drawings and the curve of her cheek, her neck, and sloping down to her shoulders. And the signature on the bottom

right there? Ah, you've noticed that, have you? Yes, it appears…
-CLICK-

Bones ache and muscles twinge and eyesight blurs and only the taste of memories lingers on. She considers a cruise or a walking holiday or any of the plethora of 'Getaways for the over sixties…seventies…eighties' as advertised in the lifestyle pages of the Daily Telegraph but they are not for her. Solitude is more than just a living arrangement; it is a companion.

-CLICK- …So you have some hacks for us today, don't you? Yes, I do, because people often have these at home, gathering dust on their kitchen counters because they've run out of things to do with them. Not putting them to their full potential? Yes, exactly, now if we… -CLICK-

There is a faded sepia photograph on the mantle – a large man and a slight woman stand, beaming, on church steps. He wears a morning suit and black bow tie; she wears a calf-length dress in white silk with a veil and train which falls to her feet in twists and turns, and they look *so* happy. A happiness that only exists in the dust of darker recollections now. Another photograph sits at the other end of the mantle – a black and white print of a serious looking girl of eleven or twelve stares at the photographer from the back of a seaside donkey. Agatha no longer remembers the name of the little girl, does not know who she is or was but some tenderness for the child remains and so her photograph remains upon the mantel, beside the vase Agatha received from British Home Stores as a gift on her retirement two decades before.

And only if one were to look carefully, would one notice an absence on the mantle. There is a gap between ornaments where silent chimes sound out from a carriage clock that has been hidden away for over half a century, unseen but not unnoticed. Its tinny little bells weigh heavy in the air even now. Ask not for whom they toll.

-CLICK- ...With two hundred pounds each, both our experts are travelling across the West Midlands on the hunt for bargains and hoping to make those ever-elusive profits... -CLICK-

One grey October morning, Agatha wakes to a chill in her bones and a darkness on the horizon. She does not eat breakfast – the idea of eating brings with it the sensation of gentle nausea – but contents herself with a cup of sweet tea before a morning of pottering about the house. There are chores to be done, household tasks and bits and pieces to tackle, and she does them slowly, with an odd sort of melancholy buffeting her from room to room.

It is an uneasiness which fails to shift by the time she makes herself a second cup of tea at half past eleven and sinks gratefully into the old armchair in the living room.

-CLICK- ... doubled his money and he's very happy with that. So, is this the start of a winning streak? Hillary, you inherited

these pieces from your great aunt, didn't you? Yes, many years ago now. Ever worn them? When I was younger, yes. Well, they're going under the hammer now, let's see... -CLICK-

A stray thread from the frayed arm of the armchair brushes against the side of her thumb and she plucks at it without thinking while idly cycling through television channels with the remote gripped tightly in her other hand. Bright colours flicker across the screen, snatches of conversation, of music, of life catch her attention momentarily but she does not register the different programmes to any real degree. She winces at the tightness in her midrift and reaches for her tea. She shifts in her seat, attempting to make herself more comfortable, and briefly wonders whether she has a stomach upset. Her mind cycles though her last few meals in search of a potential culprit. Sweat prickles across her forehead as she takes a sip of tea, taking no comfort from the brew sliding down her throat like shards of ice.

-CLICK- ...mortgage lending agreements, and that's before you've even set foot inside the property itself. Yes, but we're here to lend a helping hand and shed some light on the often difficult process of... -CLICK-

The volume of the television wavers – raising and lowering of its own accord. The images darken as well – or is that the sky itself darkening, shrouding the room in a flickering gloom? Agatha feels a cold pressure in her chest, fit to burst, and her eyes grow wide in realisation. Breaths come short and rasping as the mug of tea tumbles from her grip, hitting the arm of her chair, hot liquid splattering across her shins and feet and pooling at her feet like effluent. Her hand raises to her chest and the unbearable *coldness* within, and, for a moment, I swear our eyes meet.

The old lady who lived in my house – the old lady who had once, many years before, been my sister - dies.

-CLICK- ...so you see, Detective, Mr O'Shaunessy couldn't have been in his office when his wife made the call. As hard as it is to believe, he had to be in Jonah's apartment at the same time. And I think you'll find the bullets found at the scene of the crime are a match for that pistol. You don't mean to say...? I'm afraid so, they are both guilty of murder... -CLICK-

It is strange how quickly her body becomes an empty husk. In the space of a fraction of a second, she takes her last breath and a fraction of a second after that her heart falters and beats one last time and a fraction of a second after that any cobwebbed trace of life and spirit she may once have had is gone. I stand watching her for several days, marvelling once again at the absence that is the human body without soul.

Light flickers across her face, bringing unnatural life where there is none. As rigor mortis sets in across her body, her hand tightens its grip upon the remote control in mockery of the arthritic weakness of her later years. As the muscles in her cold dead fingers stiffen, the corpse cannot help but squeeze down on the buttons and the television proceeds to click through show after show. Agatha makes do with a choir of daytime television hosts to herald her into the beyond - a poor replacement for the choir of angels which are suspiciously absent from their posts.

-CLICK- ...next guest is a real trailblazer when it comes to talking about menopause and bringing into the open all the positives and negatives that come with this change in life experienced by, let's face it, half the population of the world. She's released a new book on the subject, and is here to... -CLICK-

Of course, she is not *really* an empty husk. I fancy that I can hear them now: the billions of microscopic bacteria released from servitude by the cessation of her blood flow are even now beginning to feast on the woman, cells rupturing and blisters forming within and without.

-CLICK- ...if you are a proud owner of a blender, you are... Are you making the most out of it? Now I missed out on these when they were on sale. Did you? Yes, and now I can't get one for love nor... -CLICK-

For the first time in the last eight decades, I find myself alone and I don't know what to do with my new-found freedom. Already I feel the house settle about me, its final sigh escaping into the ether, and I wonder what binds me to this place. I spend a day or two within the walls of the house themselves, the gossamer warmth of the brickwork moving in and out of my own insubstantial flesh. Perhaps, I think, by entwining myself in amongst these bricks and mortar I can better understand the hold they have on me. I hope to discover their reasons for chaining me so, but I remain without answer by the time I leave the brickwork, unchanged save for the mould spores tangled in my hair.

-CLICK- ...became my goal each day, walking to the corner shop and back. So just setting yourself small, achievable goals then? That's right, Jen. I was able to build up from that, until eventually I was able to overcome my anxiety and... -CLICK-

The television continues to flicker in the living room, and my sister has taken on a shiny, swollen look. Two or three large bluebottles feast upon the bloodied foam which drips from her nose and mouth to splatter upon her sensible cotton blouse. The air about her has taken on a distinctly unwholesome pallor. There is no real reason for me to spend any time with her, and if it weren't for purely scientific interest, I would not. However, I have not seen a body decay before.

-CLICK- ...I mean, I knew he'd be flirting with her, you know? I mean, I understood... that's, like, the point of the whole thing.... but I was sat right there, and it was like.... Babe, that's well out of order, you don't need to take that. You're like, a goddess, and if he doesn't appreciate that... -CLICK-

Well, I suppose that is not entirely true - to live among humans *is* to watch them decay. Every breath, every flutter of pulse brings with it the scent of the grave. From the early morning flicker of eyelids to a late-night yawn before sleep, each day brings with it decomposition in slow motion.

-CLICK- ...and a very beautiful one at that... but I still think that you should be going out with fellas your own age. Phillip, I'd much rather be with you, you know that. But what will people think, Laura? What will they think of us? I don't care what other people think, Phillip, they don't matter to me. You're the only one... -CLICK-

Yet I have never seen one weep so, nor blossom with as much colour as my sister. Those who have died in the house in years gone by have been whisked away briskly, lest the house be contaminated by the black cloud of death. Even the cat had been removed in a hurry, what little of it there was left after I tore it apart.

-CLICK- ...ost Families coming up next on Paranormal UK. Weak, limp, lifeless? Surely there's more to life than this... Now, with Proteritol Vibranol, our new formula brings the bounce back into your hair and into your step. Seventy-five percent of women surveyed said that... -CLICK-

But this body sits here still, swelling and sagging and darkening before my very eyes. An educational experience, right here in the parlour.

-CLICK- ...I want to give women freedom, I want to help...guide them, I suppose...to a place where they do feel good about themselves and their bodies. Because we've all been through this, haven't we? Precisely! We've been through it...been through some dark times, actually...but I think that... -CLICK-

It is around the time when the electricity in the house fails and the television finally ceases to entertain the maggots and bluebottles feasting on my sister's face that I realise that no one cares that she is dead. Could it be that hers is the one death within these four walls that does not scar the family in some terrible way? Of course – there is no family left to be upset by her death. She has passed into the world beyond with the family name for a shroud, taking it with her for all eternity. Amen.

My sister's skin begins to liquify and soak into the fabric of her armchair.

Not only is she without family, but there are no friends either. No acquaintances to check on her absence from the world this last month or so. The clattering of the letterbox brings with it only takeaway pizza menus and final demands for electricity and water bills. Occasionally the telephone rings but the salespeople and confidence tricksters on the other end of the line show no concern when it remains unanswered. It does not occur to them to care – they have targets and deadlines and better things to do than worry about old ladies who do not answer the phone.

There are no longer milkmen or grocer's boys to spot something amiss when a weekly order remains untouched upon the doorstep.

Even the next-door neighbours are too focused on their own lives, and if they do briefly wonder when the last time was that they saw the old lady next door, they are too concerned about being seen to be making a fuss to go and check, and so the momentary concern flickers from their mind, un-regarded.

I suppose I have never considered the loneliness of death because it has never *been* lonely to me. If anything, it brought me closer to my family, not that they knew it. But my sister sits – slumps – swollen and leaking and blackened, without anyone to mourn her passing. It never occurs to me that *I* should mourn her, and I'm not sure I would know how to anyway.

Perhaps this is why I soon find myself falling back into familiar beats. I watch the wisteria plant curl and climb outside the spare bedroom which once belonged to me, in the dim and distant past. I close my eyes and listen to the sound of woodlice in the earth under the house, the gentle creaking of floorboards beneath my feet.

There is a small hole at the bottom of the back door which occupies a great deal of my time. For whatever reason – perhaps the growing humidity within the house – a family of slugs appears to be using this hole to gain entrance to the kitchen. I sit and marvel at the way they scrawl their shining trails across the kitchen floor, glistening in slow hieroglyphs which spell out strange and secret stories as they travel. Small and pale, they glide in exploration, and I wonder if they can sense me; I wonder if they fear me – some unknowable beast looming above them as they travel in supposed safety through this still and silent house. How long would it take, I wonder, for them to completely take over and redecorate my former home in moonlight silver? What poetry could they write upon every surface?

I take enormous pleasure in crushing them one by one, feeling the thin membranes between their outsides and their insides bursting under the pressure of my thumb. I wonder if they cry out, if animal instinct sends waves of terror streaming between parent and child. I wonder if it hurts them.

Absorbed as I am in my pest control duties, I am not immediately aware of the knocking at the front door. In fact, it is not until the knocking becomes actual hammering on the door that I am roused from my task and take an interest.

There is a commotion at the letterbox, and for a moment I presume that the postman is dealing with a particularly challenging letter, when suddenly I hear a voice from someone evidently kneeling at the slot.

"Ah, Jesus. It stinks in there."

Whomever the unseen voice is talking to, I do not hear their reply through the door. Only:

"You want to get down here and get a whiff? They were right, you know…"

The voice drifts away as the speaker stands up and moves away from the door. I walk over to the front room window and peer out, just in time to see two men in dark blue boilersuits slam some sort of battering ram into the front door, sending it shooting open with all manner of splintering wood and clattering metal. As the door bounces back against the wall, it sends the hallway mirror crashing down onto the floor where it shatters into shards of silver and glass. Thousands of tiny reflections of boilersuits and heavy boots shimmer back at me like twinkling stars from the depths of the carpet and my sister's dead body is discovered.

Do Not Go Quietly, My Love

Do not go quietly, my love demands,

Do not stay silent - desire seeks a voice,
The blessed pulse within commands:
Do not go quietly, my love

And should you find yourself in need of rest,
Throat in ragged strips and blooded shreds.
Steal yourself to carry this request:
Do not go quietly, my love

For if the gentle sweetness of your love begins to fade,
Silence rolling through this darkened life of yours
Rejoice in echoes that linger in the shade
Do not go quietly my love

Fight and fight and fight some more
Rend cloth and flesh asunder with your sweet rage

Swallow down the blood or spit it 'pon the floor
Do not go quietly, my love.

It is raining

It is raining.

Except the word does not do justice to the state of the skies outside. Plum-hued clouds press down upon the Earth with such a weight that if I stood with my arms raised to the heavens my fingertips would brush against storm-head cotton.

There is a window at the turn of the stairs that offers the most marvellous view of next door's front garden and the street outside. I stand there now, watching as the grey-flecked world beyond the glass becomes nothing so much as a chalk drawing, colours merging and fading and slowly washing away, down the sputtering drains and ultimately out to sea…

The ferocity of the downpour is such that the lime trees which line the street are left unseasonably bare, with leaves and spindly branches battered to the ground to join the tidal flow of rainwater. Grassy path walkways and neighbourhood lawns become swamp-like beneath the onslaught from above.

As a child I would sit on the stairs during weather such as this – not that I can recall ever seeing weather *quite* like this before – wrapped in the eiderdown from my bed, feeling so safe and warm and content. I can remember the scent of the soft fabric and my own warm breath as I contemplated the rolling clouds on the other side of the glass.

Now, however, I feel unsettled. Of course, I feel no warmth nor have any breath; there is no comfort I *can* seek, other than those moments when my darling Hannah is at my side. But it is not this lack of comfort which sets me on edge, rather that I do not feel that this storm can safely be contained out there. Tendrils of it writhe through the air like roots through the earth, seeking a cold mischief of their own design. I fear that the glass in the windowpanes will not stop them for very long.

All about the house the air hangs heavy and oppressive - a headache stretched from room to room. There is a tension which has sent each member scurrying off to separate rooms about the house, the idea of closeness too much for them to bear. A sense of someone trying to hold your hand on an unpleasantly hot summer's day, or the weight and body heat of someone pressing down on you, smothering you, crushing you and removing any sense of safety and comfort you once had, in the dark and unknowable hours of the night.

Underscored by the low rumble and pitter-patter of this late evening rain, my darling sits in the parlour, tapping away at the laptop computer which seems to have been a permanent fixture before her this last month or so. I do worry that the harshness of the light may bring about lasting damage to the deep copper of her beautiful eyes and wish that I could soothe her tired eyelids with gentle lips and sweet words.

She sits and frowns at the writing that dances across the screen before her, fingers poised delicately above the keys, when a momentary flicker of darkness fills the room and the house descends into darkness for a fraction of a second.

"Mum?" she calls, nervously.

"Don't worry, Han," her mother calls back from the dining room, "it's just the storm."

"Should I save my work?" There is a pause – silence from the other room. "Mum?"

"Yes, I would." Her mum's voice is harsh, annoyed, but if Hannah notices, she doesn't react. Her eyes grow wide in momentary panic as the lights flicker again before returning once more.

Hannah's fingers skitter across the keys again and she lets out a sigh of relief. As the screen fades to black, she closes the lid of the machine and stares out through the parlour window, into the glistening darkness of the premature night brought forth by the storm. She bites at the skin at the edge of her thumbnail and worries. There is lightning in her eyes and she is beautiful.

In the dining room, Debbie glares briefly up at the lampshade above her, her eyes narrowing accusatorily. Before her, spread out on the table, her dream garden lays in scattered photographs and magazine pages, gardening books intermingling with packets of seeds. Looking back down at the organised chaos, she tries to choose between galvanised lawn edging or willow hurdles, before giving up and closing the catalogue in defeat.

For a moment, she stares at her reflection in the darkened dining room windows, the glass turned mirror-like by the lamp light above her. For a moment, she fancies she can see the flickering motion of her own heart beating within her chest reflected back at her, before a low heavy rumbling and crack of lightning illuminates the garden, painting the branches and leaves in a flash of ozone white.

An odd sense of irritation fills her mind as the garden becomes dark once more. She takes a final gulp of tea in an attempt to clear her mind of negativity and makes her way to the kitchen.

Terry does not notice his wife as she enters the room behind him. He does not hear the clatter of ceramic as she places her mug in the dishwasher beside him. He does not feel her hand as she slides it around his waist.

He stands at the sink, a soap-sud speckled baking tray air-drying in his hands, and stares into nothingness. There is an abyss before him, black and tantalising, and the heavy sound of raindrops fills his mind with a dark music indistinguishable from the storm outside.

After a moment or two he realises that his wife is speaking to him, and it takes all of his strength to pull back from the darkness to look at her. He frowns in confusion.

"Hmm?"

Debbie goes to speak, goes to chide him for ignoring her, when the room is plunged into darkness once again. Not in a flicker, however. This time, the lights stay off.

She blinks in surprise as a gentle panic grips the back of her mind and scolds herself at such an unhelpful reaction.

"Mum?" Hannah's voice quivers from the parlour.

"It's just a power cut, nothing to worry about," Debbie replies, managing as best she can to keep her voice even and calm as she stares once more into the storm-toss'd garden. "Can you go upstairs and check on your sister?"

There is a gentle grumble from the other room, and she hears her eldest daughter pad upstairs to check on Lily.

Peering out of the window, Debbie is surprised by the brightness of the garden despite the darkness of the clouds overhead. Slowly, an uneasy realisation begins to settle over her. Leaning past her husband to get a better look, she notices the lights are still on their neighbours' houses.

"Number three's still got power…" she mutters, more to herself than to her husband. She looks up at him. "D'you think it's a fuse or something?"

"The shelter," he murmurs hoarsely.

A swell of anxiousness rises in her chest as she looks from the glassy expression on her husband's face out through the kitchen window. There, at the bottom of the garden, sits the dark shape of the recently uncovered air-raid shelter.

It glistens like a large and ominous toad, beneath a slick, black tarpaulin which has become untethered at one corner and flaps back and forth in the storm revealing the slightest hint of a deeper darkness within. Debbie clears her throat and when she speaks, there is more of an edge to her voice than perhaps she meant there to be.

"What are you talking about?"

"It's the shelter… I need to…" Terry trails off.

"Terry, it's nothing to do with the shelter. Are you going to check the fuses or do you want me to?" She places her hand on his arm briefly, before pulling back. "What the hell, Terry? You're freezing!"

Before her husband can reply, certainly before she has a moment to process, the sound of a door slamming open echoes from upstairs.

"Mum!" Hannah shouts from the top of the stairs, "Mum, it's Lily, quick!"

Her first response is to look to her husband, look to the man she has been married to for twenty years - the father of her children - for a reaction. She searches for some sign that the fear in his daughter's voice has triggered some base parental instinct deep beneath the mire of his fugue state. But she sees all too readily that he cannot give her the reaction that she needs.

"I… I'd better go and check on the shelter…" Terry mumbles, with something close to shame in his voice. He does not look her in the eye.

"What? Terry, no! No!" She hits him on the shoulder in frustration and fear as he pushes past her and makes for the kitchen door. Debbie's mind reels at the sight of her husband abandoning his family and for a moment she contemplates going after him and dragging him back inside.

"Oh for *fuck's* sake!" she spits to the night sky, before flinging open the cupboard under the sink, grabbing a torch and rushing upstairs to her daughters.

***

Well?

I dont want to

What do you mean you don't want to? We are Warrior Queens, remember? I thought you were braver than all the others.

not like this

YES like this! I thought you wanted to be in control of your own destiny? My Warrior Queen, don't you see? You are twelve now, no longer the child that once you were. They know – they ALL know and it will not be long before you are sought out by others. Maybe even by your own...

but it hurts! Everytime i do it it hurts even more!

Hurts?! More than the empty loneliness of your days at school? More than empty days stuck with this family of yours? There are none that care for you as much as I do – do you really think it will hurt more than the pain of us losing each other?

what do u mean?

If he gets his hands on you then we can no longer be together. I can feel it, the dark lust within him. Within all of them. You think this hurts? Hah, you have no idea. Let me protect you! Take charge of your own destiny, my Warrior Queen! Fight back and live on your own terms with me! For me!

but this isnt what I want. You want me to do this. I dont!

i dont!

r u still there?

***

The rain is heavy against his neck and back, sharp and quick like marbles pelting his skin. It runs in strangely warm rivulets beneath his clothes, slicking his thinning hair down against his scalp and obscuring his vision.

The garden has become alive in the storm. The trees quiver in the wind, the few surviving autumnal leaves that still cling to bare branches rattle like teeth in an empty skull – a gentle beat-keeping percussion to run beneath the ever-present music of the night. Deep purple clouds crown the skies and loom down with a stillness which jars against the frenzied motion of the garden

Terry walks in darkness. He does not look up at the lights still shining in his neighbours' homes, nor does he notice the black emptiness that looms in the windows of his own. He does not notice the way the rain soaks into his pyjamas or the sodden way his slippers slap against the garden path as he makes his way towards the back of the garden and the partially uncovered shelter.

It beckons him. The corner of the tarpaulin which has been pulled away from its mooring flaps and waves in the storm like the greeting of an old friend. Terry suddenly feels cold, goosepimples standing up on his skin, and he longs for the protection from the elements that the old shelter will afford him. He can see the emptiness revealed with each shift of the tarpaulin, and fancies he can already feel the dry space around him, keeping him safe from the storm.

Because, he realises, that's all he has ever wanted – shelter from the storm. He smiles to himself and shakes his head as if amused by his own stupidity. Clouds seem to part in his mind, and for once the gentle sounds of swing music on the edge of the wind do not upset him.

Terry stumbles from the path onto the lawn as he heads towards the air raid shelter. The lawn gives way slightly beneath him, the already patchy grass made fluid in the rain. Each step he takes sends his slippers sinking deeper and deeper into the mud, thick little waves of it slopping over the top of them and seeping into the hem of his pyjama trousers.

But still Terry's focus is on the warmth and safety of the shelter. He walks towards it with a rain-slicked grin plastered across his face and even as he sinks to his ankles beneath the lawn he does not falter. The mud clings to his every step, making his journey forward harder and harder. Slowly he begins to *wade* through the dirt which is now up to his shins and soaking into the fabric of his trouser legs but still he continues forward.

It is only once the filth beneath him begins to encroach on his thighs does Terry seem to falter in any way. He looks down, baffled, before looking back up at the shelter with a puppyish longing. Whimpering, he tries to shift himself, but the mud is thick and sucks him back with each attempt. He reaches out a hand in desperation towards the blackness of the shelter, stretching out as far as possible and gasps in frustration at the distance still to be covered between the tips of his fingers and his goal. He cries out in rage and curses those unmoving clouds above for their unchecked cruelty.

Grunting, Terry begins to scrabble at the mud at his thighs, scooping out huge, damp handfuls of earth from around him, clearing a path. With each sopping wet handful cleared he jerks and wriggles his legs, but the rain pours so hard that each space cleared soon fills with water and dirt and his legs just *will not shift*. He screams with the pain of the unjust as he rakes his hands through the swirling slop which was once his back garden. He feels the pebbles and roots beneath the soil as they coil and bump against his fin-gertips and then – inch by inch – he seems to make progress. Slow going, yes, but there is no doubt about it, he can move his left leg forward by a fraction, then his right leg in turn. It takes all his effort, but Terry finds himself able to move through the mud which now hungrily grasps at his waist. He pushes forward, straining every tendon and muscle in his body, until once again he finds himself tangled in the roots of some long-buried tree beneath the soil.

But this is different somehow. As he plunges his hands into the murk around his waist to pull himself free, the roots seem to entwine themselves around his forearms. He pulls at them, lifting them free of the earth, and looks down in horror at the mud-slicked skeletal fingers gripping him tightly. Terry shakes his head, a low keening sound coming from the back of his throat as the arm - yellowed bones cleansed bare by the hammering rain - grips tightly to his own in a crude handshake.

He claws at it, desperate to prise those sharp, blank fingers away. He shakes his arm in desperation, but the strange visitor merely flops insolent along with his own harried movement, digging itself into the soft flesh of his own wrists.

Pain shoots up Terry's arm and he slips in the mud, his feet no longer able to find solid ground beneath the swamp of his back garden. As he falls into the dirt his forehead collides with something hard and as he blinks the stars away two empty eye sockets stare up at him. Dark they are, and mocking, staring at him from a skull which grins as it floats, stark white against the liquid mud of his back garden.

Those two dark holes stare into his soul. Terry can feel fingerbones crawling up and down his body now, pulling him down into the mud, pulling him down towards that waiting skull. He struggles to get away, struggles in the cold and wet and filth, streams of water filling his mouth and nose and he begins to scream and scream and scream.

***

"What's wrong with her, mum?" Hannah looks up, panic stricken, as her mother enters the room.

A small lamp in the shape of a cat - presumably battery powered - sits upon a shelf above Lily's bed and casts a pale orange glow over the room, painting deep shadows beneath Debbie's eyes and in the hollows of her cheeks.

She doesn't immediately answer, but walks hesitantly towards her youngest daughter, sat bolt upright in bed. Eyes red and tired looking, her skin porcelain brittle, sweat-slick and pale against the pink of her pyjamas. She is still, barely breathing.

"I...don't know," Debbie manages, pushing back the strands of hair that stick to Lily's forehead, feeling for a temperature. "A seizure or something?" Her fingertips trail around her daughter's face, feeling for a pulse. "She feels... she's not got a fever or anything..." Debbie gently shakes her by the shoulders. "Lily? Lily, can you hear me?"

Her mind races as she looks at the girl, at the dark circles under her eyes, her sore, cracked lips. Were they new – a symptom of the strange illness which held her in its grip – or did she always look like this? Debbie didn't know. She couldn't remember the last time she had spent any real time with her daughters. She couldn't remember the last time it had felt like they were a real part of her life or she a part of theirs.

Lily rocks back slightly at her mother's touch but does not respond. She does not blink and barely a flutter at her chest suggests she is breathing.

"Mum, what's going on?" Hannah mutters, from her position at the edge of her sister's bed. "First the lights and now this…"

"I don't know, okay?" Debbie snaps, adrenaline and dread coursing through her veins in equal measure. The glow of the fairy lights catches the edge of Lily's hair giving her a halo glow in the darkness, and Debbie looks from her to Hannah, whose tears glitter like silent jewels on her cheeks. She takes a deep breath, trying to keep the panic out of her voice. "It's nothing, Han… It's just a coincidence… shit timing, that's all."

Debbie looks back through the open bedroom door towards the darkness of the hallway. She rubs her eyes in frustration before looking back at her youngest daughter.

"Lily, Lily! Can you hear me? It's mum!" she calls gently.

Hannah watches her mum in silence for a moment, and then whispers, in a voice heavy with concern. "She hasn't done anything stupid, has she?"

"What do you mean?"

Hannah does not say a word but points with a perfectly almond-shaped nail towards her younger sister's arms and legs, where thin lines of pain have left delicate scabbed trails across her pale skin. Debbie's eyes grow wide in horror. She lets out a low, animal groan of anguish.

"Oh Lily…What have you done to yourself?" She looks over at Hannah. "Did you know? Did you know she was doing this?"

Hannah shakes her head and shifts back on the edge of the bed, away from her mother.

"No, I swear I didn't."

"For fuck's sake…" Debbie grabs Lily gently by the shoulders and pulls her still, silent daughter to her chest, rocking back and forth.

And then.

There is a hammering sound from below. Slow but insistent, it echoes up the stairs and through the open bedroom door. The darkness at the top of the stairs looks deeper than ever, even the moonlight through the landing window merely highlights the gloom.

The hammering rings out again and Debbie realises that she is holding her breath. She lets it out in one long uneasy sigh. Decisions weigh heavily in her mind and in her soul and she can feel something almost curdling within her. A tiredness perhaps, or an inevitability. All the same a heaviness shift inside, a heaviness that she has felt since the day she first stepped over the threshold of this house and set about attempting to make it something it could never be – a safe and loving family home. Her mind begins to crystalise, holding panic and other unhelpful emotions still and stopping them from taking charge.

"Mum?" Hannah whimpers, confused.

Debbie does not meet her eldest daughter's eyes as she leans forwards and kisses the top of her head. Before she can say anything, the hammering begins again.

"Stay here with Lily, okay?" she murmurs, her voice low and harsh. "Call an ambulance. I'm just going to check to see what that noise is, I'll be back in a moment."

Hannah grabs her mother's arm. "Mum don't."

Debbie smiles weakly. "Don't be silly, Han. You look after Lily. I'm just going to check downstairs, that's all."

She gets up and crosses to the doorway. Before she leaves the room, Debbie looks back at her daughters. "Just… block this door behind me," she says. "Pull something across it… the chest of drawers or something. I'll be back, I promise."

Hannah nods, the colour draining from her cheeks as she watches her mother leave. Night has so perfectly taken the landing that she has barely stepped out of the room before she is swallowed by the darkness. Debbie closes the door behind her and is gone.

With a squeeze of her younger sister's cold hand, Hannah slides from the bed. Her eyes are glued to the back of the bedroom door, expecting at any moment for it to burst open.

But it does not. The door remains resolutely closed and so, heeding her mother's words, Hannah crosses the room and begins to tug at the chest of drawers which sits against the wall. Various bits of cheap jewellery, makeup and other youthful detritus tumble from its surface and scatter across the rug.

Eventually, with much heaving and juddering across the carpet, the bedroom door is successfully blocked. Beads of sweat have blossomed on Hannah's forehead, and she takes a deep breath. A sort of blankness takes over my beloved's mind – a compartmentalising of terror and fear which she has subconsciously learned from her mother. She turns to face her younger sister, still sat bolt upright amongst brightly patterned blankets and old soft toys.

"Right," Hannah mutters quietly to herself, "ambulance."

She scans the bedroom thoughtfully for a moment, before her shoulders drop in tragic realisation.

"Of course."

Of course. Her mobile telephone is downstairs in the parlour, safe on the table where she left it, blank and black and good for nothing and a million miles away at any rate.

The thought of shifting the chest of drawers back and venturing downstairs in the darkness to retrieve her telephone doesn't even bear thinking about.

Then her eyes alight on her sister's phone - half hidden beneath the bed, having evidently slipped from the young girl's hand when this strange seizure had taken its grip.

Dropping to her knees, Hannah scrabbles under the bed and retrieves the phone from its hiding place. As she does so, it turns on and the last few lines of conversation glow obscenely from the surface of the screen.

Despite the urgency of the situation, Hannah's eyes cannot help but scan the little lines of blue and green. A frown crinkles her perfect forehead and her thumb slides down the screen, sending the text skittering across the glass.

"Oh Lily..." she groans quietly as her younger sister's pain and loneliness are laid bare before her. "Who is this? Why...why didn't you say?"

The phone feels heavy in her hand, a brick thrown through the window of her mind, and a wave of nausea washes over her. She shakes her head, hoping to shift the hateful conversations between her sister and this stranger from her thoughts. Without any real conscious decision, she clears the messages from the screen completely before scrolling to the keypad and calling the emergency services.

A dial tone, and a click and a hiss of static, before a sensible sounding female voice answers.

"Emergency, which service do you require, fire, police or ambulance?"

"Ambulance," Hannah manages to say.

"Speak up, dear."

"Ambulance, please... it's my sister..."

"I see. May I take your name and address?"

Momentarily blank, Hannah manages to stumble through her answer, reciting the information with the slow deliberation of an unfocused mind.

"And what is the emergency, dear?"

"It's... it's my sister. She's... I don't know... having a seizure, I think? She's all still and hardly breathing. Please, you have to hurry!"

"Don't rush me, young lady," the voice at the other end of the phone snaps. There is a long pause, and for a moment all Hannah can hear is the strange clicking and hissing sounds which pulse down the line like a heartbeat. Slowly, the sounds seem to build in intensity, and when the woman next speaks, she has to raise her voice above the noise.

"Don't act as though you're in any sort of a hurry to help your sister, young lady. After all, you found time to have a snoop through her messages, didn't you?"

Hanna freezes, her mouth dry. "I...what? What are you talking about?"

"The thing is, young lady," the neat, clipped tones at the other end of the phone continues, *"there is no help. There never is. Not for your sister. Not for you. Certainly not for me. It is a simple fact that we all need to learn sooner or later: Life hurts and life* should *hurt. It hurts, young lady. It huuuuurrrts..."*

These last few words grow loud and harsh, the sound stretching out into a low groaning sound that goes on and on, louder and louder, seeming to reach out and drive sharp, dirty fingernails into the soft parts of Hannah's brain.

She pulls the phone away from her ear with a yelp and throws it across the room. It hits the wall with a loud crack and slithers to the floor. The sound of impact echoes around the darkened room, seemingly hanging in the air a beat longer than expected, and with it, Lily rouses from her fugue state.

Hannah does not notice at first, still fixated as she is on the terrible black screen of the phone across the room, and it is only when her sister gasps that she turns to see.

"Lily!" she cries, wrapping her arms around her sister's slight frame.

"Where...? What's going on?" the young girl asks from the centre of her sister's embrace, a look of panicked confusion in her eyes. But then, a growing sensation of pain within robs her of further words. A pressure that builds inside and suddenly, in her sisters' arms, she lets out a piercing scream.

Hannah moves back from Lily in shock, just in time to see the horrified expression on the young girl's face. For the briefest of moments, she searches for the cause of her distress, before red lines begin to slowly gouge their way along the soft pale skin of her sister's cheeks. One, two, three, they form - deep and dark - like scratches from some monstrous cat. Lily screams again, recoiling as though slapped by some vicious, unseen hand, and when she turns back to look at Hannah, three more slash marks scar her other cheek. Almost lazily, blood begins to flow, streaking down her face and spattering onto her nightdress.

She reaches out for Hannah who grasps at her sister in misguided protection. As she does so, the young girl shrieks again, open wounds appearing on the bare flesh of her arms.

She judders in shock sending more splashes of red over her sister and the now-ruined bedcovers.

Hannah holds the panicked girl against her breast, and I cannot help but feel a pang of jealousy. I wish I could be held in those arms of hers, rest my cheek upon her breast, be calmed by the caresses of her hand. I wish it was my blood upon her skin, baptising her in the warmth of my body.

You are the heat within my veins, Hannah, my love.

As Lily screams in pain in her sister's arms, her skin criss-crossed with open wounds, blood dripping from the tips of her bare toes, I cannot stop myself from reaching out to run my fingers through Hannah's thick, mahogany-brown locks. The sharp scent of her fear brings forth a fluttering in my chest.

Outside the bedroom door, a floorboard creaks.

Let Me

S top.
    Let me.
Let me look at you.
Really *look* at you.
From here to the end, let me gaze in adoration at each
breath you take, each smile and flush of cheek. And if
the future brings a shroud upon my eyes,
Be the light which guides me home.

Let me.
Let me know you.
Let me face the world beside you, protecting, protected.
Let your depths be mine and in the darkness when they
are
    your all, let me gaze at each minute and mirror'd glimpse
and hope – in some way – to *understand* them for you.
And offer comfort.

Let me.
Let me show you.

Just a tiny fraction of my admiration as you stand before
me – so wonderfully full of life and hope, sadness
and beauty.
Perfection, in a million ways or more and all of them
unknowable, unthinkable to you.

Let me.
Never let me
Stop.

Reunion

Debbie is well aware of the sheer absurdity - the *drama* – of the situation as she leaves her daughters behind. That awful fear we have of making fools of ourselves and overreacting – of going too far and embarrassed by stepping beyond the boundaries of social norms. She'd told them to block the door behind her, for goodness' sake. With each careful step downstairs in the darkness, she cannot help but shake the sensation of un-realness that rolls against the back of her neck like the breath of an unwelcome lover.

Nonetheless, she takes the little bronze statuette of man and woman entwined from its place upon the landing win-dowsill and holds it in her hand. Its welcome weight against her palm keeps her balanced, keeps her centred, as she makes her half-light descent into the downstairs hallway.

The heavy sound of hammering has stopped now, she has not heard it since she left Lily's bedroom. The sound of the storm, however, is louder than ever. It brings with it a coldness, a damp chill which seems to wash through the hallway, breaking in waves against the bottom of the stairs.

Then all of a sudden, there is a bang. Different than before, less purposeful. It is the simple sound of wood bouncing off plaster which echoes above the sound of rainfall and makes her jump. It is all she can do to stop herself from dropping her makeshift weapon. The sound rings out again and Debbie gasps, before catching herself and swearing under her breath, irritated at her own jumpiness.

It is not until her feet touch the hard wood of the downstairs hallway that she realises the source of the clattering sound. Such an everyday sound - alien in its normalness in the strange, sudden darkness – the sound of the back door caught in the wind, banging against the kitchen wall.

The back door caught in the wind.

The *open* back door.

Debbie looks up to see a dark figure standing in the kitchen doorway, silhouetted against the faint light from the window behind. Large, with hunched shoulders and a lolling neck, it takes a moment before she realises that it is her husband.

"Terry?...Terry, are you okay?" she manages to ask.

Her husband does not answer, but looks over at her with a blank, glassy expression. He shuffles slightly, on unfamiliar feet, and turns to face her. His clothes are glossy and hang heavy about him, slick in places where the wetness of them clings to his skin. Dark splatters across his neck and cheeks stand in stark contrast to the whiteness of his eyes.

"What's happened?"

"My…darling…" Terry's voice is a low growl, hesitant and painful. It sounds inhuman, and Debbie tightens her grip on the statuette in her hand.

"Terry?"

Her husband smiles at her and takes a heavy step forward. It takes its toll – an effort to put one bare, muddied foot in front of the other – not helped by the pools of brackish-looking mud which drip from him as he staggers, pooling beneath him on the parquet floor. One more step forward and he slips slightly, landing heavily against the door of the downstairs toilet with a thump which echoes about the hallway. He does not take his eyes off his wife.

"Terry, you need to stop," Debbie says as she watches him push himself up and away from the toilet door, leaving behind a smear of dark filth across the wood. "Don't come any closer. Just… just go and sit down in the living room, okay? Go and have a rest." She stands firm by the stairs, stopping her husband's access to the rest of the house. Her heart flutters wildly, but a maternal strength runs through her like steel.

"I wish… to see my daughter," he manages to say, thickly. There is something strange about his voice, as ragged as it seems, there is something *else* there like music half-heard from a nearby room. There is something strange about the way he stands as well. No, not strange – *familiar.*

And then, in a heartbeat, it is Terry standing there once more, dripping mud on the hallway floor.

"My…kitten… I wish to see her…"

"Terry, no."

"My… darling wife… You have no right to stop me!" he shouts, his voice bouncing off the silent walls. "This is…MY house! MY family!"

He lunges forward, pulling himself along the wall to give himself momentum as he attempts to push past Debbie.

Debbie, however, will not let him pass. Cannot let him pass. Her husband is a big man, given further strength by the strange rage which has struck him, but Debbie pushes back against his chest, her fingers digging into the mud-soaked fabric of his t-shirt. She scrabbles and claws at him, sending him staggering back slightly, skidding in the puddles of his own filth. As he stumbles, Debbie manages to swing her arm up and the statuette in her hand clunks against the side of his head.

Terry roars in pain but the hallway is too small for the swing to have much force behind it. Despite the blood – a glossy black in the darkness – which bursts from his temple beneath the ornament's metal figures he manages to push back at her. As he reaches up towards the banister to steady himself, she clings to his other arm and uses all her weight in an attempt to pull him off balance.

They dance together in the darkness. A whirl, a dip, there is music in the raging storm outside and Terry and Debbie find the pulse, the *fury* beneath the rhythm as they find themselves in each other's arms in perverse, manic togetherness. Debbie tries to sink her teeth into her husband's fleshy shoulder, but he manages to grab at her arm and *pull*, sending her spinning.

Debbie sobs, desperately trying to keep her grip on him as she stumbles. Gasping cries and furious admonitions flutter from her lips and fill the empty hallway as her hands slip in the mud that coats his skin. He looks down at her, his eyes a fleshy white, and cries out:

"I want…to see…my daughter!"

He sweeps his arm around and in one solid swoop hits Debbie with the back of his fist. His knuckles clunk heavily against her cheekbone and she tumbles backwards, hitting the wall behind her, her head bouncing obscenely against the hallway radiator as she slumps to the ground at her husband's feet.

What is that in his milky-blank eyes as he stares at his wife's body, crumpled at his feet? Anger? Love? Confusion? Whatever it is, the moment passes, and Terry lumbers on.

He begins to climb the stairs, up to the top floor of the house and his daughters' bedrooms.

Except.

Except it's not Terry, is it? The figure seems to *waver* as it takes step after painful step upstairs. Terry brings his mud-soaked foot down, but it is ragged, clacketty fingerbones which grip the banister, scoring lines in the white gloss paint of the handrail. The light from the landing window reflects in the mud covering Terry's arms, dripping heavily from his water-logged clothing, splattering onto the stairway carpet, but neutral pebble-painted wall can be glimpsed through a flicker of chipped and mould-studded ribs

In one moment, it is Terry's wide-eyed face that looms into view as he climbs the stairs, and then something skull-white glistens in the darkness, something with deep, empty eye sockets. *Something* smiles an endless smile, filth-streaked and impossible.

But behind all that there is *another* something. One that makes my heart race. As I stand at the top of the stairs, the floorboards outside Lily's bedroom door creak beneath my feet and the air fills with the scent of my father's aftershave and the ever-present cloud of cigar smoke. Between the flickering faces of Terry and the skeletal unknown, my father's heavy features become visible.

The realisation hits me like a flash of lightning and for a moment he fills the whole world. Large and broad of shoulder, the same dark, mischievous grin across his face, the same bear-hug presence of a man. Somewhere far away, the scratchy sounds of Benny Carter play on an unseen record player.

And from his lips he calls to me:

"My daughter, my daughter."

His voice is thick with emotion, his accent heavy with tears of remorse that glisten on his cheeks and in the bristles of his moustaches. And I am sure he notices me, he *sees* me. For the first time in decades, I hear his voice and feel something close to joy.

Despite the ever-present flickering between other lives and bodies that share the same soul-space upon the stairs, I know that my Papa has come for me, to hold me in his arms. Finally, I am not alone!

My mind races, and it is all I can do to stop myself from rushing to him, tumbling down the stairs and greeting him with a hug.

But that would not do. I am a woman now, not a child, despite the quickening of my heart. And I know, *I know* there is anger in him; there is a rage within him that darkens the skies and seethes foul cruelty into every room in this house, but despite all that, he is still my Papa.

After all, death changed me, so would it not change him? Tempered the darkness, shaped the blackness within him into something that more resembled a soul.

My non-existent pulse races at the sight of him climbing each stair, and as the top of his head crests the landing, I bask in the fact that – for the first time since the spirit of my sister's dead cat left me – I have someone to share this time and space with.

My father reaches the landing and pauses for a moment, staring down at me. His chest rises and falls like cresting waves. I look deeply into his eyes.

"Papa," I whisper, and in his eyes I see

nothing.

I have become far too accustomed over the decades to the coldness brought about by the lack of care and attention of others for this moment to hurt. The skin of my cheek has been cooled for too many years – untouched by others – for this spirit's blank stare to hold me in its grip for too long.

But as this empty father of mine reaches *past* me and takes hold of the doorhandle at my back, I am overcome by such weariness. These spectral bones of mine ache so, and the weight of them almost brings me to my knees. A sudden wave of nausea washes over me. I look about me and I am disgusted by the rags of life which even now cling to me like

a rotting shroud, and I long to close my eyes and sleep forever and a day until the world is dust about me.

I walk away. From my father, from Terry, from whatever
this creature is; from Debbie, bruised and bloodied, at the
bottoms of the stairs; from Lily, scarred in scarlet, foaming
and screaming like a Victorian lunatic; from Hannah, my
love - her mind white with terror like the signal of an un-
tuned television set, trapped in a nightmare of unknowns. I
cannot even bring myself to pity them.

I walk away, my back to them all, towards my old bedroom. There are noises behind me: cries and screams and
the sound of straining wood, but they are nothing.

My old bedroom is cool and dark and comforting. Hannah's life sits upon the shape of mine once lived as though is
a skeleton, and she the muscles and tendons which bring it
warmth and motion.

I think, perhaps, that I have lived my life through others
for too long now. Do I blame myself? No, not at all. Do I
hate them for it? Yes, I think I do.

When I was younger, before Agatha was born, I would
find myself alone on many occasions. Times when my father
would have gone to work and my mother was busy with her
housework in the kitchen or parlour.

Out of sight and out of mind, for a short while at least,
I would sit on the floor of my bedroom, hugging my knees
and burying my chin into my chest. In the tiny little uni-

verse of my balled-up body, there was only the darkness - almost dazzling - behind my tightly closed eyes and the warm woollen scent of my stockings and the rhythm of my young heartbeat.

Sitting here, in my old bedroom, my darling Hannah's bedroom, I am connected to my younger self with a glowing thread that ties us together through time. I find myself drifting, calm and quiet, my youth and back again, and I realise the strange emptiness I feel has always been with me. Before today, before I died, even.

I think of myself rushing back and forth at play with my sister in the garden, running though the lapping waves at the seaside, dancing with my father in the parlour and can see, at this distance, what I shadow I was even then.

Perhaps my soul has always been an empty husk, and what little life I spent upon the earth was all that had filled the rattling emptiness. Twelve years of life in a shell designed to hold decades – no wonder I died so young.

So I tell myself: no more. No more pointless searching for connection or fulfilment. Clearly, I have walked this spirit realm looking for something that I did not even realise I was missing and I am sick to the stomach with it all. How naive I was, how blind to my own self. These people in my life, these families amongst whom I find myself in constant entanglement, they are no more real to me than wooden figures in a child's dollhouse and I refuse to let myself be hurt by their dreary nonsense any longer. I am ever so tired of everything, tired of these lives so full.

I tell myself that I am done with them all.

And I know am lying to myself.

A scream rips through my hard-won solitude, and I look up from my position on the edge of the bed. I reach my hand to the mask that covers my face. The cardboard feels cheap and flimsy beneath my fingertips as I pull it up and take it off and a quiet voice at the back of my mind wonders why I ever bothered wearing it at all. For a moment I imagine I feel the cool breeze on my skin, imagine the relief and sense of release after so many years imprisoned, but I understand that this is mere fancy. I feel nothing, as always.

I am used to seeing everything at once. Time and space have meant nothing to me in the years since my death. A connecting thread there may be to the girl I once was, but it is one I spin myself, from the cotton fibres of the vastness of existence. Yes, I am used to seeing everything at once, but now, there are some things it seems that are hidden from me. Lily's bedroom crackles in my mind in darkness, an ache behind the eyes. Hannah and her sister are pinpricks of light in the dark, but nothing else, and I no longer see the way they cower from the blood and violence of the evening.

Perhaps in spiteful retribution for me closing off my mind to the emotions of the world around me, the world itself has started to close itself off to me.

Another scream from the landing draws my attention briefly and I look up to see my father pounding on Lily's bedroom door. His broad hand slams against the wood, sending mud and filth splattering across the surface. He roars - an echoing, rattling sound that seems to come from many throats - and slams his shoulder into the door. My father shimmers as he does so - becoming Terry once more, then something else skeletal and foul and curiously *real* in the darkness.

Suddenly, with a splintering noise and the sound of tearing carpet, Lily's door shifts beneath this demon's weight, first one inch, then another. I hear Hannah screaming again from within the room, and picture her, flushed and panicked, desperately holding back the shifting door.

"Come to me, my kitten," this flickering shadow thing grunts. Veins and tendons twist violently about its neck and shoulders as it forces its weight against the door. Dark red ribbons form on its forearms as the pale flesh begins to split, crushed as they are against the surface of the door.

And then, a shift. The door crunches inwards and with a yell of triumph and pain, my father falls to his knees in the bedroom doorway. The thing inside of him looks up through borrowed eyes, ragged patches of blackened skin mottling a bare-boned grin lit by the lamp-light glow of Lily's bedroom.

"My kitten, my darling girl," it sputters in a voice which no longer sounds like my father's, nor Terry either, for that matter. It is a sound from beneath the earth, a voice of rock and soil, of tangled roots and crawling things. A voice that is wet and dark and old. A whisper at the centre of the raging storm. A whisper of bones beneath the soil.

"Go...go away," I hear Hannah scream from the other side of the doorway, her voice angry and thick with tears. "Leave us alone, dad, or I'll… I'll call the police."

"You wretched, jealous little whore," he grunts, a trail of mud-speckled, pink-hued saliva dripping from his injured lips. He grabs hold of the doorframe and hauls himself to his feet. "You cannot keep me from my daughter!"

I study him from my position sat on the floor of Lily's bedroom. The heaviness of him, the effort it seems to take to hold himself upright. Himself? Themselves. The three figures which seem to take up the same space upon the landing flicker worse than ever between each, although something tells me that only I can see the layers of the man. Hannah, I think, sees only her father, muddied and torn, standing in the doorway of her younger sister's bedroom.

Standing in the doorway, yes. But despite the eagerness with which his fingers grasp out towards the girls, he makes no move to enter the room. There has always been creeping darkness in the back bedroom, one which has so often prevented me from dallying there for longer than a moment. I am puzzled to see it push my father back as well. I would have gathered darkness spoke to darkness and would welcome him to its shadowy bosom like an old friend. It does not seem to be the case; the monster cannot cross the threshold and enter Lily's bedroom.

Terry looks down at himself with an expression of sadness and frustration etched across his face despite the blankness of his eyes and lets out a roar of anger like that of a wounded animal. He flails his arms in momentary wild abandon – or so I suppose – but then he takes a sudden lunge at Hannah as she blocks the doorway. His speed takes her by surprise as his filthy hands slam into the side of her head.

"We will dance, my kitten and I. We will dance again," he rumbles as he brings his clenched fist up towards his face, dragging Hannah with him. Her auburn hair is entwined between his fingers and he drags her forward, pulling and struggling in his grip.

"Dad, get off me!" she cries out, her feet skidding against the carpet. She tries to keep balance as she is lifted, desperately clawing at Terry's hand in an effort to release herself. The sound of her sobs and struggles rings out across the hallway as the girl fights, hammering against her father's chest and arms, but he holds her before him, gazing down into her angry, panicked face.

He stares at her in deep contemplation, the emptiness returning to his eyes, the speckles of mud and filth across his cheeks. There is something that could almost be love there – the last shreds of Terry's consciousness perhaps, staring out of the horrific legion which has taken the reins.

"I'm sorry, *mein Liebe*," he growls, holding Hannah close enough that the smell of his sour, copper-scented breath fills her nostrils. "There is no place for you here anymore. We make a home here together, my daughter and I."

At this, he closes his free hand over Hannah's nose and mouth, clamping his fingers tightly across her tear-stained cheeks. She tries to shake her head free of his grasp, but he holds her in place with the fingers of his other hand digging into her scalp and he *pushes* and *pushes*. Blood-tinged foam flecks his teeth as he smiles blankly down at her, and with her pulse clanging rapidly in her ears as it desperately tries to deliver the last dregs of oxygen left in her blood stream to her brain, Hannah at last sees the stained, mould-patched skull of the creature flickering beneath her father's grim features.

Her body judders in his grasp, but still he holds on tight, stealing her life away. Blue-black lightning begins to crackle at the edge of her vision, framing her view of the monster before her.

Standing behind my father, I dig my fingers deeply into the flesh at either side of his neck and wrench them back, my nails scoring glistening trails through his skin which begin to flow blackly down his chest and shoulders. The meat of him feels cold beneath my fingers, unresponsive and dead, but I guess he senses my presence now as he rocks back in shock, dropping Hannah who slumps against the doorframe of Lily's bedroom.

My father roars and tries to turn, lashing back at me blindly. I dig in deeper as he does so, pushing down until I am knuckle-deep between the sinew and muscle at his throat. Putting all my weight behind me, I lock my fingers within his flesh and pull the beast back, away from my love, away so he can hurt her no longer. The liquid darkness from his neck begins to soak into the sleeves of my dress. He is heavy, but the suddenness of my weight behind him catches him off guard and together we stagger backwards across the landing towards the top of the stairs.

We grunt and struggle together in the dark as I pull my father back, away from Lily's bedroom. The stink of blood and soil befouling the space at the top of the stairs. My father splutters and gags, black clots spraying from his lips, from Terry's lips, from between the teeth of the fleshless creature within my arms.

And as we struggle, I am afforded the briefest of glimpses of my beloved Hannah, tear-flushed and gasping but wonderfully - cruelly - alive, crouched fearfully at the threshold of her sister's bedroom. I wonder for a moment if she sees me.

Would that make everything better? Would that have made the blessed, hollow monstrosity of my life worthwhile? Would every dust and pain-filled second of my imprisonment within the lives of these people have counted for something if - even for a heartbeat - she could look into my eyes and see *something*? Is her acknowledgement of me what I have been waiting for?

Even as my father shakes and bucks and thrashes about in a vain attempt to dislodge me, a fluttering rises in my chest at the thought. I fancy I can hear the swell of strings in the air as Hannah looks up from her crumpled position, her hate-filled eyes gifted glorious beauty by her tears.

I am a silly girl once more, my mind filled with these romantic affectations which bring a weakness to my knees. I shuffle my feet back to steady myself beneath my father's bulk.

The carpet drags under my feet briefly and then there is nothing beneath them but air.

My foot treads heavily down into the emptiness of the top stair and we hang suspended for a moment, my father and I. Then, sensing my hesitation, he swings his arm back one last time, striking the side of my head and we are sent tumbling back together, down the stairs, one on top of the other on top of the other.

I never see my darling Hannah again.

***

There is no sensation quite like falling down stairs to remind you of your own humanity – even if you *have* been dead for almost a century. My elbows jar and knees clatter against wood and carpet. My neckbones crunch and backbones clang and stars blossom before my eyes and amongst all that, the muddy weight of the thing that was once my father crushes down upon me with every turn, knocking the memory of wind out of me with each and every collision.

As we come to a halt in a pile at the bottom of the stairs, the back of my head strikes the parquet flooring with a clunk that makes my teeth clench. I stare up into a face that is at once oh so familiar and yet more alien than I ever thought possible. Beneath those heavy eyebrows and thick moustaches his skin is sunken and sallow. Corruption blossoms in the hollows of his cheeks and shadows rim his milk-white eyes.

For a moment he looks as stunned as I by our sudden decent down the stairs – although perhaps it is my presence before him that is the cause of his confusion.

Whatever its reason, the moment of puzzled calm is merely that, and suddenly the thing on top of me growls and lunges forward, bloodied yellow teeth champing down through the air towards my face. I shriek, despite myself, and twist my head away, just in time to see Debbie standing unsteadily over both of us. With a grunt of effort, she brings the metal statuette of entwined lovers down hard on the back of Terry's head with a damp sounding crunch.

The impact drives him down on top of me - face first - and with a kiss, the world goes black.

The Music Stopped Today

The music stopped today,
    The tables bare and chairs in disarray.

Gone, the rhythms and the rhymes,
Rusted still, each beat an ancient gate entwined

Secrets held in whisper's grasp
Unspoken, threads of memories fade fast.

Heartbeats calm
And rendered sluggish still in turn

The melody of day and dawn unspun,
With pearls of birdsong scattered underfoot, unsung.

In which I die

The year is 2022. I am ninety-four years old. I am twenty-one years old. I am twelve years old.

The world is dark.

The year is 1933. I am five years old.

I stare down into the deep, glossy eyes of my little sister, held tightly against my mother. The baby smells unpleasant – powder and milk and human waste. I notice with alarm that my mother has the same scent. I wrinkle my nose in disgust.

The year is 1920. I have yet to be born.

My parents, still in the first flush of marriage, slumber beneath the eiderdown. The sour scent of alcohol hangs upon their breath; they will sleep until lunchtime. A fresh bruise blackens about my mother's eye. She will never speak of it to anyone.

The year is 2021. My darling Hannah is eighteen years old. I have fallen in love for the first time in my life.

Hannah sits at the edge of her bed in a room which once belonged to me and sorts through cardboard boxes. She idly runs her fingers through her dark hair. There is a deep unhappiness within her heart, but she does not realise it yet. I imagine spending the rest of her life in blissful togetherness. I worry that I hate her for this.

The year is 1951. My sister Agatha is eighteen years old.

She lays a faded eiderdown upon the parlour floor and sets about rolling the bulk of my father's cooling body onto it. Blank and purposeful, she ignores the splashes of red which speckle her stockings as she shifts the man. Her back will never be the same.

The year is 1939. It is my eleventh birthday.

My father turns off the wireless with a gentle click. The Prime Minister has just informed us that the country is now at war with Germany. My parents' expressions are nervous behind fragile smiles. The gift that they have bought me sits on the dining room table between us, unopened. I worry that – were a Nazi bomb to fall on the house – it would forever remain unopened.

The year is 2021. I have been dead for over eight decades.

The parlour is warm. My sister sits in her armchair, several days dead. Sunlight shines through the windows, plucking at dust motes that hang in the air. The stillness and silence of the house fill me from top to bottom, glowing through me as though I am a piece of stained glass.

The year is 1937. I am nine years old.

The house is filled with people. The house is filled with life and music and cigar smoke. The laughter of friends and neighbours spills out of every window into the night air. I sit on the stairs and watch enviously as my mother and father dance in wild abandon. I cannot wait to grow up.

The year is 2022. I am ninety-four years old. I am twenty-one years old. I am twelve years old.

The world is bright again.

***

I do not know where I am. The space about me is huge and a strange *pulling* sensation like the one that comes from peering into the darkness at the bottom of an old well tugs at me from all directions, towards walls that are far too distant to be seen. At the same time, there is a strange sense of coming home. Familiar shadows lurk at the edge of my vision, as though I am surrounded by the ghosts of things I once knew.

The gentle sound of rushing wind fills the infinite space around me, but the air itself is still. I look down and notice that I am standing on the bloodstained rug from the parlour and, somehow, this feels right.

From across the nothingness, a figure staggers towards me. For a moment it seems as insubstantial as smoke, but it takes on colour and shape as it steps onto the edge of the parlour rug, and I find myself staring at my father once more.

And it really is my father. Not the shadowy half-man I watched him become in the years after my death – haggard and corrupt. His sunken cheeks seem fuller now, the sallow skin re-pinked. Wherever this place is, for a moment it seems to have brought my father back to me. No sign remains of the snapping, skeletal creature that walked in strange synchronicity with him upon the stairs in Hannah's house. No rot or filth or blood befouls his clothes.

He stares at me curiously, a frown creasing his heavy brow. When he finally speaks his voice is low and hesitant.

"I know you," he manages.

"Yes, Papa. It is me, Matilda," I reply.

His eyes are dull, and he turns his head this way and that, as though examining my face. I suppose I should be hurt by his lack of recognition, but then again, he has not seen me since I was twelve.

"Matilda? No, you are not my Matilda. You died, kitten. You… died…"

I nod my head in agreement. "We all died, Papa."

He seems to fade for a moment, his head hanging heavily as though the puppet string holding him aloft has been cut. He seems smaller than I remember him, older.

"It does not matter if we are alive or dead," my father mutters, quietly. He lifts his head, and now his eyes glisten - an ocean of sadness and joy, "Not when you are here, Matilda!"

He takes a step forward and claps his hands together in joy. "Oh, my kitten, it is you, yes! I see it now, this young woman who stands before me – my darling girl!"

After several decades of being a mere observer of the lives of others, I find myself taken aback at the sensation of being on the receiving end of such emotion.

"I missed you so much, my darling girl!" my father continues. "After you…" he shakes his head and winces slightly, before starting again. "There was never any dancing, kitten. No one wanted to… dance again, when you were gone. The music was never loud enough, you know? The light was never bright enough to illuminate the darkness."

Until this moment I had presumed that I would feel warmth, perhaps even love, for my father were we ever to meet again. Perhaps a longing for the comfort I lost so many years ago. But now that we stand on equal footing – no matter where this place might *actually* be – I find myself filled with nothing but sadness.

"You made your own darkness, Papa."

He looks up at me, wide-eyed. "No, no! I did not," he splutters, shaking his head as if clearing it of troublesome thoughts. "It hurt *so much* when you were gone, kitten. And they blamed me." His voice becomes quiet, venomous. "Not in words, no, but I could see, behind their eyes, they… hated me! Can you imagine how much that hurt?"

As he pleads, I see for the first time that he is not as solid as I am. The edges of him, his skin and clothes, seem to be crumbling and drifting off into the air in tiny fragments, perhaps in rhythm with the crumbling of his mind. Like sand across the dunes, there is a continual degradation of his outline.

He does not seem to notice.

"And so, yes - I drank, and I…" he drifts off again. "It was never enough, kitten. Nothing ever washed away the filth and the hate and the *pain* of it all."

He speaks of pain to me, this sad little man. As if I were not witness to the corruption which he wallowed in over all those years. A loving family, suffering one hundred tiny deaths each and every day at the hand of a man both monstrous and pathetic in turn.

"What do you want from me, Papa? Forgiveness?"

"I do not know, kitten. You said it yourself – we are dead. What value is there in forgiveness now? We are as motes of dust in the eyes of infinity, are we not? Let us drift together, dancing until the end of time."

"The thought sickens me."

"It does?" My father smiles, watery with tears. "How long have you been alone here, kitten? And who was it who came back for you, eh? Me, not your mother. *I* came back for you, my darling." He holds out a hand to me and whispers:

"Come, dance with me, one last time, Matilda. And then? I will go, if that is what you wish."

I look down at his hand. Like the rest of him, a thin film of dust seems to be sloughing off from the surface of his skin. There is soil beneath his nails and ingrained in the whorls of his fingertips, but I cannot help but reach for him. There *is* music in the air, but it is distorted, as though coming from far away and deep underground.

Everything hurts so much. Would one last dance really be anything more than a single drop in the ocean?

"You just can't stop the lies, can you, Papa?" A voice echoes strangely about us. A voice I know, a quiet voice which nevertheless sets my ears ringing. My father's eyes narrow and I feel a presence behind me. Across the infinite void or at the very edge of the parlour rug, it is difficult to say, but there is someone else here with us.

For a moment there is the sensation of something towering behind me, like a tidal wave looming overhead. When I turn to look, however, there is simply a small, frail-looking elderly lady stepping calmly towards us. I recognise the face of someone that I have lived with for the better part of a century. The old woman who lived in my house. Agatha, my sister.

I know her – from the way she shuffles across the rug, to the slight tremble of her slender arms, I see her, and I *know* it is my sister. But there is something monstrous about her.

Her eyes are a deep, translucent red – the colour of uncut rubies and blood blisters – and she exudes a power unlike any I ever felt in all the years we shared a home, before or after my death.

I look back at my father, who no longer has eyes for me, it seems. He glares over my shoulder, transfixed in a kind of curious rage, one hand still reaching out to me.

"Are you going to tell her, Papa? Are you even capable of telling the truth?" My sister's voice is as frail as ever, but there is an edge to it. "You didn't come back for Tilly. You didn't even know she was there, did you? All those years amongst the dirt and earthworms and it didn't even occur to you that your other daughter might walk the spirit realm. So blinkered by your hatred for me, Papa. Even now, you see her as what, another obstacle?"

My father grunts and shifts slightly. His other arm – the one not outstretched to me - is twisted behind his back unnaturally. For the first time I realise there is something clenched in his fist. His eyes flicker back to me, a grin spreads across his face, and he opens his hand. A blood-stained carriage clock drops to the floor with a metallic clang which echoes about the eternal nothingness. The sound fills the space for a close, hot moment, a flush of blood rising in my cheeks as I realise his intentions all along.

My mind feels like the surface of a pond during the first thaw of spring. The snapping, cracking sound of unseen ice defrosting after a long winter's sleep. My mind clears, my emotions becoming more fluid than I ever thought possible. There is so much I need to say to my father: how much I hate him for the multitude of ways he ruined my sister and mother's lives; how much I wish to seek comfort in his arms. How disappointed and disgusted I feel towards him for the shit in which he wallowed all those years after my death; how angry I feel for the ways he had tormented Hannah and her family.

But after all this time, words fail me. They dry in my throat and my emotions remain unspoken.

The vapour trails they leave behind, however, are as strong as they have ever been and coil about my bones and tendons like serpents. Their strength feeds me, and in a moment, I find myself blindly leaping towards my father, fists clenched.

I may not be strong, but my father is old, and I have the element of surprise on my side. As my fist collides with the soft roughness of his cheeks he stumbles backwards, crumpling to the floor. He yells out in pain and shock, and my weight carries me forwards and I find myself tumbling to the ground with my father for the second time in forever. The world slowly turns red and shimmery as my fists make impact again and again and againandagainandagain.

I cannot tell if the streaks of warmth that run down my cheeks and chin are my own tears or my father's blood, nor whether the grunting sounds of agony are his or mine. Each strike of temple or cheekbone reverberates up my arms and my knuckles shine blackly. Beneath me, my father's face changes; it is not just the broken nose and purpling eye beneath my fury, but a significant stuttering too: one moment it is my father, the next it is Terry. Another moment after that, clumps of decaying flesh detach and float into the air with every thump of my fists against green-hued bone.

And the strangest thing of all? My father takes it. His hands lift weakly in a vain attempt at fending me off, but there is no real effort behind it. Perhaps he understands that he deserves this, perhaps he does not have the strength to fight back. I hit him and I hit him and I hit him until the price has been somewhat paid and an atonement has begun for each bitter, unspoken word.

It is not until I taste blood in the back of my ragged throat that I realise I am screaming as I strike him. My knuckles begin to ache, and I start to slow. My shoulders sag.

I feel Agatha standing behind me, her eyes boring into the back of my head, and I cannot help but wonder what she must think of me. On the ground, my father groans.

"I think that's enough, Tilly," my sister says quietly.

I am still her elder by five years, but Agatha has lived every bit of her age and then some, and I nod weakly at the authority of her words. I clamber off the groaning body beneath me, but cannot bring myself to stand, half-sitting, half-collapsing on the parlour rug beside him. Like a petulant child, my cheeks burn with anger and shame, and I cannot look as my father gets to his feet, his eyes swollen near closed, his lips torn and ragged.

But if I had thought for a moment that the thrashing he had received from his eldest daughter would have the slightest impact, I was wrong. Smaller than ever, older than ever, the bruised and battered man shakes his head.

"Enough?" he shouts, standing there hunched over like an aged heavyweight boxer. As he speaks, droplets of blood sparkle into the void from between chipped and broken teeth. "Enough? No, you do not get to say that, Agatha." He chuckles, a low rumbling sound in his throat. "I know you see only weakness in me but no, you are not…you are not in charge here!"

He staggers forward slightly, an image from a faulty projector. His eyes roll wildly in their bloodied sockets. "Leave your sister alone…didn't I…didn't we tell you?" He slams his hand against his chest and shakes his head again as if trying to rattle his thoughts into order.

"*Enough*?! I am your father; you do not speak for me!" he angrily jabs a finger towards my sister.

Perhaps it is the battering he has just taken, or something more spiritual, but my father is barely holding himself together, and here and there a deep red glow is visible beneath his skin. Even his finger appears to be crumbling, a smoke trail of dust drifting from the very tip of his nails.

"I will say when this is over!" he spits, reaching forward suddenly and grabbing my sister by the wrist.

"I. Will. Say!"

He pulls Agatha towards him and for the briefest of moments there is a look of triumph on the man's face. Beneath the blood and decay he seems victorious, and he searches my sister's blood-red eyes for some semblance of supplication. There is none to be found, however - she stares back at him, deep into his eyes.

Even from across the void I can feel the power behind her gaze, feel it rooting around our father's mind and seeking out his sins. I can feel the well-earned hatred - the anger - within my sister, a cracked and broken darkness in stark contrast to the dull perversions of evil within my father.

And slowly, his eyes begin to widen in horror.

My father makes a tiny spluttering noise and both he and my sister look down at his hand which is gripping her wrist tightly. He jerks his hand back with a cry, trails of blood and pus spattering in the air. Large pale blisters have begun to rise along his fingers and thumb, his dirt-encrusted fingernails cracking and blackening as though they had been thrust into the centre of a crackling fire.

Eyes terror-wide, he staggers back from his daughter, stumbling to his knees. No sooner has he landed on the ground, than thin black tendrils begin to sprout from wound-like slashes which appear around him, their pointed tips searching the air like roots searching through soil. Like dark veins come to life, they search blindly, scraping at his legs and feet before surging over him.

They quickly climb over his feet and calves and thighs, binding him to the ground. He tries to pull himself away but it is no use, the roots are, by now, well entwined about him and hold him fast. He screams in fear and pain as the probing things begin to *dig* into him.

Despite his struggles, they hold him so tightly that the surface of them seems to burn through his clothing and soon chunks of raw-looking flesh from my father's legs tumble away into the nothingness.

He looks up at Agatha.

"Kitten, it hurts…stop this…"

"It's horrifying, isn't it, Papa? Being at the mercy of something over which you have no control at all. Wishing that the pain would stop, if only for a moment. And knowing that it never will."

My father makes a choking sound as the black tendrils creep their way up his body – around his torso and up into his chest cavity. Hidden from view, they begin to take hold of his lungs. Dark red bubbles form at the corners of his mouth.

"I would have stopped," he splutters. "I would have…"

His voice trails off with a crackle and a tear runs down what remains of his cheeks. He struggles to breathe through the cage of black roots which now hold him in their grip, biting into him with blind, unseeing hunger. He tries to shake his head, his eyes wide and pleading.

There are parts of him – his legs and the lower part of his trunk – that are now bound so tightly by these strange black veins that there no longer seems to be space for flesh or bone.

"You let the sickness in your heart run roughshod over this family, Papa, and you did *nothing* to hold it at bay. *You should have been my protector, but you might as well have plunged a knife into my heart for all that you chose to end my life that night you first entered my bedroom! You ended me! You deserve nothing but pain!"*

These last words, hoarse with emotion, reverberate about the infinite void around us and it is not until millennia have passed and civilisations have risen and fallen and distant suns have blazed in glory and cooled into darkness and the last tattered threads of emotion have faded into silence that Agatha finally looks at me. Her chest rises and falls, her expression cold.

Between us, our father's body twitches. Thin, gnarled branches sprout from his nostrils and from between his lips, his mouth open unnaturally wide and his eyes stare glassily into the distance. Between the unholy tendrils, whorls of red and black specks drift in the gently moving void.

The scent of blood hangs in the air.

"Is he dead?" I ask.

"You said it yourself - we all died."

I look at my sister, annoyed. "You know what I mean."

"In pain, I hope, but dead? I don't think so."

"What did you do to him?" My words hang there for a moment, unanswered. Then Agatha sighs.

"It wasn't me. It is just something that happens here, I think." She waves a hand to indicate the strange hollow world around us. "The burning of his skin was a judgement of sorts. A weighing of sins. I guess the vines are his punishment - trapping him here until the end of time."

I look around at the strange and distant space which we find ourselves in.

"Do you think this is hell?"

Agatha shrugs. "I don't know. You've been dead for longer than I have, shouldn't you have it all figured out?"

There is no answer to that, and silence falls between us once more. My sister and I stare down at the strange, trapped figure of our father and watch as part of his cheek becomes detached and crumbles away.

"He never said he was sorry," I whisper.

"I wouldn't have wanted him to. Cheap words mean nothing."

After a moment, my sister sniffs and rolls her shoulders awkwardly. "I...I missed you, Tilly."

I can't help but smile. Beneath the aged skin and still-raw scars, my sister stands before me. Memories of tea parties in the back garden and hand-stitched doll's clothing flood my mind. Children's Hour and Just So Stories and Cat's Cradle on the stairs. A warmth blossoms beneath my skin as I stand there with my sister.

"I never went away, Aggie," I manage to say. "Not really. I was always with you."

"Always," my sister mutters, managing a smile. She looks at me. "You never stopped him though, did you?"

A lump rises in my throat. What warmth I had begun to leech from me.

"What do you mean?"

Agatha shakes her head - that small, calm smile still on her face. "That feeling…shame. Such a hot, angry emotion. After a while, when I knew that he was never going to stop, I could feel it begin to seep into my bloodstream, a poison mingling with the blood in my veins, slowly contaminating every muscle and organ. And when he *was* gone, when I finally had time to heal…that shame was all that I had left inside me.

"The only thing that allowed me to live each day, Tilly. The only thing that stayed my hand from pressing that razor blade *just a fraction deeper* each time, was that fact that the shame was *inside*. Inside, locked away, no one knew. I may have been able to see all that filth when I looked at myself in the mirror, but with Papa dead, at least everyone else's eyes were clear.

"But then *I* died, Tilly. And do you know what I realised then?"

I have no words. All I can see are my sister's blood-tinged eyes and that neat, *dangerous*, little smile. I feel small beneath her thoughtful gaze.

"I realised," she continues, not waiting for me to respond, "that you had been there all along. You had seen what that man did, you were *complicit* in his crimes."

"No, Aggie, no! I cannot tell you how it hurt to see you suffer, do not call me complicit. What could I do, what influence could my spirit have had upon the mortal world?"

My sister laughs. "Influence, Tilly? You skinned my fucking cat, or have the years faded that memory from your mind?"

They have not. I still remember the slippery warmth beneath my fingers, but I am not going to say as much to my sister. The sense of violence and the ease with which its skin separated from muscle and tendon. The jealousy I felt, *still* felt, at the time my little sister got to spend with my mother, no matter how short. I am not sorry for what I did.

"I am so sorry, Aggie," I lie, knowing that my words mean nothing. It does not matter - they fall upon deaf ears.

My sister shakes her head slightly and walks away from me, across the infinite expanse of the parlour rug and the endless void.

It is difficult to gauge how far away Agatha is – space does not work as expected here, but when she speaks again, her voice is as loud and sharp as if she were standing right in front of me.

"And even then, I don't think I *hated* you, Tilly. Not really." She paces back and forth, her mind frothing and foaming in rage. "In death I became monstrous because *why should I be the only one to live a life of pain?* I thought, perhaps, we could be monstrous together - the Mueller sisters - without a care in the world, making the bastards pay, hurting them all, and then..."

My sister stops her pacing and turns to me, her voice soft and quiet. "...and then you stop him from hurting *her*. You see she is in danger and you step in. And in that moment, I realise that you are far more of a monster than I could ever be, Tilly. You watch your sister being abused for years and you do nothing, NOTHING! But the moment he tried to lay a finger on that *whore*, you do not hesitate to wrench him from the earthly plain."

"That's not fair!" I cry, shaking in anger and fear. "Things were different then, he was dead..."

I do not have the words to explain to her; do not understand this world I live in – lived in – any more than she does. The strange energies that seem to ebb and flow in a spirit, that dampen emotion one moment, only to drag them forth a moment later, stronger and more urgent than ever.

The ragged wounds upon Agatha's arms and chest begin to open as she talks, as though the humors within her veins are increased and pushing out through her skin. Trickles of blood begin to flow down her arms, droplets glistening in the air as she gestures towards me.

"I was jealous of you when you died, Tilly."

"Jealous, why?"

"Because you didn't have to suffer the way we did, you stupid girl. A life of hurt which *you* were not condemned to suffer alongside the rest of us. They mourned you, our parents, every bloody day of their lives. And they *hated* me – the daily reminder of the daughter they lost."

"Aggie, you cannot say that!"

My sister glares at me, then lifts her arms in profane beatitude. The sleeves of her cardigan are soaked through and heavy with blood.

"Fuck off, Tilly," she mutters, and turns to walk away.

She strides past the shrivelled and blackened remains of our father. I follow after her, without really understanding why. What can I say to her, when the violence and anger of her words are run through with so much truth.

Did I rage like this in the first few months of my death? No, but then again there had not been the same suffering in my short existence to twist the soul and blacken it so. Life had not delicately etched its hate into me like a master craftsman at his most creative as it had done to my sister. I had watched the pale shoots of unhappiness grow within my heart like a plant receiving too little light. I had seen...

"Stop!" I call after her, before the thoughts have fully formed in my mind. To my relief, she ceases walking away, although she does not turn to face me.

"You won, don't you see?" I say to the curve of her back. "You beat the bastard, literally. And when he came *from the grave* for revenge or whatever it was that he sought here, did he find succour? No, he found punishment. *Judgement.* You have such power within you, Aggie." I sigh, desperate for my sister to understand. "And yes, I witnessed unimaginable horrors - being a spectre in that house for all those years - but I also witnessed you growing up. I witnessed the woman you became. A pillar of strength and independence who never let another person write her story for her or take her along a path she did not wish to tread.

"Do not let his hate be *your* epitaph. Do not let the sourness of our father poison *your* heart! Yes, the monster…*violated* you and killed me, but we do not get to sow that hatred further still. I see that now. Please come back to me – you are so much better than this!"

She turns slowly, her elderly frame straightening as she does so. The blood that runs down her arms does so in torrents now, each fingertip a candlewick twist of scarlet as it falls, pitter-patter, onto the rug.

"A strong, independent women, eh?" Agatha nods her head coldly, not looking me in the eye. "That's what the young people say these days, isn't it? A strong, independent woman." She gives a cynical chuckle. "Sounds like a bit of a curse, if you ask me. Not that anyone ever asked me. *A path I did not wish to tread?* Don't make me laugh, I was dragged along my path by the actions of Papa and Mama and you, Tilly."

Her hand swings up to point at me and even at this distance I feel the warmth of her blood splash across my face.

"And YOU!" she shouts again. She begins to walk back to me, staring straight at me now, her eyes acid-pits of fury. They seem to boil and spit as she gets closer and closer to me, her arm still outstretched in judgement.

"So, you can *rot* here with him, Tilly. Father and daughter, trapped in the endless void *and you can just think about what you've done, YOUNG LADY!*" Her voice becomes monstrous and uncomfortably loud. Every fibre of my being wishes to flee – although where I do not know – but I am rooted to the spot. *Something* has wrapped itself around my feet and binds me tightly, and there is nothing I can do to stop Agatha and the judgement she feels she is owed.

Perhaps she *is* owed it. Judgement, revenge - call it what you will - for a life painted in such shades of darkness. Perhaps I *am* complicit, although it is hard to express to Agatha the greyness of one's mind in the spirit realm, the disconnect you feel.

I fear she would not accept that as an excuse anyway, even if I had the words to make my meaning known.

I worry for the state of my sister's mind once she has handed down this sentence. Will her bloodlust be satiated, or will she apportion blame for her corrupted life ever further until, finding no others left to blame, she turns her gaze inward in a black-hole of penitence and punishment?

I see bleakness in my sister's future.

She stands before me now, her hand hovering over my forehead like a priest about to give blessing. I am surprised to see tears in her eyes and there is part of me that hopes there is regret somewhere in this terrible thing that she has become.

"You were both responsible, Tilly. I am sorry." She presses her hand to my forehead. "I love you."

"I love you too," I manage to say.

Agatha's palm is hot and wet against my skin, and I close my eyes as her blood runs through my eyebrows and drips down onto my cheeks. I take a deep breath and steel myself against the oncoming pain.

I feel a shift around my ankles as whatever is binding me to the spot – the same black tendrils I had seen about my father, I suppose – ready themselves to burrow into my flesh.

There is a beat longer, just a breath, but the wait feels almost farcical.

My sister's hand lifts from my face and I open my eyes.

Agatha stands before me, arm still outstretched. She shakes her head, bemused.

"Of course," she murmurs, before looking up at me. "*Auf Wiedersehen*, Tilly."

For a moment I don't understand. Then her hand quivers and I see, beneath the blood, her fingers seem misshapen and deformed. The same blisters that had formed on our father's hands line her fingers and palm, swelling before my eyes.

As they grow larger and paler, I can see other blisters forming on Agatha's wrist and creeping up her arm, disappearing up underneath the sleeve of her cardigan. By the time the first blisters on her fingertips burst, the whole of her arm is covered, and the painful swellings have begun to form over her shoulder and across her chest.

It is not until the first blister bursts, however, and the first lump of the skin from her finger has floated off into the abyss, that Agatha makes a sound. She begins to laugh – a high-pitched chuckle of amusement. The blisters on her skin grow larger still before they rupture, with one particularly sticky looking clump of flesh detaching and tumbling away, leaving a red raw hole in her forearm the size of a ten pence piece.

Before my eyes, my sister begins to bubble and burst and soon ribbons of pus and blood and meat spiral out into the void like they had from our father.

She does not sink to her knees, however. She stands before me, laughing defiantly as chunks of her throat and her décolletage start to detach in a cascade of dripping rose petals

By the time the blisters reach her face, my sister has stopped chuckling, although the ragged holes in her half-destroyed throat gurgle and splutter in a way that suggests she would still laugh if she could. One red-tinged eye rolls wildly in its socket before resting its gaze upon me. It dawns on me that this is the second time in my life that I have had to bear witness to the rotting away of my sister – three times if you count the eroding of her soul – and this is the quickest of the lot.

"I'm sorry, Aggie," I manage to say, although whether there is anything left of her to hear or not, I cannot say.

By the time the words leave my lips there is little left of her, and by the time I take my next breath, all that remains on the parlour rug is a pair of blood-stained carpet slippers and the rich scent of burnt sugar.

A familiar little tune rings out and I look over at the mantelpiece where a carriage clock sits, gleaming in the early morning sunlight. I stand in the parlour proper, the rug beneath my feet no longer stretching off into endless space but firmly hemmed upon the parquet floor.

The house is empty.

There is no need to search the place from top to bottom, I sense the absence of both the living and the dead like the passing of a headache which no longer throbs at the temples or the cessation of a beat that no longer plays two rooms over.

The thrum of life which had passed me by unnoticed for all those years now rings conspicuous by its absence.

Instead of life, it is the creeks and groans of an empty house that I listen to. The warmth of the dawning sun caresses my face, and I try to hold it in my mind as the familiar emotional numbness of the restless dead begins to creep over my mind again like late Autumn frost. I try to hold that warmth for a beat longer and relish it. Its strange sense of safety and contentment.

I gaze wistfully out of the parlour window and a tear rolls lazily down my cheek, forging its own little path through the filth and the blood.

I wonder what my darling Hannah is doing now.

I wonder.

***

Perhaps lives such as ours are not meant to be under constant scrutiny. The observation of the day's minutiae stunts each moment's growth. A soul under an ever-watchful eye is stretched too thin and, in its turn, becomes flabby and weak.

Hannah and her family, my parents, my sister, I watched them all and watched them wither. Lives that died on the vine, seeking the sunshine of anonymity, and failing – for I stalked the hallways and bedrooms of this house, seeing all, knowing all, judging all.

Perhaps I should feel guilty. But, my darling, I don't feel anything at all.

I close my eyes and breathe in the silence; feel it soaking into my skin. A weight lifts from my soul, and I am...

...home.

When I open my eyes, I catch a glimpse of the mirror hung above the mantelpiece in the parlour, and the young woman who stands within.

She has a large smudge of ash across the upper lid of her left eye and a smaller one on the upper lid of her right eye. She has 43 splashes of blood of varying shapes and sizes across her nose and cheeks, although there are slightly more on her left cheek than on her right.

They will soon be hidden behind a cheap, blue horse mask made of cardboard.

I wish she was at peace.
Like me.

Epilogue

The Little Boy and The Dark Forest

A long time ago, and a long way away, there lived a little boy. He was a lonely little boy – dark of eye, red of cheek and stout of stomach – who lived with his father in a little apartment above a tin merchant right in the heart of a little village in the countryside. His mother had been a beautiful, delicate creature, with skin the colour of fresh milk and lips like rose petals. Never had there been a more perfect soul in the village or for miles around for that matter, and when she had died in childbirth, the whole world had howled like a wolf in the moonlight and her husband – the little boy's father – had turned to the bottle before her body had yet cooled.

And so, the little boy grew up with a drunken tyrant of a father and a cloak of sadness about his heart and a way of looking at the world around him as though always on the lookout for God's next mean trick.

The watchfulness in the little boy's dark eyes made it difficult to make friends, and the few other boys and girls who lived in the village took great amusement in teasing the little boy. They would mock his clothes and his hair. They would mock his terrible father and his absent mother. They would mock the pinkness that rose in his cheeks when he tried to play and the stumble of his footsteps as he tried to run.

Of course, this made the little boy very sad indeed. But more than this, it made him angry. The poor soul had been robbed of the chance to learn the twin arts of kindness and forgiveness from his mother, and the only gifts bestowed upon him by his father were those of impotent rage and railing against the petty crimes of others.

When the boys and girls from the village tormented him, the little boy would stamp his feet and curse and shout, and of course the other children thought this was jolly fun and would make a game out of the boy's frustration. They would tease him in turn, their hearts giddy with joy at the sight of the blush rising in his cheeks and the tears springing in his eyes, and when his fury could no longer be contained and broke free in a frothing, hissing explosion of self-pity, they would scatter away down the streets of the village laughing and braying in the summer sun.

Now every year, at the coming of the Harvest moon, a small carnival came to the village. Not as large a one as may have graced the nearby towns but thrilling enough of a distraction to bring the villagers out of their homes, clutching their hard-earned coins, eager to take part in the festivities. There were games to be played and sideshows to be viewed – coconut shys and sweet biscuits for sale, feats of strength and curios from around the world. For a day or two, the villagers could forget their worries and enjoy themselves, their lives scored by the ever-present calliope music that filled the air.

The little boy desperately wanted to visit the fair. Through the dusty glass of his bedroom window, he had watched stalls being built and tents being pitched in an empty field at the very edge of the forest on the outskirts of the village and the desire to walk among the bustle of people burned like a flame at the centre of his little round tummy.

He knew there was no use asking his father to take him to the fair. Such joviality did not sit well with the hammering inside his father's head or the sourness of his liver. If he were to attend the fair, the little boy decided, he would have to go by himself.

The little boy was hesitant to go during the day, however. He often found himself unable to set foot outside of his door without the watchful eyes of the children of the village upon him, waiting to have their cruel fun at his expense. Such a gathering as the fair, the little boy felt, would surely draw every boy and every girl from their gardens and bedrooms, each of them just as likely to occupy themselves in poking fun at him as in the merriment of the fairground attractions.

And so, it was not until after dark that the little boy managed to pluck up enough courage to leave the relative safety of his home. With his father's drunken snoring rattling the glass in the windowpanes, the little boy wrapped up a few silver coins in his handkerchief and skipped off merrily through shuttered streets guided by a firelight glow in the night sky to the wonders that awaited him in the field at the edge of the village.

The night was warm, and braziers flickered at the makeshift entrance to the fair. Some stalls had closed as the darkness had descended – Hercule the Mighty had swapped his dumbbells for a tankard at a nearby tavern and the donkeys from the donkey ride stall have been stabled for the night – but there was a buzz about the place even so. The little boy walked with stars in his eyes and a sickly kind of joy in his heart as he walked amongst the straggling villagers and tired fairground-folk who populated this night-time attraction. He gripped his 'kerchief of coins tightly to his chest, knowing that – with such limited funds – he would have to be judicious in his choice of fun.

He bought a sweet biscuit from a disinterested young woman who cradled a whimpering babe at her side and chewed it thoughtfully as he made his way over straw-lined pathways to see what further fun there was to be had. A coconut shy beckoned, as did a tired looking dobby set, before a chance turn around the corner of a hoopla stand brought something more exciting into view.

The tent itself was small but magnificent looking. The purples and reds of the hanging canvases practically glowed in the darkness. The words *Fortunes Told* had been painted in fine golden script on a board which hung above the entrance to the tent. The twisted twin scents of incense and copper hung heavily in the air and, the decision made, the little boy approached the tent with a strange thrill gripping him.

The interior of the tent was warm and dark, little glowing stubs of perfumed powders glowing here and there to illuminate the gloom. There was a man sat behind a table on which sat something large covered with a black velvet cloth. The man, small and pale, looked up at the little boy as he entered as though he had been waiting for the child his whole life. A thin smile crept across his face.

"It is not often that I have visitors as young as you," he whispered in an accent that spoke of far-off lands. With a gentle wave of his hand, he indicated that the little boy should take a seat before he continued. "Does the young gentleman wish to have his fortune spun?"

The little boy nodded; his voice lost in his throat.

The fortune teller spread the long fingers of his hand and to the boy's horror and delight the image of an open eye had been delicately tattooed in the centre of the man's exposed palm. "Do you have sufficient funds for this journey into the unknown, my boy?"

Wordlessly, the little boy shook the handkerchief out over the man's open hand and out tumbled his coins. The tinny sound of metal upon metal as the coins fell sounded too loud in the close, dark space and, absurdly, the boy felt a blush rise in his cheeks.

With a nod of his head, the fortune teller removed the velvet cloth from the object on the table before him, and a brilliant crystal ball was revealed. With a wave of his fingers, he invited the little boy to peer deeply into the abyss within.

At first there was nothing except his own distorted reflection staring back at him, and the little boy felt the blush in his cheeks burn ever brighter. An annoyance, an anger, bubbled in his stomach and for a moment he considered demanding his money back before *something* swum into view beneath the curved glass surface.

And then, the little boy saw…
…every spiteful pinch he had ever given a classmate when the teacher's back was turned.
…every little girl's dress he had ever peeked up.

…every insect he had crushed beneath his thumb.

…every rock thrown at a stray dog in the park.

…every drop of liquor he had ever snuck while his father snored drunkenly in his armchair.

The whirlwind of cruelty and petty meanness laid out before him horrified the little boy. What cruel trick was this? His head spun and his throat felt thick and sticky with saliva. He wanted to scold the fortune teller – look him in the eye and reprimand him for such cruelty, take him to task for spying on little boys. The urge to rage at the man began to build inside him.

Then the image within the crystal shifted. There was a sense of diving deeper and deeper into the very centre of the swirling memories. What followed next were not images as such, but sensations which seemed to box his ears – anger, fear, desire, hatred. Each one swelling inside him like a rising tide, only to dissipate and be replaced by the next. The sounds of sobbing, of screaming, of whimpering.

And then…

A figure in the darkness of the glass raised their hands in anguish and pain, and the flow of blood and the sting of death rang out as clearly as the chiming of a clock. The little boy's mind reeled at the sound of screaming and…

He pissed himself.

The little boy recoiled from the crystal ball in horror, pushing himself away from the table and staring up at the fortune-teller with wild eyes.

"*Was ist los, Kind?*" the fortune-teller asked in a different, more natural voice than before, but the little boy's mind spun, and cold terror gripped him and with a cry of despair he was out of the tent, leaving the canvas flapping behind him.

If the little boy – sweating and sodden – thought that fleeing the tent would be the end his torment, however, he was out of luck. Whether they were figments of his imagination or not it was difficult to say, but as he stood, bewildered, on the straw pathway outside the tent, it seemed that every little boy and girl from the village were standing in audience. Fingers pointed and little pink tongues jutted from between chipped and missing teeth and the children laughed and laughed and laughed at his disgrace.

Forgoing his usual attempts at raging the humiliation into submission, the little boy became consumed with shame and embarrassment. Turning this way and that he ran, seeking refuge from the braying laughter of his peers, until his fat little legs brought him to the forest that ran along the very edge of the field in which the funfair sat.

With nary a second thought, the little boy plunged head-first through an opening between the ragged trunks of two large beech trees and into the darkness of the forest itself.

The dried leaves of a warm summer crunching beneath his buckled shoes, tears of embarrassment streaming down his ruddy cheeks, the little boy ran for as long as he could. He left behind the laughter and the mockery for the towering trees which seemed to glide overhead and the shrubs and bushes which whipped against his bare legs in the darkness and scored little lines of red through his pale skin. The little boy ran.

He ran until his breathing became ragged and wheezing in his over-worked lungs.

He ran until his heart beat fit to burst.

He ran until little red spots flickered across his vision and he wondered if he was going to pass out.

He ran until his body would let him run no further and he stumbled and collapsed, exhausted, into a heap amongst the exposed roots of an old oak tree.

Now brought to a stop - and once he had caught his breath - the little boy looked about him. He was no stranger to sneaking about after dark, away from the cruelty of other children and the coldness of uncaring adults, and so the darkness of the forest held no fears for him. The moon shone big and bright in a star-speckled night sky far above the canopy of knitted branches overhead and painted the trees and roots about him in edges of silver. The night was warm and still, and as the adrenaline began to leech from his system and his ragged breathing became more regular, the little boy felt his eyelids growing heavy and he soon drifted off into a deep, dreamless sleep.

***

He awoke with a start in the dawn's early rays, to the sight of a pair of large brown eyes peering at him blankly. Head still muzzy, the little boy scrambled back against the trunk of the tree as his mind attempted to understand what he was looking at. Like an optical illusion swimming from one image to another, he suddenly became aware that he was looking at a large bird which had perched on one of the lower branches that hung overhead.

The little boy laughed at his foolishness, although his heart continued to beat rapidly in his chest. The bird was a strange one, unlike anything he'd ever seen before, with dark brown plumage and large eyes like that of an owl. Its head twitched slightly, as if trying to get a better look at him.

"Dummer Vogel," the boy muttered, before repeating himself, this time in a louder voice. *"Dummer Vogel!"*

It sounded good to hear his own voice in the deeply wooded forest and as he got stiffly to his feet, he couldn't help but feel a little foolish. He picked up a small stone from the forest floor and threw it lazily at the bird. The thing ruffled its feathers in avian indignation, but merely shuffled along the branch slightly, out of reach of further projectiles.

The little boy shook his head and raised his eyes towards the sky. The weak light of the dawning sun told him that he had a few hours until his father would become conscious, and so he set off in the general direction of home.

By now, the branches above him were so crowded and the view of the sun so sporadic that it wasn't until he felt the first twinge of hunger in his belly that the little boy realised he had become turned around somewhere along the way. It dawned on him that his journey to the edge of the forest had taken far longer than he had planned.

He kicked a tree root in frustration at the world, and looked about him, trying to get his bearings. The forest here was so thick, however, that it was difficult to see much more than a few feet ahead. Adding to his irritation, the bird that had so rudely startled him appeared to be one of many, because here and there in the branches of the trees the boy could see dark brown feathers and those blank, watchful eyes peering down at him. They were like ants at a picnic – first he would spot one, then another and another until the hairs on the back of his neck would rise at the realisation of quite how many there were, dotted hither and thither above him.

More than once he was reduced to shouting: "*Dummer Vogel!*" and swearing with all the anger he could muster just to disturb their calm watchfulness, if but for a moment.

But still they seemed to flock to the trees and branches around him. With every step he took, every minute, every hour he found himself still lost in the forest, more and more eyes seemed to stare down at him. *Judging* him.

The little boy had thought the laughter of the children back at the village bad enough, but the round brown blankness of these eyes felt as though they were burrowing into the back of his skull. As if the rough thirst in his throat and rumbling of his empty stomach were not maddening enough, every step he took that seemed to lead him deeper and deeper into the forest was met with a constant assessment on the part of the hundreds of birds which covered every inch of the canopy above him.

He felt them in his mind, silent, ancient. He felt them as he tripped over moss-covered rocks and pushed through bright green shrubs. They were all there was, and all there would ever be, they peered out though *his* eyes, their feathers filled him.

By the time the trees began to thin out and a clearing of sorts opened up before him, the little boy no longer knew who he was or how long he had been in the forest. The bird's eyes had maddened him. There never seemed to be a change in the half-light that dappled his face through the gaps in the branches above, but nonetheless, he felt as though he had been trapped in the forest for days. He was dirty, he was hungry, yes, but above all the thickness of his tongue and throat spoke of a thirst which threatened to end him.

The clearing into which he had stepped was barely worthy of the name. The surrounding trees had thinned out, perhaps, the overhanging leaves sparce enough to allow more of the summer's light through, but there was no sense of openness or freedom amongst the woodland. A large, gnarled oak tree – long dead – stood at the centre of the clearing but it was not this that drew the little boy's attention.

A large black horse had become entangled amongst the branches of the tree. It looked to the little boy as though the creature - in its panic - had gotten its bridle trapped within its twists. The leather cord dug deep into the flesh and muscle of its broad, velvet-dark neck, garrotting it where it stood.

A thin line of steam rose from the wound at the horse's neck and the little boy supposed that the injury must have been fresh, although he was surprised that he had not heard anything on his approach to the clearing. Deep furrows had been carved out in the ground below where the horse's powerful-looking hind legs had kicked and skidded in its struggle to get free, churning the dirt and grass beneath hooves the size of wastepaper baskets.

The dirt beneath the horse was a glossy black, and as the little boy stepped closer and closer still, he could see this steamed gently too. In its desperation to get away, the creature had churned its own blood into the dirt. Now mere inches away from the creature, the little boy could see the wet stream that flowed down the front of it and reddened the tips of its hooves.

The little boy's stomach growled. The little boy's thirst grew. He felt as though he had been without sustenance for days and little lightning bolts crackled at the edge of his vision. The scents of perfume and copper tainted the air.

The little boy laid a hand upon the horse's broad neck, feeling the warmth of it, his fingers staining scarlet from the blooded coat. His mouth began to water and before he knew what he was doing, he crammed his fingers into his mouth, sucking them clean of the warm, salty blood.

His stomach rumbled in appreciation but there was not enough. He reached his chubby little fingers up to where the leather cord dug deep into the horse's neck and pushed against the wound. Blood bubbled to the surface, coating his hands once more, before the boy gladly returned them to his mouth. His tongue darted and caressed each knuckle and nail, tasting every morsel that he could find. Blood covering his chin and lips, he glanced up at the birds in the trees, each of them studying him carefully, glossy round eyes above sharp grey beaks.

"What?" he called out to them, thickly. "You have something to say to me?" He pointed a pink-stained finger out accusingly. "You did this to me!" the boy continued. "You brought me here!"

Not waiting for a response from his audience, the boy pushed himself up on tiptoes and clamped his lips around the wound. With childish glee he began to guzzle, his lips forming a seal about the open wound lest any of the precious blood be spilt upon the ground.

But the little boy grew greedy. In his haste to feed, he began to *bite*. He was tempted to *chew*. He was driven to *devour* and as his teeth made contact with the muscles and tendons of the horse's neck the beast's eyelid fluttered open and one large black eye rolled wildly in its socket. It searched madly for the source of the attack, its mouth beginning to foam around its bit.

So intent was he on the task at hand that at first the little boy did not notice the horse's awakening, and it was not until it gave a braying, gasping snort that he stood back from his feast in surprise.

Red of face and damp of shirt the boy gawped as the beast seemed to shiver and rock against the tree, until a flailing fetlock struck the boy on the side of his head and sent him sprawling across the clearing and down into a deep sleep.

When he was found, several hours later, by the local Holzfäller who lived on the outskirts of the village, all sign of the horse and the blood had vanished. The little boy was sent home with a sugar biscuit from the funfair and troubling sense of unease, to a father who beat him until he was sorry, and beat him because he loved him, and beat him because he didn't know what else to do with a wayward child.

That night – when he was in bed and the lamplight was low – the little boy tried to remember what had happened in the forest. But there in the dark, only the sharp taste of blood on his tongue remained. That, and the sense of eyes watching him. Watching him and *judging* him – now, and forever more.

Now, and forever more.

Prologue

A young girl lays on her bed. Her eyes are closed in a slumber so deep that it is only the gentle rise and fall of her chest that gives life to her form. In all other aspects she is as still as the grave.

Her bedroom is prettily – if cheaply – decorated. It is a room that is loved, that holds within it so much more than mere ornaments and trinkets. This is the room of a girl who enjoys reading and loves writing poems. The room of a girl not yet grown tired of dolls, yet with one speculative eye on entertainments more befitting her years to come – balanced as she is between the child and the adult.

The room is airy and warm, the plain linen curtains at the window are drawn, but the fabric is thin enough that the day's light illuminates the room. Certainly enough to see that, despite the girl's nightgown, she is not in a state of natural rest. If the darkness under her eyes was not enough evidence, there is also a nest of bandages at the back of her head.

The door to her bedroom opens slowly, and a head appears, staring wildly at the slumbering girl - her sister. They share these same features, these girls, the same dark hair, the same eyes the colour of a moonless night sky. This one, younger, has her hair in plaits that frame her serious little face. From behind her, the sounds of life within the home rustle along – a clatter from the kitchen, quiet strains of music from the wireless, the dull, deep hum of her parents' voices.

"Tilly?" she whispers, furtively. She has been given strict instruction to let her older sister rest and under no circumstances to disturb her. But the day has grown too long for this young girl, and she is unaccustomed to entertaining herself. Pushing the door open wider, she drags behind her a wicker basket from her bedroom.

"Tilly, play with me."

Standing beside the bed, she stares at the patient. Silently, she reaches out a hand to touch her sister's bare arm. It feels warm to the touch, almost feverish.

She gives her sister a good-natured, sisterly shove.
"Wake up!" she hisses, but her sister remains unresponsive.

The little girl bites her lip thoughtfully, and clambers up onto the eiderdown beside her sister, dragging the wicker basket behind her.

"Come on, we can play Happy Families or Old Maid," she says, taking a pack of cards out of the basket and briefly searching for a place to lay them before putting the pack carefully down on her sister's blanket-covered thighs.

She proceeds to pull out the contents of her toy hamper one by one, describing each one in turn and examining her sister's face for any sign of interest. A French knitting bobbin follows a small china tea set follows a snakes and ladders board follows a selection of animal masks follows a doll with a miniature straw hat and a knitted ballgown. And maybe, just *maybe*, the girl places each item down with a little more force than necessary. And just *maybe* she glances furtively up at her sister each time. But these siblings are no stranger to the rough and tumble of childhood play, and after all, their parents have other things on their minds than the scolding of youthful bad behaviour.

The girl is old enough to know that something is wrong, despite her attempts to stir her bedridden older sister. She saw her sister strike her head upon the hearth, had watched her mother tend to her wounds. Had heard her parents arguing and laying blame – their daughter's injury merely a catalyst for another airing of petty slights and historic injustices.

The little girl picks up two of the cardboard animal masks and briefly considers which is her favourite. Pulling the elastic strap of the orange cat face over her own head, she clambers up to her sister with a blue horse mask in her hand.

"Come *on*, Tilly," she mutters as she clumsily pulls her sister's head up from the pillow, attempting to loop the mask's elastic around with her other hand. She fumbles, and the mask drops from her fingers. A warm flush of annoyance hits her cheeks. "*Stop* it," she hisses through gritted teeth.

Her parents' voices float up from downstairs and she rolls her eyes.

"This is *your* fault," the girl says, struggling with the mask once more. The elastic snaps into place and she lets her sister's head fall back onto the pillow. She adjusts the blue horse mask, pushing her fingertips roughly around the eyeholes, around the nose. The sound of her parents grows louder. She pushes harder, jamming her sweaty little palms against the blue cardboard, feeling the shape of her sister's skull through the thin material. "This is your fault!"

She pushes her hands down hard, feeling her anger coursing down her thin arms, tears flowing hotly down her flushed cheeks. She wants to scream, wants to shriek until her throat fills with blood at the injustice of it all, but instead she pushes down and down and *down* until the pain goes away.

Chest heaving, she sits back, looking down at the mis-shapen mask that covers her sister's face. She goes to move it but stops. Through one of the creased eyeholes, an eye shines with a bloodied sheen that was not there before. The atmosphere of the room has changed; the hairs on the back of the young girl's neck begin to rise.

She climbs down off her sister, consciously ignoring the still figure. She begins to collect up her toys and tidy them away, one by one by one.

Not looking back, she carefully closes the door behind her as she leaves. After all, her parents had given her strict instructions to let her older sister rest.

Addendum - Table of Births and Deaths

Name	Date of Birth	Date of Death	Cause of Death
Herman Mueller	28/06/1892	16/03/1951	Subdural haematoma /suffocation
Sarah Mueller	11/04/1908	04/08/1945	Intentional self-harm
Robert Bullen	21/10/1919	24/04/1945	Penetrating Abdominal Trauma
Matilda Mueller	03/09/1928	02/11/1940	Subdural haematoma
Agatha Mueller	10/07/1933	19/09/2021	Heart attack
Charlie Owens	06/09/1958	31/07/2022	Intentional self-harm
Jill Simmons	27/01/1964	20/03/2047	Malignant neoplasm of breast
Terry Lawson	17/03/1979	21/07/2032	Failure to thrive
Debbie Lawson	24/09/1980	25/09/2051	Cirrhosis and other diseases of liver
Rajput Rathkuuli	23/07/1998	08/05/2022	Land transport accident

Name	Date of Birth	Date of Death	Cause of Death
Patrick Rayn	24/12/2003	18/02/2039	Death by misadventure
Hannah Lawson	07/02/2004	29/01/2065	Accidental poisoning
Callie Smith	16/04/2004	21/01/2097	Heart attack
Aaron Starr	16/05/2006	16/05/2032	Intentional self-harm

About the Author

TJC Howard exists above and beyond the spiritual realm. Is he proof that there is life beyond our ken? Perhaps. Certainly he has been known to manifest behind a keyboard from time to tome in order to tap out messages from the beyond upon a glowing lap-top screen. The blood running down your walls has nothing to do with him.

TJC Howard lives in West London with his wife and two chil-dren.

He may or may not be dead.